I0675058

Mage Confusion

Books by Virginia G. McMorrow

The Mage Trilogy
Mage Confusion

Coming Soon!
The Mage Trilogy
Mage Resolution
Mage Evolution

The Firewing Trilogy
Firewing's Journey
Firewing's Shadow
Firewing's Hunt

Novel
Upstaged by Betrayal

For more information
visit: www.SpeakingVolumes.us

Mage Confusion

Virginia G. McMorrow

SPEAKING VOLUMES, LLC
NAPLES, FLORIDA
2022

Mage Confusion

Copyright © 2004 by Virginia G. McMorrow

All rights reserved. No part of this book may be reproduced or transmitted in any form or by any means without written permission.

ISBN 978-1-64540-734-8

For Kevin, with love.

Acknowledgments

Thanks to my agent, Cherry Weiner, for her encouragement and guidance.

Chapter One

My first mistake was to let the flameblasted idiots standing outside my cottage door know I was awake.

"Stop knocking!"

Muttering, I scrambled in the dark for a match and a lamp, snagged my bare foot in the heavy wool blankets, and tumbled onto the icy floor.

The knocking increased in volume.

"I heard you. I'm not deaf or dead, though you'll wish you were both if the racket doesn't stop."

I groped for the match and lit the lamp with another curse as I shook my foot free. Fumbling for the rumpled tunic and trousers I threw aside hours ago, I tugged them on, picked up a boot, and discarded it in disgust.

"Stop knocking!"

They did, the very moment my other boot smacked against the wooden door with an echoing thud. Hastily running fingers through tangled, long dark curls, I rubbed bleary eyes and shivered.

"Who's out there?"

Cautiously prying the door open a crack, I waited for an answer as a pale sliver of moonlight traced a delicate line across the ground. I may have been half asleep and dreaming, but I wasn't stupid.

Silence. Then, finally, a low sigh, aggravatingly familiar. "Alex, it's me."

My second mistake was to let the flameblasted idiots come in.

Me. Jules. At this uncivilized hour and with barely restrained amusement in his tone. *Damn idiot.* I flung the door wide open, slamming it against the wall so hard a dish rattled behind me somewhere in the pantry.

"Do you know what time it is?" I planted one hand firmly on my hip, in case he missed the point. "Do you?"

"All too well." As he yawned, moonlight illuminated light brown hair, catching the glint of mischievous humor in sleepy green eyes.

"Then what . . ." I caught his subtle glance and ever so slightly cocked eyebrow to the deep shadows at his side. "You'd better make your dying peace with the lords of the sea if you've shown up in the middle of the night with another potential husband for me."

Something, or someone, moved in the darkest part of the shadows and laughed in a rich tone I hadn't heard here in Port Alain in a very long time. Far too long. "Still as cranky as a beached whale on a stifling summer's day."

"Elena?"

A dark-clad, slender figure crept from the gloom to stand blinking in the meager light from my lamp. "May we come in? Please? Or must I trudge up to the Hill and wake Jules' family for a warm fire and comfortable seat?"

Utterly caught off guard, I inched back to give them enough room to come inside. Shivering again, though from more than just the frigid floor beneath my bare toes, I knelt, head bowed, keeping sight of Elena from the corner of my eye.

"Majesty."

"You're not serious?" Throwing her woolen hood back, Elena Dunneal turned dark blue eyes to Jules with a sharp look of disgust. "She's not serious?"

Lords of the sea, but I was. How could I not be?

"Alexandra Daine Keltie at your service," I murmured, bewildered at Elena's unexpected appearance after long months of uneasy silence.

"Alex. I'm tired, cold, and far more thirsty than anything else. I brought a peace offering for waking you so rudely in the middle of the

2

night." She thrust a bottle of Marain Valley wine under my nose, forcing me to look up.

"Well, all right then." I grinned as Jules yanked me to my feet. Hugging Elena close, I stepped back to study her delicate features. It'd been almost a year since she came south to Port Alain. Elena was in high spirits then, happy to escape the stifling politics of the fortress in Ardenna, the heart of Tuldamoran. At least until swift change overtook her peaceful, happy life. Four months past, Elena was thrust onto the throne. Shocked at the sudden death of her father, the king, there'd been no time for private words, and she'd withdrawn from every one of us.

Except Jules.

Which was something Jules' wife tried very hard and very often to put in perspective—not always successfully. I didn't blame Lauryn for the failure. I blamed Jules.

Framed by long, thick black hair, Elena's face was strained, exhausted, and royally annoyed. "I won't have you doing that," she said quietly.

"Waking up grumpy at such an uncivilized hour? Can you blame me?" I led her away from the door into the small parlor.

Cozy and very much suited to my needs, the cottage was my home, though it didn't have to be. Rosanna, Jules' mother, respected my beastly need for privacy and solitude. But it bothered the old seawitch because she knew all too well what kept me away.

Elena waved a slender hand to catch my attention. "Kneeling and bowing and all that submissive nonsense. I get enough of it in Ardenna, and very little is meant with respect."

"You thought I was being respectful? Good, then I can still fool you. Anyway, you are my queen." I arched a brow at her. "Or have you decided to run away and leave the crown to little Brendan?"

"Little?" An unroyal snort followed. "Do you mind if I sit?" She yawned, looking very much like the old Elena who ran barefoot with the rest of Rosanna's hooligans. "I really am tired."

"Do queens need permission? Or are you just being polite for old times' sake?"

Elena sent a poisonous look my way before glancing curiously around the cluttered room, and then past Jules to my small bedchamber, tucked away at the back of the cottage.

"Did we interrupt anything?"

"Would it matter?"

"I'd be far more apologetic."

"And curious," I added dryly. "Here." I gestured her in the direction of a low armchair, carefully setting a well-thumbed pile of books on the floor. "Jules, is it beneath your pompous dignity as Duke Barlow of Port Alain to build up the fire while I open this bottle of wine?"

"Not if I do it for an old, cranky friend." He scampered well out of reach, not an easy trick in my cozy, cramped cottage.

"Old?"

"You are a bit older than me." He tossed his light woolen cloak onto the pile of books, toppling them over. "Sorry."

"Liar." I smacked his hands away from my precious books and pushed him in the direction of the cold fireplace. "Two months only in age, but twenty years' worth in intelligence." Rummaging around the pantry, I found the sharp, thin blade I kept for such important tasks. Gripping the bottle, I neatly plucked the cork free and sighed as I caught a whiff of the rich aroma.

"Must I share this?"

"I'm afraid so." Elena flung her own cloak on top of Jules', creating a mound at her feet. "I've been dreaming of it all the way from Ardenna." Accepting the glass I offered, she raised it with a calculating grin. "To my older friends."

Jules lifted his glass, as I did mine. Smooth as silk. Definitely worth being summoned out of a warm bed in the middle of the night.

"So, Elena." I plopped down by the now-blazing fire, resting comfortably against some old, faded pillows Rosanna embroidered for me. "Why are you here in the uncivilized middle of the night?" As she sent Jules a guarded look, I added, "Not that I'm unhappy to see you, of course."

And not that I hadn't missed her terribly.

Dark blue eyes studied me, very cool and calculating; suddenly demanding in an unfamiliar way. "Jules is in a bit of trouble, which might include you."

She was flameblasted serious.

Jules shrugged at my baffled expression. "Elena came to warn me."

"Couldn't she send a courier?"

I thrust cold, bare feet toward the fire's warmth, wiggling my toes. What had I done? And to whom?

"Alex. This is serious." Elena kept her eyes fixed on mine.

"I don't doubt it."

She stared at Jules for a long moment and then past him when it became obvious he wasn't going to explain the situation. No surprise. Jules always avoided confrontation unless it was to his distinct advantage or unless, as was usually the case, he was backed into a corner.

"I don't know who to trust in Ardenna," she admitted, after a strained, uneasy moment. She reached for the half-empty bottle. The Dunneal ring, gold crown set in a circle of sapphires, caught the fire's roaring blaze as she twirled the bottle in her hands. "With my father gone so suddenly," her voice was hushed in the tense silence, "none of his counselors are ready to deal with me, despite all the preparations he made over the years to ensure a smooth succession. And with mother gone these past few years, he hadn't been quite himself."

I murmured something comforting, acknowledging her still raw grief, which prompted a sad smile to her face.

"The counselors are somewhat better now, after months of my hard-headed manipulation, but they don't truly see me as an adult. I'm surrounded by sweet-talking, deceitful, self-serving diplomats and retainers full of politics and full of themselves. And what they managed to sneak behind my father's back—"

"I can't imagine."

"Then try and imagine the worst. They weren't ready for me, and I wasn't ready for them." She shook her head in disgust. "Besides," she smiled shyly, "part of the reason I came tonight was to see Brendan."

"As though I'd mistreat your brother," Jules complained. "You have very little faith in me."

"I miss him. I'm alone all too often." Elena met my intent gaze with a flush of embarrassment. "And I've no one but myself to blame for hiding when you and everyone here wanted to help me. You don't have to remind me, Alex." Before I could add anything pointedly related to Jules, and the fact Lauryn had been fretting, Elena changed her tone, setting the bottle on the table beside the armchair. "But that's not why I'm here. There've been rumors Jules is under suspicion of treason against me. It's so ridiculous, I shouldn't even respond. But the Ardenna Crown Council of Mages wants him closely watched, and that means I have to take the rumor seriously. They're watching me, too, and trying to destroy the only solid link I have with the Tuldamoran duchies."

"Jules?"

"Don't be snide. Yes, Jules. You know how influential he is with the other dukes."

"I'll have to keep that in mind."

"Alex—"

"Sorry. Go on."

"The Crown Council of Mages doesn't like my politics any more than they liked my father's, which only adds to our mutual distrust. I can't help being suspicious . . ." She caught herself, and waved a hand in frustration.

"About what?

She shut her eyes for a moment. "I can't shake the feeling they had something to do with father's death, as well as mother's accident years ago. But it's something I don't think I'll ever be able to prove."

I glanced at Jules, who shrugged. "You never said anything."

"Nothing to tell," he said quietly. "As Elena said, we've no proof."

"It's not important now," Elena intervened.

"It may be if they're looking to get rid of you."

"They think Brendan's easier to manipulate, if only for his youth, so, yes, maybe it's true. There've been rumors Jules is plotting with some . . ." She glanced his way, and I couldn't read their exchange. "Well, some interesting parties to get the Tuldamoran throne back into his family's possession."

I turned from watching Elena and stared at Jules, keeping my tone bland. "There's usually a thread of truth in any rumor. Guilty?"

"Of course not," he snapped in hurt annoyance, pushing light brown hair from his rugged good-natured face. "Why would I want to be bothered with that nuisance, anyway? Governing Port Alain is enough trouble."

"I was just looking after my queen's interest, and protecting you from your mother's wrath."

"Alex."

I ignored Elena. "Whom are you supposed to be conspiring with?"

"The Meravan government, for one—"

7

"Meravan? That's absurd," I protested, recalling what I knew of the neighboring kingdom. "They're too desperate for our trade to keep their people fed and clothed. With their erratic seasons, they depend on us. We're their closest trading partner and, unless I've misunderstood your father's policies, Elena, we've never taken unfair advantage of them when any other country would."

Elena turned to Jules with a smug look. "Even when she's not in the schoolroom, she still sounds like a schoolmistress." Before I could defend myself, she turned back to me, still smiling. "You're right. But the Crown Council of Mages seems to think Meravan's monarch is becoming greedier."

"Is that new?"

"No. They've always tried to change our agreements and never open-ly admit they're fair. But they are fair."

"And the Meravan monarch knows what Elena thinks about the cur-rent trade agreements because she's reminded their ambassador several times," Jules defended his queen.

"Diplomatically, of course," I slid in, earning a grin from Elena.

"That won't stop the Crown Council from suggesting to Meravan perhaps a new face on the Tuldamoran throne might present an oppor-tunity for more favorable trade. At some risk to our merchants, though the Council would never admit to it." Jules shrugged in an offhanded fashion, though his eyes were grim. "Nor do they care."

"Absurd," I muttered, tucking my bare feet beneath me and stretch-ing for my glass, all but unforgivably forgotten. "All right, my queen, whom else are you plotting with?"

Elena met my gaze without blinking, and I suddenly tensed. "That brings us to your part in all this."

"My part?" I asked slowly. "What? Am I guilty of infiltrating trea-sonous thoughts into the children's lessons?"

"You're not exactly guilty of anything," Elena hedged. "The Crown Council wants the local mage council here in Port Alain to keep a close eye on you."

"What in hell for?" I demanded, quite aware why they might have an interest in the local schoolmistress, whose long-dead mother had been a rogue seamage.

"Good question." Elena exchanged a furtive glance with Jules. "That brings us around to the other party tangled in this plot."

I crossed my arms to avoid pulling the words from her royal tongue. "The Crownmage."

I laughed outright in relief. "The Crownmage doesn't exist. Everybody knows that. So there, see how easy it is to prove our innocence." Still chuckling, I put the glass back down, almost missing the dark look that flashed between my two friends. "Please don't tell me you believe in the Crownmage."

Elena leaned forward in earnest. "The Crownmage exists. The Council's convinced—"

"That's even more absurd, Elena. I expected better from you," I said in disgust. "The one political group you distrust the most believes in something probably conjured out of a child's bedtime tale, and you fall for it like a frightened infant."

"Alex—"

"The Crownmage is a legend. The last one appeared five centuries ago, according to unverified records. If he really existed. There hasn't been one since. And," I said firmly, "there won't be another." I clenched my fists in irrational annoyance, trying to sound convinced, desperately trying to persuade them so we could chat about something less distressing.

"How can you be so absolutely sure?" Elena asked; a dangerous, unsettling look in her dark blue eyes. "Your mother—"

I scrambled to my feet, scattering pillows across the floor. "Leave my mother out of this nonsense."

"She was a seamage from Port Alain."

I quickly cut her off and grabbed the wine bottle. "Yes and her mother was a seamage. Neither of them left anything in their rather long-winded notes and studies that ever hinted at the possibility of another Crownmage. I know it doesn't prove anything," I said defensively, as Elena's raised eyebrow spoke eloquently, "but something as important as a Crownmage would have to be discussed somewhere."

"Your mother kept records—"

"Yes, she did, for all those renegade mages who refused anything to do with the mage councils. She was damn curious and had sources all over Tuldamoran who sent her information. I know, flameblast you, because I have it all. And I've read every last word," I said, catching surprise in Elena's blue eyes. "If there was a Crownmage to be found anywhere, my mother would have known the moment he took his first breath and cast his first spell." I poured more wine all around until the bottle was empty, silently cursing my shaking hand. I gave it a mournful glance before tossing it aside.

"And you?" Elena's voice was a trace too casual.

I spun around to face her. "What about me?"

Elena held my gaze without mercy or remorse. She'd learned a lot these last four months in the capital, and I wasn't sure I liked what I saw. "What kind of mage are you?"

Royal flameblasted seahag. "Are you blind? Elena, you grew up with me. You spent summers here for as long as I can remember. You know I'm not any kind of mage. I never had—"

"Lies." She calmly tapped slender fingers against her glass. "Well, all right, Alex, maybe not lies. Denial perhaps. I remember some rather strange incidents when we were children," she added smoothly, slanting a furtive look at Jules as she took another dainty sip of Marain wine. "Apparently, so does the Port Alain council of mages."

A knot formed in the pit of my stomach at the thought of the local council. "I remember, too." My face flushed scarlet in betrayal. "Whatever I managed to do was a childish trick. I had no control over anything. Water, air, fire, earth. Not over any of them. You should remember very well."

"Alex—"

"You pushed me to keep trying until Jules . . ." I looked down at my hands, unwilling to pursue this conversation. "Forget it."

"How can I forget it," Elena's voice softened, "when you've never quite forgiven me for that incident?"

I looked up. "Jules could have been seriously hurt."

"But he wasn't."

"He was lucky."

"And you were scared." The softness vanished, her expression now cool and unreadable. "You were frightened then, and you're frightened now."

"Damn you, Elena. I wasn't a mage then, and I'm not a mage now." I faced her stubbornly across my tiny cluttered room, feeling claustrophobic. "I'm not." After an uncomfortable silence in which neither of them offered sympathy, I grumbled, "And even if I were, which I'm not, and I don't know how to convince you, what does that have to do with Jules' trouble?"

After eying Elena's composed face, Jules drained his cup and set it down on the table. "If I'm plotting treachery with the Crownmage and the Meravan government, the Crown Council in Ardenna will have our local Port Alain council of mages keep an eye on me. Since they're watching you, too, I thought—" Jules flushed scarlet.

"We both thought," Elena added quietly, taking pity on him, "if you'd been developing any mage talent, you know, Alex, on your own without telling anyone, you might be able to help."

I sat in rigid silence.

"But as you haven't..." Jules shrugged uneasily, his expression letting me know he was still unconvinced. "I'd just be grateful if you kept your eyes and ears open without getting into any trouble with the council. I need proof of my innocence, any way I can get it, or the Crown Council of Mages will all too happily hang me."

"Maybe they should," I said in retribution for the wound he ripped open and the dreams I knew would return the moment I fell asleep.

"Alex, please—" Elena's plea cut through my bitter thoughts.

Lords of the sea, it was the middle of the night, and I was never any good at thinking with a muddled head.

"How do they imagine your treachery, Jules? Rather, your alleged treachery," I amended dryly at Elena's sharp glance. "Let me make an intelligent guess. Meravan raiders start creating diversions and trouble, possibly even using their own mage talent, for poor, insecure, newly crowned Elena, who has no choice but to turn to the Crown Council of Mages for help." When neither of them said a word, I continued, "Then the legendary Crownmage comes out of hiding and, on behalf of Jules' claim to the throne, offers formal Mage Challenge to Elena's mage of choice because the traitorous duke has been secretly conspiring with the Crownmage."

"Now listen—"

"Am I supposed to be the liaison between you and the Crownmage?" I ignored Jules' murderous expression, knowing it would only get worse. "Here's the part I don't quite understand. What's your motive for wanting to take the crown from Elena? Oh, wait," I slapped my head, "how could I forget? It's so simple, even your twin boys could unravel this puzzle. Vengeance for a love gone wrong, but not quite forgotten, isn't that right? You've always wanted Elena to step beyond friendship, and you still do. But she wasn't interested, Jules," I said, adding cruelly, "and still isn't. So I presume that's why you're allegedly seeking vengeance."

I refused to soften my words. They didn't bother to soften theirs.

"Am I right?"

"That's not . . ." Jules' started to protest, but his words trailed off in embarrassment as he turned away from me and Elena. She had been grief-stricken at causing him pain when she rejected what he offered a lifetime ago.

"That's what my sources are reporting," Elena answered calmly for Jules, though her cheeks were flushed as she glanced at his averted face. "Apparently, it wasn't as much a secret as we'd hoped."

"Too bad. It's not something you'd want your enemies to know," I murmured. "Not when they can use it against you."

"Too late for that," she said regretfully. "There's more, Alex. There's already been trouble along the Belbridge coast. That's why you—"

"Tell me something, Elena. What's my motive in this sordid affair? Am I siding with Jules because he's convinced me over the years you're not fit for the throne? Am I jealous?" The specter of an orphan child reared her ugly head in my mind, though I tried to banish her. "Power hungry? Or maybe I'm just a spineless coward, lacking the guts to go after power of my own—"

Elena raised a hand to stop my fevered words. "I don't know, but with Jules under suspicion, and perhaps you, too, I'm pressed to keep a balance in how I deal with both of you. With Brendan squiring here at Port Alain, I have to make it appear our relations are somewhat normal."

I laughed, not bothering to hide my bitterness.

"But I'm forced to show some distance between us if I'm to trap whoever's behind the rumors. I don't trust any of the four mages on the Crown Council. Please understand, Alex." She was practically pleading again.

"That you're in a very uncomfortable position? Comes with being queen," I said wryly. "But for you and Jules, and maybe myself, well, damnation, you know I'd do anything to help you." Caught between laughing and crying, I added, "Almost anything. So if you want my help, and I can't think what help a schoolmistress can give, well, all right." I stared at them, all traces of my humor vanished. "But I don't trust either of you. You're the dearest people in the world to me, but that won't matter."

Elena's flush deepened, staining her cheeks. "How can you say that?"

"Because you're holding something back from me. Or maybe you're both just a little mad. I don't know, too much Marain wine maybe."

"Alex—"

"If I get caught in the middle of some nightmare you've kept hidden from me, I'll hound you both until the end of your days. I promise you."

Chapter Two

The nightmare returned to haunt me as soon as my head touched the pillow and I fell into an uneasy sleep. Fire and ice once again. Meaningless swirls of black and red, spiraling wildly. Enfolding me, spinning me around. Pressure. Intense pain. Always intense pain. Fire and flames, and a cold blast of wind slapping my exposed nerves like a wall of ice, numbing every last pitiful inch of me.

It always ended with a scream of heartbreaking anguish and despair. The scream lingered on, echoing in my head long after it forced me awake.

I woke trembling, drenched in sweat, and furious. I tried to convince myself a long time ago the dreams had vanished. Not very flameblasted likely after Elena prodded the old guilt and pain awake, and yes, the fear. I was never free of the dreams, but there were some few blessed moments when I could pretend I was. I muttered a string of rather imaginative oaths about the royal idiot and her lovesick duke, both of whom, most likely, slept without any trouble. Exhausted, I flung the few blankets I hadn't discarded during sleep from my shivering body.

Sleep? Barely two hours, and I knew it was useless to try again.

Squinting tired, aching eyes against the sunrise, I shook myself free of the lingering nightmare, cursed Jules and Elena again, and puttered around like the village idiot until it was time for the children's lesson up on the Hill.

* * * *

"Alex was very sleepy today."

Coming toward the schoolroom along the path that connected the small building to the manor, Lauryn Barlow, Jules' wife, shot me a look filled with sincere apology at her five-year-old's brash comment.

"Maybe Alex was up all night with nightmares, worried she'd have to see you and your brother so early today," she suggested mildly to Carey. "Especially since you're the only two who ever cause her any problems."

Hunter, inseparable from his twin, sighed in absolute disbelief. "Alex loves to teach us."

"Indeed," she murmured, ruffling her hands through identical curly hair. "Now the truth." Lauryn turned gentle light blue eyes to me. "How unruly were they?"

The twins lunged for me, each possessively grabbing one of my hands and holding on as though a ravenous seabeast had caught their scent. "Alex!"

I hid my grin behind a cough. "Remember our agreement," I whispered, tugging at their arms. As they nodded solemnly, I winked at Lauryn, who matched my tone with a stern expression. "They were your children today. Perfectly behaved. Not at all like Jules."

"Then I trust they'll continue their good behavior for Brendan." She nodded in the direction of Elena's younger brother, coming to capture the twins and whisk them down to the stable.

"They wouldn't dare behave otherwise." Brendan came down the path, his smile so like Elena's, still fresh in my mind from last night's uncivilized visit. "They know I'll simply call the queen's guards." He stood ramrod straight and cast a stern look at the twins. "I have a fair amount of influence with the queen."

Lauryn smiled gratefully at Brendan before turning back to me. "Jules said a courier arrived from Ardenna late last night."

"A courier?" I asked unwittingly, catching the barest flicker in Brendan's dark blue eyes before he gathered up the protesting twins and led them away, not looking at either of us, particularly me.

But Lauryn must have noticed his expression, too. "Odd he left so fast."

"If the courier had nothing for him, Brendan wouldn't interfere in our conversation," I said swiftly, trying to control the rising panic in my head. What was Jules thinking, not to tell his wife Elena came in person? "Brendan was brought up with manners. What news did the courier bring?"

"Elena fears some Meravan trouble is brewing and wants us to watch the coastline for raiders."

"As though we don't." I rubbed my eyes, gritty from lack of a decent night's sleep and sighed. "Port Alain, if our revered monarch minded her school studies, is strategically located at the point of land closest to Meravan across the Skandar Sea. We'd be idiots not to watch the coastline."

"Stop sounding like a schoolmistress." Lauryn's eyes took on a mischievous glint as she unknowingly repeated Elena's words. "She meant for us to watch closer than we do now."

"I see."

Did I, really? Lords of the sea, what were they plotting? Was Brendan the only one who knew his sister visited in the middle of the night? Why didn't Jules tell Lauryn?

"Alex—"

At Lauryn's swift, insistent pressure on my arm, I looked up barely in time to find the intricately carved gate leading to the manor's main entrance mere inches from my face.

"You are tired." Lauryn frowned in maternal concern, though she was no older than me. Like a sentinel, she stood in my path as I turned to face her sheepishly. "Are you ill?"

"No." I shrugged moodily. "Trouble sleeping."

"You'd better not tell Jules. He'll start nagging you again to find a husband. As though that would solve your restlessness."

"A dull man just might put me to sleep." I pushed an escaped strand of curls behind my ear. "But I won't tell him. I'd like at least one peaceful week without his annoying comments."

"He forgets to mind his own business. But he means well," she said quietly, searching my face for reassurance. "I'm sorry he's such a nuisance."

I shook her arm playfully. "I'm entirely used to his interference. Besides," I added breezily, as she started to walk away. "You know I usually ignore him."

But not this time, damn him. Jules' clandestine midnight visit with Elena started the dreams again. What I needed was a sensible talk with the only other sensible person in Port Alain besides Lauryn.

Rubbing my eyes wearily once again, I stared at the manor house before stepping inside. It had been my home from the day I was born. Warm and familiar and spacious in the eyes of a child with a hundred thousand secret places to idle away the hours. Either alone with my dreams or heartaches, or hiding with Jules or his sister, Khrista. The best was hiding with Elena from both of them on hot, drowsy summer afternoons.

Before the dreams started.

I sighed heavily, with no small amount of trepidation. Scanning the length of the three-storied manor house, I ran my hand with affection along the rough stone. Admiring its modest grandeur, my roving eye rested on the corner turret with its balcony overlooking not the bobbing masts in the Port Alain harbor, but its owner's precious gardens. That turret, and the apartment within, meant home and comfort to me years and years past. With a last lingering look at the house I'd chosen to leave for the privacy of the cottage, I stepped inside, up the elegantly carved stairway, and headed for the turret and its guardian oak door.

"You look as though you tossed and turned in your sheets all night." A suggestive twinkle appeared, out of place on the plump face appraising me from the other side of the oak door. "I hope whoever kept you wide awake was worth all the trouble."

I grumbled an unintelligible greeting as Rosanna Barlow waved me into her bright, sun-warmed sitting room.

"That should stop my son from pestering you about a husband."

I sank onto a pile of embroidered cushions she kept piled on the floor especially for me. "No one kept me awake."

"Too bad." Jules' mother studied me for a long, appraising moment as she stood motionless by the door.

Instinctively, I dropped my gaze and toyed absently with my comfortable, worn leather boots.

"The dreams are back again, aren't they?"

My head snapped up so fast my neck hurt. "How did you know?"

Rosanna's smile was gentle, soothing, a trace mischievous, well, more than a trace, as she shrugged. "I can always tell with you. Don't ask me how, because I don't know. But you're troubled again. It's fairly obvious."

"Your idiot son is troubling me." I smacked my fist against my boot heel. "He thinks I'm keeping secrets from him."

"Friends shouldn't keep secrets from each other, is that it?" She settled herself in the rocking chair by the window overlooking her beloved garden. As Rosanna's silk gown rustled, old familiar memories crept in uninvited.

"Certain friends shouldn't keep certain secrets from Jules that Jules feels he should know about," I corrected sourly, pushing the memories away.

"He is duke of Port Alain," she teased, though turned serious at my frown. "What on earth does he think you're hiding?"

I tugged off my boots, tossing them in a corner. "Mage talent," I nearly spat out the words. "So does Elena." Plumping some well-worn pillows behind me, I settled back opposite Rosanna.

"Are you?"

"You, too?"

"No," she said reasonably, reaching over to pour us both some cool Marain wine. "Have a sip. It might help your crankiness. Now, I wasn't implying I think you're doing what Jules thinks you're doing. I was just asking for the truth. In case," she added slyly, "you don't want to admit to him you really are doing what he thinks you're doing."

"Beastly old witch." I took a lingering sip of the fruity wine. "No wonder your son is so treacherous. Listen, I'm not hiding anything. Jules knows better. Having mage talent in my bloodline is no guarantee I'll have it."

"I distinctly remember an incident—"

"Yes, the day Jules aggravated me so badly I tried to turn his wooden chair to sawdust, with him in it, and managed to turn it into a puddle of muddy water instead."

"That's the one."

I took another sip, inhaling the rich fruit, remembering the bottle Elena brought, and the dream; and that day so long ago. "Then Elena wouldn't leave me alone until I tried again. Somehow, I changed wood to fire and almost burned Jules to death."

"You could have refused."

"I didn't want to disappoint Elena. I wanted her to be my friend."

Rosanna sighed. "She was your friend long before then—"

"They know I couldn't control a damn thing." I rolled over her words, trying to banish the uncomfortable thoughts accompanying them. "If I were really a mage, I'd have succeeded in controlling whatever element was in my bloodline, which should have logically been water, as my mother was a seamage. But I couldn't do it then. And I can't now," I whispered, turning away from her all-too-knowing eyes.

"Have you tried recently?"

"No."

"Then how do you know you can't?"

I slammed the delicate glass down on the floor by my bare feet, surprised it didn't break. "Has Jules been talking about me?"

"No. I'm just speaking the truth." She raised a hand at my growing indignation. "You know in your heart if you'd only take the time to look and," she said evenly, not the least bit fazed, "be honest with yourself."

"I came here for sympathy."

"Which you always get when you're not feeling sorry for yourself," she scolded, smoothing the sleeve of her silk gown as though she hadn't inserted a dagger in my heart.

"Is that what I'm doing?"

Rosanna suddenly smiled with the warm affection that was my earliest memory and reached over to pat my cheek. "I'm never exactly sure what you're doing. But at times like this, when you're so very stubborn and willful—"

"And not too far removed from that pitiful orphan child you raised."

"Now you're feeling sorry for yourself." Rosanna shook a finger in my face. "You weren't a nameless orphan. I knew your parents and raised you as one of my own wild brood, young lady. Until the day he died, Jules' father felt the same. We loved and disciplined you as though you were blood kin to Jules and Khrista. Very willingly."

"I know," I whispered, looking away in embarrassment as I fought the memories that stubbornly crept back into my awareness. "I've always been grateful."

She sighed irritably. "You're trying my patience."

Confused, I looked up, caught by surprise at the tears in her eyes.

"I don't ever want to hear how grateful you are. You should know that by now. Those are words I'd expect from a courteous stranger for hospitality. You're family. My family. And it will always be that way." Rosanna scowled, more perturbed than I'd seen her in a long while. "I know that's why you sometimes stay away. I just wish you'd stop being so needlessly independent. It isn't something new. You're twenty-five years old, Alex, but sometimes I make the mistake of thinking you're an adult."

I answered her accusations in the only way I could, straining to keep my expression neutral. "But that means I'm kin to your son. And if you think I'll claim kinship with that sneaky, monstrous, idiotic excuse for a duke," I started to grin, "then I'd rather have been raised by a seawitch."

She smiled back, fully aware I sidestepped dangerous ground, and reached out to keep me seated as I went to grab my boots. "You're avoiding the point of this conversation."

I sagged back against the embroidered pillows in defeat. "Maybe I was raised by a seawitch."

"You came to see me, remember?"

"To complain about your son, remember?" Crossing my legs and tucking bare feet back underneath, I drained my glass.

"Listen." Rosanna paused, choosing her words with care. "The lords of the elements grant mage talent where they will. Power over fire, air, water, earth, wherever and however they see fit. If you're lucky to have any talent, whether it's in leather crafting or mage skills, or gardening, though everyone knows you've none of that," she said dryly, "it's wrong to ignore it."

I clenched my fists in my lap. "If a person has it."

"Yes. No matter how little or great that talent might appear. And it's just as wrong," she added firmly, "to not even try to uncover whatever talent you may have, regardless of its unconventional nature."

I grabbed my boots and stuffed my feet into the worn leather. "It's just as wrong to almost destroy someone with uncontrollable talent."

"True."

I glanced up suspiciously to find her staring at me, gray head leaning back against the padded armchair.

"And even more wrong to run away from it when you could learn to control it. But you're afraid." Her gaze was serene, her challenge blatant.

I tucked my woolen trousers snugly into my boots as fast as my shaking fingers allowed and walked toward the oak door and freedom. "Thanks for the wine."

"Alex—"

One hand resting against the smooth wood, my back to Rosanna, I whispered, "You're so sure of yourself." Turning to face her, I was immediately sorry at the sight of her troubled expression. Haunted, almost.

I did the only sensible thing. I fled.

* * * *

"Jules lied to me." Lauryn cornered me in my cottage later that afternoon.

"About?" I paused, holding the teakettle in mid-air, one eye warily on my friend's deep scowl.

"Don't play innocent. Jules confessed he and Elena came down here in the middle of the night. Or did he lie about that, too?" Lauryn's expression shifted subtly from anger to pain, at the thought of Jules' possible betrayal.

"No. They woke me up. I didn't think Elena wanted anyone to know. I wasn't even sure she'd taken the time to see Brendan."

"I knew his quick departure was suspicious."

"Don't tell him. The poor boy will be devastated." When Lauryn remained silent, I sighed with remorse. "Listen, I'm sorry."

"I'm not blaming you for lying."

"Why not?" I remembered the tea kettle in my hand and poured us both a cup. "I didn't tell you Elena visited either."

Lauryn accepted the offering and sat in one of the armchairs. "Elena wanted her visit kept quiet."

"So why be angry at Jules?"

"Because he still loves her."

Damn. Damn. Damn. "He married you."

"She wouldn't have him."

"He loves you. Don't deny he loves you."

Lauryn set her teacup aside and started to leave, but I grabbed the sleeve of her simple wool dress and held her back.

"He does love you."

Slowly, she nodded. "I know he does. I do, Alex," she hastened to reassure me. "But he'll never get over Elena. And it's not her fault. She can't help being aware of his desire any more than I can."

"You're imagining things."

Lauryn laughed, sadness etched on her face. "There's no escaping the truth, Alex. You, of all people, should know that by now."

Chapter Three

Idiotic, really, to think I could escape. I knew better. The dreams abandoned me for three nights. Instead of catching some rest, I avoided sleeping. I'll admit it. I was afraid. The fourth night, smugly thinking myself safe, I threw aside the children's lessons I'd been preparing, and crawled under my wool blankets exhausted, grateful, and naive.

And very flameblasted sorry.

The dream jolted me awake well before dawn, soaked in sweat and tears, with echoes of the scream lingering in my head. By the time I managed to still my trembling limbs and calm my heart, the sun had risen. The bright rays of light streaked through the window of the bedroom and nearly blinded me.

I needed to leave the confines of the cottage, though had no clear destination in mind. If I wandered north for about half a mile along the cleared forest path to the Hill overlooking the harbor, I'd find myself at Rosanna's turret. After our recent conversation, that option was out of the question. Wandering south about a mile along the same cleared forest path led to the port itself. East or west, I'd wander aimlessly through woods and fields. What I needed, or convinced myself anyway, was the calming breeze of Shad's Bay against my skin, ruffling my hair free, soothing my hurts and craftily painting an illusion of normalcy.

An impossible task.

Tugging on a comfortable, baggy woven tunic, trousers, and light woolen cloak, all in mismatched shades of blue and green, I grabbed some coins and made my way south along the forest path.

Jules' father, the old duke, set his laborers to clear the path for me, north and south, when I'd announced my rebellious plans to move to the old abandoned cottage in the forest some seven years past. Before his regrettable death, he made sure the cottage was sturdy and as new as his laborers could make it, with never a word of regret or admonishment. The old man instinctively knew I needed to find my own way, though Rosanna never forgave him completely for not discouraging me.

My suggestion I earn my keep for all they'd done saddened her. She relented and pushed aside her regrets, which were only for the demons tearing at my heart, and gave her blessing for the schoolroom. Setting his laborers busy again, the old duke made sure the schoolroom matched the cottage in sturdiness and comfort. It was the only time he scolded me, insisting he'd converted the unused space only to make me happy. He never took a single coin. I still missed him.

Wiping away traitorous tears, I tripped over a fallen branch. Swearing viciously, I shoved aside those memories and concentrated on the leaf-strewn path ahead. It was early, the air cool and crisp. Glad for my woolen cloak, I set a fair pace to warm my chilled bones and reached the outskirts of town before very long. The shopkeepers, many of whose children I'd taught, greeted me with a wave or sleepy nod. Several three-masted trading ships had recently arrived from Belbridge Cliffs up the east coast and Bitterhill toward the west. There was also a pair from Meravan, south beyond Shad's Bay, some days' travel across the Skandar Sea.

Arriving within smelling distance of the bakeshop, I inhaled the rich, sweet aroma of fresh-baked loaves of brushed oats and apple muffins. Jan's pudgy, flour-sprinkled face smiled a greeting and pressed a half loaf of brushed oats into my hands, refusing payment. Nibbling absently at a small piece I'd broken off, I wandered through the streets until I stood uneasily opposite the large stone building set in the center of the port's activity.

The one building I was determined to avoid. Port Alain's own Mage Council Hall, the duchy's gathering point for mages with any of the four elemental talents.

Unsure of my motivation, I sat on the low, rough seawall that lined the coast road for miles east and west of the harbor, thinking. My mother, a seamage, despised the council for their political posturing and blatant push for power by advising Tuldamoran nobles. There'd always been renegades who rebelled against their hypocrisy. My mother had been one of the more well-known rogues, a fact that never quite reconciled the Port Alain council to my presence, no matter how harmless I might appear.

"You don't typically hang around this part of town, Mistress Keltie."

I slowly turned my head, surprised to see Neal Brandt, seamage and chief of the Port Alain council, standing at my side, arms tucked beneath his wool cloak. I blinked. "Pardon me?"

The elderly man, mage pendant sparkling in the sunlight, narrowed his eyes. "Thinking about joining us?"

I studied the tidal crest etched on the copper pendant. "I have no reason to."

"Your mother—"

"Never passed on her talent." I shrugged. "Selfish, don't you think?"

"Indeed." The mage leaned over and scooped up a handful of stagnant water from a shallow puddle left over from an earlier rainstorm. Holding the water cupped in his palm, he smiled benevolently as the liquid evaporated.

"Lovely trick."

He didn't blink, bent again to scoop another handful of water, and held it out to me. "Care to try? It may turn to fire in my hand if you do."

"I doubt it, Mage Brandt."

"Do try."

"I'd only disappoint you."

"Surely if your mother were alive—"

"She wouldn't even waste time speaking to you." I returned to my breakfast, ignoring the mage, and privately amazed at my boldness.

"Should you find yourself with unexpected talent, do call on me." His smile was predatory as he brushed off my rude remark. "I'd be delighted to teach you."

"I'll keep that in mind."

"Do." He nodded, heading toward the hall where he vanished inside.

"Interesting choice of companion, Mistress Keltie," a familiar voice whispered in my ear. "Or are you spying for me?"

Startled, I nearly dropped the nibbled loaf of brushed oats at the sound of Jules' amused voice. Annoyed he'd managed to sneak up on me, I slanted the duke a dark, menacing look, holding out the loaf. "Care to join me?"

"As long as you're in a pleasant, generous mood." He broke a sizable chunk from the loaf and handed the rest to me, taking a seat on the seawall. Tucking long legs beneath him, Jules opened his cloak to catch the early sun's warmth and smiled. "Well?"

"Well what?"

"Are you spying for me? Or betraying me to Seamage Brandt?"

"I came to Port Alain specifically to avoid you."

"Oh." He took a bite. "Sorry," he mumbled, looking not the least bit apologetic.

"Why are you in town so early?" I asked, munching contentedly on the brushed oats, gazing out across the bay already filled with sails, catching the early tide and buoyant breeze. Bright-hued merchant sails broke the monotony of the fishermen's white canvas, crisscrossing paths along the bay.

"I have an appointment with the Darby Trading Company and thought I'd be considerate and meet them in town rather than on the Hill."

"Keeping close ties to your people, my lord, to inspire trust and confidence?" I asked dryly.

"Sure."

"You'd better try harder."

"You haven't a drop of respect in your veins. But listen, I hear there's a handsome new captain working for Darby, and—" When I tried to snatch the loaf from his hands, Jules pulled away, laughing as he bit off another piece of bread. "With all this nonsense of Elena's, I thought to see if there were newer rumors of any peculiar Meravan behavior here or up the coast."

"Ah." I squinted as the sun glimmered on the water. "Spying."

"Someone has to do it, since you're being so damnably difficult." He reached out to grab another chunk from the little remaining of my half.

I snatched it out of reach. "Why am I being so damnably difficult? Because I've disappointed you? Damn it, Jules, I'm sorry I don't have the least bit of mage talent to help you in whatever manner you and our glorious monarch have imagined, but there's nothing I can do!"

Jules nimbly caught the edge of my cloak as I jumped from the seawall and held me back. "Have you ever tried to tap into the talent again?"

I yanked my cloak from his fingers. "Yes. Ten years ago. Nothing happened. Jules, I don't know what to do or say to convince you and Elena. Nothing happened. I can't do a flameblasted trick or even feel any inkling of mage talent inside me."

"That was ten years ago."

"It could just as well have been yesterday."

"All right." He shrugged casually. Too casually. "You don't have to say anymore. I believe you."

"You are such a liar." I stared at Jules until he blushed and turned away, gazing seaward, eyes following the graceful flight of scattered seagulls. "Speaking of lies, why didn't you tell Lauryn Elena delivered the message in person?"

Jules winced, face still averted. "She came to see you?"

"You didn't answer my question."

"Elena didn't have a lot of time. She didn't want Lauryn or my mother going to any trouble playing hostess."

"Why not tell your wife what you just told me?"

Jules shrugged sheepishly. "It was a mistake."

"It was a stupid mistake."

Cool breeze ruffled his light brown hair, blowing it back from his handsome face. "What did the old mage want?"

Uncomfortable with the touchy topic, I didn't resist his obvious ploy to talk about other things. "Mage Brandt found it curious I was hanging around, spying, as it were."

"Understandable, from his point of view. Why are you here anyway?"

"I got lost."

Jules turned back to face me and rolled his eyes. "You got lost?"

"If you're going to be so annoying," I cut in sharply, "at least buy me a mug of hot cinnamon tea."

"All right." He led me along, in a companionable truce, to the Seaman's Berth, a small, cozy inn we often frequented, not far from the major wharf.

"You're both up bright and early." Chester, the innkeeper, waved a greeting as he set a plate of thick sausages and fresh eggs before one of his guests, an older man, well traveled but neat.

30

"Too much to do." I grinned, taking an empty table opposite the stranger.

"Too much on her conscience."

"My lord duke, that was rude," Chester scolded, earning a raised eyebrow from the gentleman across the way.

"As though he cares—"

"Alex, really."

At the sound of my name, the gentleman turned sea-gray eyes my way, studying my face with open interest. His hair was thick and unruly, liberally streaked with gray, the face handsome in a rugged, nondescript way.

"The duke is incorrigible." The innkeeper set two cups of steaming tea in front of us. "Has been, ever since he was a boy."

"An undeniable brat," I murmured, waving aside Chester's offer of food.

"Like my little one there." Chester pointed at his young daughter, busy raising the flames in the hearth through her fledgling firemage talent. "She was well behaved in your schoolroom. Now she's being taught by the mage council—"

Those words caught the gentleman's ear, too, though he was careful to focus on cutting his sausage into even bits. I watched Chester's girl practice on the hearth, flames rising and falling inconsistently, oblivious to her father's chatter.

"She was always well behaved, and I'm sure—"

The innkeeper leaned close to our table, his face abruptly serious. "They're teaching my sweet child arrogance. Mage talent is a gift, Alex, not a reason to claim superiority." Chester edged closer, eye-to-eye with me. "Your dear, departed mother understood. I wish she were still alive to teach my child."

I squeezed the innkeeper's arm. "So do I, old friend."

The stranger's hand stood poised above his plate, and he carefully set aside his knife.

"But that doesn't mean you can't exert your influence," I told the innkeeper. "She comes home to you at night, and you're the one who loves her. Just be sure to remind her every chance you can."

"I do, and I will."

Shaken by his words, I urged Jules to leave soon after, grabbing his sleeve and dragging him a ways up the street.

"I'm coming, Alex. Hang on. Wait—"

"Did you ever see that gentleman before?"

"The one cutting the sausage into exactly even pieces?"

I laughed, reassured. "At least you were paying attention. Jules, he was listening to our conversation."

"We were rather loud." Jules studied my expression for a moment in silence. "You're serious."

"Quite. It may be nothing. I could just be easily spooked, but after that visit from Elena . . ." I shrugged, not knowing what to think.

"I'll send one of my troopers down here to keep watch, see what he does. Will that make you feel better?" When I nodded, his voice softened. "Chester spooked you, talking about your mother, didn't he? I'm sorry, Alex, especially since Elena and I did the same thing to you days ago."

"No need to be sorry. I think of my mother all the time."

* * * *

And that was no lie.

In the dark of the night when I couldn't sleep, or truly wouldn't let myself sleep, I unlocked the small carved oak chest. Rosanna gave it to me when I was old enough to understand and wonder about my mother.

Notes and books with mother's neat script, commenting on important or interesting points and people, were stacked in the chest. My grandmother's handwriting in the earlier notes was as impossible as a child's first attempt at scribbling. But not Emila Daine Keltie's handwriting. She'd taken on the task of chronicling events and setting down principles and guidelines for renegade mages who chose to keep away from the corrupt mage councils.

Some months before I was born, she'd given the oak chest to Rosanna. My responsibility, I suppose, to carry on. I wasn't a mage though, despite Jules and Elena's ridiculous insistence. Not to mention Seamage Brandt. And no renegade mage ever came to see me. Everyone knew I didn't have the talent the lords of the sea had gifted my mother.

I never knew the woman, only learned about her through her witty, dry commentary in the chronicles. Along with wispy remnants of memories Rosanna shared whenever I asked. And sometimes when I didn't ask. Emila Daine Keltie was beautiful, loving, and full of good-humored passion until the day she gave birth to me. Cursing my foolish thoughts, I blotted the tears from the worn leather cover that bound her notes. I hadn't lied to Jules, not completely. Nothing that hinted of mage talent happened ten years ago. But something peculiar did happen time and again, which taught me other things about Mother. Not through my father's memories. Sernyn Keltie died of fever soon after I was born.

No, not through his memories, but through one half of a copper pendant Rosanna had wrapped in soft black velvet. One half of a tidal crest etched delicately in copper, a seamage's token. Unwrapping it with care, I held it in the palm of my right hand, and felt strangely comforted. Felt something of my mother I could never express to Jules, or even to Rosanna. But I knew my mother, felt her affection, humor, and overwhelming compassion as the half pendant warmed at my touch.

Mage talent?

I laughed, unable to hide the bitterness even from myself, brushing away unwelcome tears. Not likely. Only an orphan child's delusion of memories, and a plea for forgiveness. Because I survived and she didn't.

Chapter Four

"I won't be able to survive another moment in his presence." Khrista Barlow, Jules' younger sister, sighed melodramatically. "I think my brother should be locked away in the deepest, darkest dungeon in Ardenna. Surely Elena owes us a favor for something or other and can arrange it?"

"And throw the key into Shad's Bay?"

"Alex, what's wrong with Jules? He's been talking about nothing except the Crownmage."

"Can you blame me for staying away so often?"

"I've been thinking about packing my things and moving down to the cottage with you until he starts making sense again. It's much quieter, and probably more civilized." Khrista handed over a cup of hot cinnamon tea, shaking back a rogue lock of brown hair. "When I finally cornered Jules this morning in his study, I demanded to know why he was so obsessed with this nonsense."

"And?" I prompted, gratefully letting the tea's warmth course through my body. I stifled a grin, sorry to have missed the confrontation in person.

"He went on so about the threat to Elena's rule and the dire troubles sure to arise if a Crownmage appeared and, worse, turned out to be a renegade. No offense intended to your mother," she added with an earnest apology in her light green eyes. When I waved away her regrets, she continued her complaint. "Jules went on in such nauseating detail. I don't know how I managed to keep myself from smacking sense into him."

A renegade Crownmage linked with a treasonous duke and a mistrusted renegade mage's orphan child would be a problem. Khrista obviously didn't know that, and I wasn't about to enlighten her.

"What I want to know," I interrupted her long-suffering sigh, "is who started this ridiculous rumor?"

"According to Jules, the Ardenna Crown Council of Mages declared the Crownmage to be a real person, not a myth. They're just waiting for another one to appear."

"Why would the council be behind such a ridiculous rumor?" *To discredit Jules or Elena, even if they didn't believe in the Crownmage? What did the council know my mother didn't? That was the scarier possibility.* "Why push a legend no one believes?"

"Ah, but people do believe, Alex, including my idiot brother. That's precisely the trouble."

"Why don't you?"

"I know better. Besides," she pointed a finger at me, her expression daring me to disagree, "you don't either. I feel safer with your logic than Jules' arguments. I'll wait until the Crownmage comes knocking at my door before I believe it."

I glanced out the window behind her restless pacing to the busy harbor below. Assuming they believed in the Crownmage's existence, did Jules and Elena want him—or her, for that matter, allied with them against the Council of Mages? I hated to admit it, but it would make sense, not that I trusted their judgment at the moment, however.

"If all four mages on the Crown Council are afraid of the Crownmage, wouldn't it serve their purpose to keep quiet about the matter and destroy the Crownmage in secret? Even better, be smart and bribe the Crownmage with the treasury Elena keeps locked away?"

"I'd think so, but I'm not a mage or a politician. To be honest, I'm glad I'm neither, particularly a mage. With all this unsettling talk, I'm not sure it's an advantage to be one these days." Khrista frowned, green eyes somber, as she leaned against the window ledge, blocking my view of the harbor.

"Why?" Not that I cared.

"Kerrie and I were speaking the other night about—"

"I thought you had better things to do when he was around." I raised an eyebrow and settled a pillow behind my back. "That is, when he's not busy playing steward to the Barlows."

Khrista's face flushed bright scarlet, though she laughed good-naturedly. "We do talk."

"I wondered. So did your mother."

The flush spread to her neck. "Is nothing private?"

I started to laugh, couldn't help it. Khrista wasn't in the least shy. There'd been so many other men lusting after her, I'd lost count. But Kerrie was different, and we all adored him. Not one of us questioned the propriety of the duke's steward courting the duke's sister. Rank or breeding didn't matter in the Barlow household. If they did, I'd never have been raised by Rosanna on an equal footing with her children, nor befriended by a queen.

"So what did he have to say?"

A sidelong glance darted mischievously in my direction. "Before or after he left my bed?"

"Whichever is more interesting."

"What if the Ardenna Council of Mages is so afraid of the Crownmage they start watching people who have nothing to do with magery or politics? Serious watch, Alex, might frighten villagers into hiding their talent or their children's talent if they thought they might be different." Khrista's expression grew pensive again.

Lords of the sea, did Khrista remember the stories about me? And how Elena pushed me until I nearly killed Jules? Or had Khrista been too young?

"Are you all right, Alex?"

"Sure." I tossed an embroidered pillow across the sitting room, narrowly missing the fireplace. And then another, followed by a third. "Damn Jules, damn the Council, damn the Crownmage, and damn Elena."

Khrista sat motionless, saying nothing. I studied her expression. There was nothing in her eyes to suggest she knew. So maybe she didn't. And maybe I wouldn't tell her. I stood and stretched.

"The dungeon's too good for your brother. Let's ask Elena to sell him to the Meravan raiders." Catching a glint of mischief in her eyes again, I added, "I'd even give him away for free."

* * * *

"Raiders, Alex! Pirates!"

I glanced up barely in time to snatch Carey in my arms before the little beast knocked over the pile of books and papers I was sorting through. "Easy."

"But Alex—" The child protested; eyes alight with unsuppressed excitement, fidgeting in my strained arms.

"Pirates, Alex!" Hunter, never far from his twin, rushed right behind him into my outstretched arms.

"Pirates?" I asked calmly, looking both boys in the eye.

"From Meravan." Hunter volunteered the information, instinctively wary of my tranquil tone.

"Did I teach either of you that heirs to the duchy of Port Alain were free to spread idle harbor gossip?" Brendan scolded from his sudden appearance in the doorway, arms folded across his chest. "Did Alex?" He met my gaze across the cluttered schoolroom as the boys squirmed, still held loosely in my grip.

I dropped my arms. "Why don't we start at the beginning? What exactly did you hear?"

Carey looked at Brendan's unyielding expression before answering in a slightly subdued tone. "Two of our merchant ships were attacked and set on fire, not far from Belbridge Cliffs."

"Who brought in the word?"

Carey shrugged, staring uneasily at his scuffed boots. "I don't know."

"One of the few survivors," Brendan said quietly. "There was only a handful. Not one of them saw any recognizable identification on their attackers." He frowned at Carey who fidgeted, knowing without looking up the disapproval was aimed his way.

"Why do you think they're from Meravan?" I asked Carey, as he shifted from one dust-covered boot to the other.

Before answering, the child exchanged a sidelong glance with Hunter, who wisely wanted no part of the trouble his twin brought down on his head. Hunter possessed Lauryn's common sense rather than Jules' impulsiveness. A twin for each of them, Rosanna often remarked.

"Father said we should watch the coast for trouble from Meravan raiders," Carey murmured reluctantly.

Why wasn't I surprised? "I see."

Carey hesitated before blurting out, "But who else could it be?"

Not the twins' fault, really.

"Listen to me." I tugged at their small, dirty hands. "Meravan has been trading with us long before your grandmother was born. They need a good amount of our food just to survive their dry seasons. But you know this, or you should," I tugged on their hands a trace harder, "if you've been paying attention to my lessons." I put a hand under Carey's chin and held his gaze. "Now why would they be so foolish to risk the queen's anger?"

Hunter touched my arm when Carey didn't answer. "Maybe they're tired of buying things from us. Maybe they just want to take it." His eyes were serious and thoughtful, so like Lauryn's when she was troubled. But Carey's expression still held barely controlled excitement.

"We don't know for sure, do we? And it wouldn't be right for the duke's sons to spread unfounded gossip, would it? After all, people believe what the duke's sons tell them." I met Brendan's dark blue eyes, so like Elena's, over their curly heads.

"Alex is right. Now if I hear another tale about Meravan pirates from either of you," he threatened, biting back a laugh at their fervent nods, "I'll send you back to Alex for punishment. Next time, she won't be so forgiving."

* * * *

"Were they from Meravan?" I asked Jules a few minutes later as he stared out the window of his book-lined study, ignoring me. Straining over his shoulder, I could see the distant masts of the merchant ships bobbing unevenly on the incoming tide.

"We're not sure." He tapped his fingers in a random rhythm against the window. "There's not a shred of proof. None of the survivors could identify the attackers. The ships were nondescript, the attackers masked and silent. No accents, no crests, no flags, nothing." Jules scowled as he turned to face me. "This incident won't help me or Elena," he said bitterly. "They'll drag me into it somehow and ruin every bit of good my family ever did for Port Alain. I don't give a damn what they say about me, but Lauryn and the boys, and mother, and you . . ."

I sat on the soft leather chair opposite his oak desk and propped a worn boot on a low wooden footstool. "They've no proof of your involvement. Or mine." At his frown, I asked uneasily, "Or do they?"

"No. Elena's not sent any word to that effect, but they could fabricate any evidence they wanted to. All too easily."

"True. But they'd still need a Crownmage to prove their point."

"They could create one," he insisted, leaning back against the window ledge, blocking my view.

"How?" I propped the other leg on the stool and balanced my weight with care. "They'd need a mage capable of controlling all four elements, which is the talent the Crownmage is supposed to have. We both know the Crownmage doesn't exist," I reminded him. "At least I do."

"If they had a seamage, or any other mage, the council could just cover for the Crownmage."

"What are you babbling about?"

"Look," Jules explained impatiently at my blank stare, "let's say they have a seamage they're claiming to be the Crownmage. Now this seamage can only use mage talent to control water in any of its forms. Right?"

"Yes."

"Then they prove he's also a firemage because the council's firemage will be the one controlling the flame behind the scenes—"

"But make it appear as though the fraud mage is really the Crownmage and controlling water and fire. And they'd do the same to show he controlled air and earth with the help of a windmage and earthmage," I finished, utterly appalled at the potential for trouble and deception.

"Precisely."

"Damn." I pounded my hand against the arm of the chair, envisioning the faces of the Crown Council's mages under my fist. When Jules turned moodily back to the window and stared out, I warned, "You'd better be prepared to defend yourself if the council really wants to cause problems for Elena."

He didn't answer.

"Jules?"

"What I despise," he said softly, still looking out over his own private kingdom, which, despite my teasing, he ruled fairly, "is they believe either you or me capable of disloyalty to Elena. The Dunneals have held the crown for centuries, winning the Mage Challenge all those years ago. As far as I'm concerned, the Barlows didn't hold the crown legitimately in the first place. My family has never sought possession of the throne again in all these years."

"There was your great-uncle James."

Jules ignored my snide comment. "That's why the Dunneal and Barlow children were always raised together, to foster friendship and loyalty. And you were thrown in with the lot of us."

"You wanted more than friendship," I reminded him quietly.

Jules spun back around, green eyes dangerous. "Not for the crown, Alex. You know that. So does Elena."

"Yes."

"But . . ." He practically snarled.

I took a deep breath, not flinching under his angry gaze. "But is that really all in the past?"

His eyes never left mine. "Of course, it is. Elena made it very clear—"

"Yet you didn't tell Lauryn Elena visited in the middle of the night," I persisted, not out of cruelty but concern. Despite my cry for independence, I perversely worried about all of them, sometimes more than others. This time was one of those moments.

Jules pushed a hand through his hair in frustration. "She'd have gone to a lot of unnecessary bother. Elena didn't have the time. I told you already." His eyes suddenly widened. "Alex, you don't think . . ."

I chose my words with exquisite care. "I thought it possible."

His handsome face clouded over with old familiar sadness. "I told you it's all in the past. It was over before I married Lauryn."

"If the council decides to use that against you, it might be a good idea to warn Lauryn," I suggested, wanting to offer something practical, something besides doubt and meaningless comfort. "It would save her needless pain."

"I love my wife, Alex. I'd never hurt her."

"I know." I smiled suddenly, easing the tension. "I just wanted to make sure you weren't in that kind of trouble."

* * * *

I decided to stir up my own brand of trouble because matters were still a little odd, despite Jules' apparent sincerity. Somehow I couldn't quite believe I was in any kind of danger. Yet instinct was screaming for caution, and I'd found out often enough the hard way it was usually best to pay heed.

So I tacked a note to my cottage door early the next morning, careful to wedge it in the very same groove I always used for such a purpose. No one should be alarmed by my disappearance. I'd vanished before when there'd been some days between the children's lessons. Then again, if Jules and Elena were plotting something nasty, they might be a trifle concerned. Honestly, I hoped they would be. With a satisfied grin, I shouldered my worn leather travel pack and set off for the one place in all of Tuldamoran that set my teeth on edge.

Chapter Five

Tramping along dirt roads to Ardenna was thirsty work; so naturally, I made sure my route passed through the lush Marain Valley with its irresistible vineyards. Row upon row of vines stretched across the valley floor as far as the appreciative eye could see. With an extra bottle or two tucked in my bulging pack, I made my way toward the Kieren River and met up with an old weathered seaman. I traded a bottle for a chilly ride upriver to the outskirts of Elena's fortress capital.

When we came in sight of the city nestled within the foothills of the Arditch Mountains and flanked by thick woods, I thanked the old man. Scurrying back to dry land, I searched, once I was alone, for traces of the old tunnel. It led from the borders of Blane Woods through the outlying districts of the city to the castle library. Through a series of connecting tunnels, I could easily make my way unseen to either the old storage rooms or the throne room where Elena held formal daily audiences. The tunnel network provided an easy way out, and in, for those granted knowledge of the family secret.

If it still existed.

I muttered an oath in frustration as darkness started to fall. Hugging my wool cloak tighter around my shoulders, I was on the point of giving up my search for the night when I stumbled over the roots of the old lightning-split oak. With a grin of satisfaction, I reached into my pack for one of the small torches I'd tucked away just in case.

Recalling the instructions, I moved a child's height to the left and two heights forward. Spun around halfway, and a half-height to the right. Then gave a stifled shout for joy as I cleared the dense underbrush from the hidden rock and uncovered the opening in the hillside. With a look around to make sure I was alone, I lit the torch and poked it through the narrow entry. Peeking in, I saw by a swift inspection of the dark, chilly shadows the tunnel appeared still passable. Tossing my pack in first, I shoved through the narrow crevice, far smaller than I recalled as a child, and into the cave. The smooth path was in good condition, untouched by weather and the constant tread of boots. I wondered whether Elena used it on her recent midnight visit to Port Alain.

Carefully placing the torch in a bracket along the smooth wall, I crawled halfway through the crevice to cover the entrance with undergrowth to keep it safe from prying eyes. Not wanting to pass the night in the dark here within the tunnel entrance, or, indeed, waste the torch by keeping it lit all night, I immediately started along the cool passage. I thrust the torch above and ahead of me, alert for bats, which I feared would get caught in my curls. Conserving my strength, I kept a steady, relaxed pace as the passage started its gradual climb.

By the time the torch was half consumed, I knew I was almost there. Determined not to waste time, and promising myself a well-deserved rest at the end of the climb, I trudged onward through the narrow passage. I was flanked by smooth walls, unbroken save for occasional traces of dampness. In a daze from the monotony and stillness, I missed my footing as three steps appeared suddenly at my feet, leading to the fortress library. Off to the side, a narrow branch of the tunnel extended left toward the old storage rooms, and to my right toward the throne room. I went right and soon found myself blocked by a similar set of steps.

With a grin of infantile spite and mischief, I inched onto the ledge and pushed the hidden door ajar. It was safely covered by the tapestry behind the throne, and I plopped wearily to the ground. With one last cautious glance around, I extinguished the torch, rested my tired head on my traveling satchel, and fell immediately into a surprisingly dreamless sleep.

* * * *

Hollow thuds vibrating beneath my head jarred my skull against the leather sack. I scrambled groggily to sit upright. Lords of the sea, I'd forgotten how Elena's steward would brutally pound the Tuldamoran staff against the dais. If I hadn't slept against the leather pack, my ears would still be ringing.

No small wonder I despised this town.

A thin slice of light from the audience chamber shone through the open door. Crawling with unaccustomed stealth, I poked my head around the doorway to confirm the thick tapestry was still in place between the throne and the tunnel. Satisfied, I rummaged through my pack for some plain bread, quiet food that wouldn't reveal my presence. Edging back through the partially open door, I leaned against the wall just as Elena settled herself, heavy silk robe of office rustling, on the throne mere inches above me.

Eyes closed, I listened as she passed judgments and controlled the discussions, impressed by her poise and knowledge despite myself. Elena's voice conveyed a calm awareness of everything and everyone in the high-vaulted audience chamber. Formal, polite, and patient, she responded without hesitation to each grievant, treating all with equal courtesy as her father had always done. It was hard not to be bored after a short time with her near-perfect royal poise and sense of fairness over matters in which I had not the slightest interest, not even from an academic perspective. I found it difficult to stay awake, particularly during a merchant's unceasing drone. How could she stand it? I fell asleep, waking shortly thereafter with a painful jerk as my head snapped forward.

Alert, uncertain whether I'd given myself away by snoring, I listened for a change in Elena's voice to indicate she'd heard any noise behind the tapestry. Her voice, however, registered barely veiled resentment and irritation, a distinct change from earlier. Curious, I listened, careful to make no sound as I inched nearer the tapestry.

"Your answer isn't very helpful, my lord mage." Elena's voice was tense with controlled anger. I was all too familiar with that tone.

"Unfortunately, no." A clipped answer omitted reference to Elena's title with rude intent.

"I was under the assumption the Ardenna Crown Council of Mages existed to provide information and counsel to the crown. Or," she paused, "have I been under the wrong impression all these years?"

At some point, while I slept, Elena lost her exquisite politeness. Not that I blamed her. But with whom was she speaking?

"You were not misled."

"But?"

An artful pause. "But we're not spies and certainly don't lower ourselves to such a pursuit."

As some of your friends do? I'd never heard of any mage reading minds, but I hastily shoved all thoughts of eavesdropping and spying aside. Just in case.

"I haven't requested you to spy, only asked your opinion of the raids along the coast of Belbridge Cliffs," Elena responded tightly.

"Didn't Duke Barlow provide that information?"

Instinctively, I braced for the attack on Jules' good name and ugly accusations of unforgivable treachery. I imagined it would be followed by slanderous remarks about me and my renegade ancestry, curious as to how Elena would manage it.

"He did, yes."

"Then I've nothing more to offer. The duke's word is trustworthy," the mage responded with cool politeness.

Where in flameblasted hells was the accusation? Or even the hint of one? Had I somehow missed it?

"Then it seems we've nothing further to say to one another, Lord Ravess."

Lord Ravess. Charlton Ravess, firemage and head of the Crown Council, long white hair, deep brown malevolent eyes. I hated the bastard since the day I clumsily walked into him some ten years ago. I was trailing happily after Elena on the way to her suite after a visit to the stables. Ravess had snarled at me and raised a hand to strike, but Elena stepped between us. Without a word, he spun on his heels, muttering a gutter insult Elena chose to ignore. I never heard the insult, only the last two words he spat over his shoulder, eyes locking cruelly with mine.

Orphan child.

I shook my head to chase away the hateful memories, but there were no more words between Elena and the mage. If Ravess believed Jules guilty of treachery, or me, how could he miss the opportunity to hurt Elena with words of betrayal by her closest friends before an audience? Lords of the sea, what were Jules and Elena plotting? And why? And given they were my closest friends, why were they keeping the truth from me?

Chapter Six

Confused and dismayed, I returned to Port Alain, pursuing some elusive truths of my own. "When are you going to hire more groundskeepers?" I asked Rosanna, a few days later, watching as she skillfully dug around some roots to tug out what I judged to be a tenacious weed.

"When I'm too old to get down on my knees," she answered, tugging harder, with no indication of any surprise at my abrupt reappearance. "Which means, not for quite some time."

"Here, let me help." I knelt down beside her in the moist earth and stretched out a hand.

"Get away." She slapped my hand back. "I know you mean well, Alex, but you don't know the difference between a weed, a winter fern, or a summer rose."

I laughed, not the least bit insulted.

When she saw I was at a safe distance from her beloved blossoms, she started digging again. "You didn't really come here to help me weed, did you?"

I took a deep breath, and let it out slowly. And another; keeping watch on her busy movements. She arched an inquisitive brow before turning her attention back to another stubborn weed. I took another deep breath. "Where's the other half of my mother's copper pendant?"

Rosanna stopped digging, spade stuck in the dirt as she leaned on it for support. She turned her gray-streaked head to give me a long measuring stare. Unreadable, almost.

I grinned, sitting on one of her decorative rocks. "If my interpretation of that expression is correct, you want to know why it took me all these years to ask."

"Precisely."

"I'm a little slow."

"And you're teaching my grandchildren."

"Well?"

"These dreams of yours are becoming a problem." She fidgeted with her old, patched, woolen gardening trousers to loosen the material at her knees and started digging again. "Not to mention your recent unannounced disappearance and how it might conceivably have spurred you to ask this long overdue question."

"I wasn't talking about dreams. And my disappearance had nothing whatsoever to do with my question about mother's pendant." I flushed beneath her slow, steady appraisal.

Rosanna rolled her eyes in weary exasperation, absently rubbing soil from her cheek, which only streaked the dirt more. "Whenever you have these dreams, you start asking me all manner of questions about your mother. And I don't believe your holiday is coincidental. Something's not quite right with you lately. I'm not sure what, and I'm worried about you."

"Why don't you ever talk about my father?"

"Has someone been sneaking spoiled honey in your tea?"

"You never talk about him. Why not?"

"You never ask, and there's not much to tell." She started digging again with renewed fervor. "He came from Glynnswood."

"Was he a criminal?"

A dark look flashed in her eyes. "Of course not."

"Then—"

"Alex," she sighed wearily, "he was a quiet, gentle man who loved your mother very deeply. But I didn't know him long. Emila grew up in Port Alain, but Sernyn Keltie was a stranger, though always courteous to me. All Glynnswood people are infallibly courteous. It's obvious you didn't inherit that particular trait." Rosanna returned her attention to the weeds.

"Where's the other half?"

"Your mother gave it to a friend. A trusted friend." At my look of impatience, she shrugged matter-of-factly. "Don't ask me who, because I don't know."

"What do you know?"

"Only that he's a mage of one kind or another. And," she added slowly, "she gave it to him in case something happened to her."

"Why not give it to my father?"

Rosanna looked away for a moment, and then back again. Her eyes were utterly unreadable this time. "Your father wasn't a mage, and Emila thought you might have a peculiar sort of mage talent, particularly since Sernyn was from Glynnswood."

"Damnation, Rosanna!" I snapped. "Even my mother was part of this flameblasted conspiracy."

"I can't believe I trust you to teach my grandchildren. Not an intelligent thought in your head. Not one. Not even a hint."

"Don't try to sidetrack me. Did he ever come to visit or ask about me?"

"Who?" When I threatened to pull out her precious blossoms, she didn't blink. "No." And waved me away with a careless gesture.

"Then why bother to give him half a pendant? Unless he came in secret and saw for himself I wasn't a mage and didn't need his help." I thought for a long moment, playing with the top of my scuffed boots. Rosanna continued weeding as though I weren't even there, humming softly. "When did she give the other half of the pendant to you? The one that I have?"

"I see we're not finished yet."

"Rosanna, please—"

"Alex. Alex." She sighed, her voice and expression suddenly serious. "Your mother gave it to me three months before you were born, along with the oak chest."

"Did she expect to die?" I tried to control the trembling in my voice and failed miserably.

Rosanna's eyes grew sad with remembered grief as she sat on her heels, appraising me in silence. "No matter their good health, many women fear childbirth. Emila was no different. She was afraid something might happen and she might not survive."

"Why not?" I asked softly, kneeling beside the older woman again, ignoring the pebbles cutting into my knees. Rosanna turned her face away, but not before I caught the gleam of unshed tears. I tugged like a bewildered child at the sleeve of her dirt-smeared tunic. "Why not?"

"She was ill in the last months, in terrible pain," Rosanna admitted slowly. "Your father sent for healers from Ardenna and Port Alain. Not one of them could determine what was causing the pain. Or stop it."

I drew my hand back from her sleeve, not wanting uncontrolled trembling to betray me. "Don't you see? It was me, Rosanna. I caused the pain and destroyed her." Standing upright, I brushed tears from my cheeks with the back of my hand like a child.

Rosanna spun to look at me, eyes brimming with angry tears. Grabbing my arm before I could step back, she pulled herself to her feet. "Stop this, Alex. Stop this, now. I thought you'd banished this foolishness long ago. Your mother would be heartbroken if she knew how you blamed yourself when you had nothing to do with it." I tried to disentangle myself, but Rosanna clung to my arm, tightening her grip. "Stop it." I refused to look at her. "It wasn't your fault," she whispered painfully, shaking my arm. "I know. I was there when she died."

"And right before she died, I was born." Prying her dirt-streaked fingers from my tunic, I freed my arm. "You're wrong. It was my fault. I don't know how or why, but it was me who caused the pain and anguish. She should never have given birth to me."

Chapter Seven

After our unpleasant little chat, I kept my distance from Rosanna. When her son approached me some days later to go riding with him, I wondered whether she'd nudged him in my direction.

"I'm going back to Port Alain tomorrow morning. If you'd like to come along and meet that sea captain . . ." Jules left the suggestion hanging in the air between us as we cantered along the road.

"The only reason I accepted your invitation to go riding is because you told me you'd be pleasant company. Obviously, you lied." I scowled at him.

My horse snorted in agreement, prompting a smile from Jules as he adjusted his bright green cloak against the breeze. "I thought the captain might make better company, but I also assumed you'd rip out my heart and force it down my throat if I made today's adventure a party of three. Or two, if I sent him without me."

"You assumed correctly." Flinging back a strand of loose curls, I added, "Though I don't usually need a reason to feel the urge to strangle you."

"Now, Alex." He reined in his horse as we neared the end of the open stretch of coastal road, well-maintained by Elena's network of local craftsman paid by our taxes. Waves crashed below, not so far we were safe from frigid, salty spray. "All right to go a little further?"

"Sure. I haven't been out riding in a while. It'll do me good to be reminded just how much my muscles can ache." I slanted a look in his direction. Jules appeared to be relaxed, a perfect opportunity to catch the devil unawares. "Has Elena sent any further word about suspicion against you or me in Ardenna?"

With a long-suffering sigh, Jules kept his eyes on the road ahead. "Only that it's getting worse."

"Anyone in particular speaking out against us?"

Jules frowned, causing lines to appear in his tanned forehead. "Every time someone mentions my name in front of Charlton Ravess, you remember him, Alex? The firemage and chief mage of the Crown Council?"

"I'll never forget him."

Jules slanted me an odd look I chose to ignore. "Ravess is the primary person swiping viciously at my reputation. He seems to be behind the worst rumors." With a glance toward the open sea, Jules hunched down into the shelter of his cloak as the breeze whipped it back.

Not when I was eavesdropping. "I should think Elena walks a fine line with Lord Ravess then," I said evenly, without a hint of doubt, "defending you without betraying her duty as queen should you be guilty."

Jules idly scanned the road ahead to the side where denser undergrowth started to line the road. "She's always defending my honor, urging Ravess to produce evidence of my guilt and put an end to his talk. You're lucky he's not focusing on you."

Maybe I slept through that part of the royal discussion, but the tone of the exchange I overheard wasn't quite as Jules led me to believe. Ravess' mockery at mention of Jules was no different than his tone when addressing Elena. He despised them both and thought them beneath him, but gave not a hint of Jules' treason.

"Can we do anything to help her?" My feigned concern hopefully masked my confusion, though Jules seemed distracted.

"I can't see what, not at the moment, anyway."

"Is she keeping an eye on him?"

"Yes. Especially since she heard there's to be a secret meeting between Ravess and the head mages of all the local councils in two weeks. You know Elena." He smiled with charm. "She'll infiltrate that meeting somehow."

"Dangerous. Should you send your own spies to help out?"

"I offered, but she'd rather I stay tucked out of sight, keeping watch with your help." Brushing a hand through wind-blown light brown hair, he turned to me, adding neutrally, "However you can manage that."

I didn't bother to reply, stifled an urge to scream, and turned away. Along the seaside of the coast road, the low stone wall ran for miles east and west of Port Alain. At this part of the stretch, heading toward Belbridge Cliffs, low shrubbery and an odd assortment of trees grew dense, making the road appear darker, more illusion than reality. I guided my restless horse forward, leaving Jules behind so I could think away from his lying eyes.

"Alex!"

I spun at the unexpected urgency in Jules' voice and watched in shock as two black-clad, masked figures toppled Jules from his horse. In mere seconds, they dragged him to the cover of the dense growth, taking advantage of the natural shadows. Turning my horse to come to his aid, I was shoved from behind and lost my seat. I smacked my side painfully against the hard ground, struggling to catch my breath as my arms were bound behind me. I kicked savagely, blindly, until I could no longer move. Fearful for Jules, I craned my neck to find him trussed as tightly as myself. Anger flared in his eyes as he struggled against the rope holding him captive, though he stopped as a sword point lightly touched his chest.

"Easy, my lord duke." The sword point glided smoothly through his open cloak to slice through the silk tunic.

Jules held himself still.

"That's better."

I strained to detect an accent or any clue to our assailant's identity. Jules met my gaze across the open ground between us. Pleading. Pleading? What could I do? I tried to move, but stopped involuntarily as my head was yanked backward. The other thug grabbed a fistful of my hair, twisting it.

"Tell your lady companion to keep still," advised Jules' assailant, tapping the sword point over Jules' heart, nearly making my heart stop.

"Alex." Jules' voice was a croak, though his eyes still pleaded.

Frantic, I tried to figure out what I could do.

"Now, my lord duke." The sword point danced along Jules' chest, slicing the tunic further, drawing a thin streak of blood along his exposed skin. "I have a message."

Jules' green eyes widened, but he kept very silent and very still.

"A warning, Duke Barlow." The black-clad assailant stepped back from Jules, running the sword point upward to his neck before removing it entirely. "We know you're anxious to slip into the queen's bed. And we know," his voice held a chilly smile, "she's just as anxious to keep you out."

Jules shut his eyes in denial and pain.

"So take heed, Duke Barlow. We've got our eyes on you, should you consider making the queen pay for your humiliation. And," the voice turned in my direction, "we're watching the schoolmistress, too. Don't be foolish. Either of you." With a muttered word to the rest of his party, the man vanished through the dense undergrowth as though it was all a nightmare.

* * * *

"If you don't stop cursing and hold still, I won't be able to loosen the knot," I snapped in frustration as the rope slipped from my aching grasp for the third and hopefully last time.

We were sitting back to back along the side of the road, still in the shadow of the dense undergrowth. Obediently, as though he were one of my young charges, Jules sat still, surprising me, though his cursing never stopped. Trying to get my smaller fingers to manipulate the rough cord, I felt the knot loosening.

"There," I grunted, sweating heavily beneath my woolen cloak from the exertion. "That should do it." I toppled to my side, unbalanced, as the idiot freed his hands. "Damn it, Jules."

"Sorry," he mumbled. "Here." He pulled me upright. "Now you hold still. I'll free your arms. There."

Briskly rubbing my arms to ease the ache and get the blood flowing again, I leaned over to untie my feet and rubbed my ankles. "Interesting message. Remind me never to go riding with you again. I'd be better off spending time with the sea captain."

"I have to warn Elena," he said quietly, ignoring my sarcasm. Helping me to my feet, Jules stood still a moment, gazing out to sea. As though in a fog, bewildered and confused, he shook his head. "I won't let them succeed. If this warning is from the Crown Council—" He stopped abruptly and walked in the direction of the horses. They had only strayed a little way up the road, munching on the nearby grass as though nothing extraordinary happened.

"What?" I pressed, catching up with him, every joint aching from the effort.

"I don't know." He shrugged. "That's just it. I don't know what to do to protect myself, and you, and Elena from this mess. If only we knew what they were planning, I wouldn't feel so helpless."

Helpless. That reminded me.

"Jules?" I said softly, tugging at the edge of his dust-spattered cloak. One hand resting on the saddle, he turned around. "You had a look in your eye when we were held captive. As though you thought I should do something. And I haven't the slightest idea what you thought I should do."

To my utter surprise, he flushed scarlet, and stiffly adjusted the skewed saddle before mounting his fidgeting horse. "I thought you could do something," he admitted, ill at ease, cringing at the sudden under-standing in my eyes. "I thought—"

What an idiot I'd been.

"You thought," I interrupted coldly, waving my arm in the direction of the incoming tide, "I should be able to call the waves over the seawall and sweep our assailants away? Or something appropriately seamage-like?" I asked, unable to keep the bitterness from my voice. He didn't answer, or even have the courage to look at me. "Well?"

"Listen, Alex—"

"No. You listen, Jules." Before he could bolt, I grabbed the edge of his cloak while he steadied his nervous horse. "I don't know how to make it any clearer to you. I'm not a seamage or any other kind of flameblasted mage. I'm sorry, truly. I wish it were otherwise, but it's not."

"Alex, listen—" he pleaded, expression miserable.

"I'll listen," I snapped, climbing onto my own restless horse, "but only when you're willing to stop this idiocy." Without waiting for an answer, I nudged my horse in the direction of Port Alain, and left Jules to find his own way back.

* * * *

For a quiet, gentle-tempered woman, Lauryn continued to knock at my cottage door, refusing to leave me alone. "I know you're in there." She started to kick at the door while she continued to knock.

I walked across my cluttered sitting room, stepping gingerly over scattered piles of books, to let her in before she damaged the door. Lauryn stood in the doorway, hand and foot upraised to strike again. In silence, she eyed me from head to toe before walking past, muttering something I couldn't quite hear. But the hint of what she might have said left me speechless. Lauryn never cursed. She gracefully removed a rather cumbersome pile of books from the armchair nearest the fireplace and sat, her whole manner radiating annoyance and disgust.

I leaned against the closed door. "Something wrong?"

"You."

"Me?"

"Don't play innocent. You haven't been to the manor in days except to give the children their lessons. Then you're nowhere to be found the very moment lessons are over. And then—"

"Lauryn—"

"Don't interrupt me, Alex," she said crossly, blue eyes flashing as I'd never seen before. At least, not at me. "Jules and the boys think you're angry at them. Rosanna thinks you're avoiding her. And no one has the decency to tell me why they think all these things. I don't know what to think. And neither does Khrista."

I started to laugh.

"What's so damned funny?" She shoved an auburn braid back over her shoulder.

"You. I'm sorry, but this tantrum is rather out of character for you."

Light blue eyes softened. "I'm worried about you. We all are."

"I'm all right."

"No, you're not. I know you often stay away, but something's not quite right this time. I wish you wouldn't forget . . ." She hesitated and looked down at her hands, which started to fiddle independently with the edge of her forest green tunic.

"Forget what?"

She paused, appraising me again. "Rosanna's never happy when you stay away so long. And it's been unusually long. None of us are happy when you do that. Alex, we're family. I think you forget on purpose because it's easier to be alone and not have to care, or run the risk someone will hurt you or make demands on you," she blurted.

It wasn't easy to keep my expression neutral when what I hungered to do was weep my heart out, or smash a hundred thousand glasses against the wall or, even better, deny the painful truth of her words. As Lauryn watched, appalled at her outburst, I knew she saw through every emotion that flashed across my face.

"I'm sorry," she said gently. "I've no right to say horrid things like that."

"You, of all people, have a right," I said slowly. "You're the least likely to make demands on me or pass judgment."

Lauryn shook her head. "I'm no less guilty, Alex. I want you mindful of where you belong. I'm Rosanna's daughter-in-law, and I'm so much a part of her family. How can you be any less?" When orphan child didn't quite trust herself to answer, Lauryn mumbled another crestfallen apology and stood to leave.

"Lauryn—"

She turned to face me, a guarded expression in her eyes.

"I'm sorry. But there are times I need to be alone. It's not that I don't care."

"Don't you think I know that?" She ignored my shaking hand as I clenched my fist and shoved it out of sight. "You're still not sleeping well, are you?"

"No," I admitted, grateful for an acceptable excuse, "and you know how contentious I get when I'm tired."

"And need a good meal," she commented, sounding nothing more than a mother. "You've lost too much weight. I'll tell Rosanna you'll join us for the evening meal tonight." Before I could protest, she added, "I'll even threaten Jules with bodily harm if he mentions the sea captain in Port Alain," she said solemnly. "Even once."

"That bastard—" As she finally laughed at my indignant outburst and released the tension, it occurred to me Jules had probably not said anything about the attack. "I'll come on one condition."

"Playing hard to catch?"

"No. It's just I'd like to disappear again for a few days, but I don't want the children to miss their lessons. Could you cover for me without telling anyone?" At Lauryn's raised brow, I added, "At least, not right away."

She tugged on her braid, thinking, eyes fixed on mine. "You won't tell me where you're going." Blatantly not a question.

"At the moment, I'd rather not."

"I didn't think so." She nodded once. "All right." One slender finger pointed straight at my heart. "But it'll cost you." I crossed my arms and leaned against the cottage wall, waiting patiently for her terms. "Dinner this evening and dinner when you return from whatever little adventure you're plotting."

I considered the trade. Not too costly. "Deal."

"Rosanna and the boys will be pleased," she said, making her way back to the cottage door. "And, Alex," she smiled with just a hint of uncharacteristic smugness, "I'm not stupid. I know just how much you can afford to pay."

* * * *

And pay I did, but everyone was well behaved, making me suspicious all around. I headed back to the path that led to my cottage after a marvelous meal of lamb roast, sweet onions, and brandied carrots. At the sound of a voice hailing me, I stopped at the gate. Kerrie, the Barlows' steward and Khrista's lover, gasped for air as he caught up to me, dark hair tousled from his scramble.

"How is it possible Khrista let you out of her sight?"

The young man grinned, flushed with embarrassment. "Only until she's read the twins a story and tucked them into bed. Then she'll hunt me down." His expression grew abruptly serious, warning me.

"You were eying me all night. Something wrong?"

"I don't know," he admitted. "I didn't want to say anything in front of the others. You know how they all fret over you."

"I wish they didn't. Not so much, anyway."

"They mean well."

"So do you. Obviously," I smiled, erasing my frown to reassure Kerrie, "since they have you fretting, too. What's on your mind?"

"Jules and I were in town earlier to look at the shipment of wool that just arrived. When we were done, he headed back, and I stopped at the Seaman's Berth."

"That where you get your news?"

"Some of it, yes. Chester asked me to pass a word on to you. There's a gentleman staying there, been there a while. Name of Anders Perrin."

I shrugged. "Don't know him."

"He's been asking about you."

I thought about the stranger who eavesdropped on my conversation with Jules some weeks ago. "Why?"

"Chester has no idea, but he's worried."

"If he's the same gentleman who was there—"

"When you and Jules stopped in together one morning some weeks ago?" Kerrie asked, nodding at my expression. "Same one. Is that good or bad?"

"I don't know, but Jules is keeping an eye on him. So far, the man's been wandering around the town, seeing the sights."

"And asking about you and the mage council. Something else, Alex. Neal Brandt's been asking Chester's little girl about you, too."

A shiver crept up my spine. "I've got nothing he's interested in."

"Chester thinks it has to do with your mother." Kerrie flushed. "Sorry, Alex. I know you don't like talking about her in connection with the mage councils, but the innkeeper wanted you to be careful."

"I will."

"Damn hard time to be a mage, if you ask me. Everyone's edgy."

"So I noticed."

* * * *

Some days later, I followed the Marain Valley route north again, back to Ardenna, but not through the tunnel this time. My destination was different. I timed my visit to coincide with the secret meeting Jules mentioned days earlier. The one Elena was going to infiltrate. I wanted to see for myself what was going on. A short distance outside the city gates, I stopped for a brief rest along the side of the road. The Dunneal fortress rose in an attempt at majesty from the heart of the city, turrets stretching to the heavens. Around the huge structure, Ardenna spread out in haphazard fashion. Merchants, courtiers, crafters, military troops, mages, whores, and visitors, all with their own brand of peculiar needs etched out their private niches.

Busy, impersonal, overcrowded, noisy, and rude, the city represented everything I despised. It took every ounce of self-control not to turn and flee back to the sanity of my simple cottage. But I was here for a number of reasons. Not only to keep an eye on Charlton Ravess, and possibly Seamage Brandt, but also to give Jules the benefit of the doubt once more. To see if I could find out anything more about his supposed treachery. That reason was far more important. I needed some final reassurance my closest friends weren't lying to me, that it was just a misunderstanding, and I had nothing to fret about.

With a deep sigh, I scanned the horizon. Shouldering my pack, I approached the south gate in time to mingle with a boisterous group of traveling actors. Trying to be inconspicuous, I kept a steady pace as I passed through the gate, heading toward the mage district and the Crown Council's lavish residences at its center. I stopped at a vendor to buy hot cinnamon bread and spiced beef, with a ridiculously high-priced glass of Marain wine. After which I waited impatiently until near dark to make my unobtrusive way to Ravess' home. Taking my cue from Jules' comments, I calculated the next night marked the clandestine gathering of council mages from the duchies. A gathering my rogue mother would've avoided at all costs, unless she wanted to spy and gather information.

Using the dark to its full advantage, I made my way over the low stone wall separating Ravess' residence from those of the other mages. Either he protected himself by arcane means, in which case, I'd never be able to tell, or he was arrogant enough to believe himself invulnerable. I took the risk he was arrogant. Creeping around the side of the house, I caught sight of a lamp shining in a back window. With all the stealth I possessed, which wasn't very much, I inched my way against the wall and peeked through the open window. The mage's distinctive thick white hair was my first sight, and then his profile. His sharply defined features were unforgettable, particularly when those rich brown eyes filled with loathing.

The mage was engrossed in a book. Turning a page, he reached for a glass of clear liquid. If I were lucky, it would be poison. Swiftly, I ducked out of sight as he looked around in an almost absent manner. Maybe he did use arcane protection.

I flattened myself against the wall and slithered farther away, still keeping the mage in sight. A flicker of lamplight caught my attention as the flame grew larger, the chamber brighter. An effortless maneuver by the firemage increased the light, as effortless as Neal Brandt's trick with water weeks earlier, as effortless as my own trickery years ago.

Were they all right? Was it fear that kept my own magic so deeply hidden, even from me? Unexpectedly, the gentleman from the Seaman's Berth drifted into my thoughts, sea-gray eyes locked on my face. Who was he? And why was he asking about me? Was the Crownmage real? Was I in danger I really didn't understand?

Heaving a melodramatic sigh of disgust, I crouched low to the ground, making my way to a safer position where I could still keep an eye on the window. I settled my cloak tighter around my shoulders, prepared for a long, sleepless night.

A long sleepless night and day later, I ached in every bone and joint of my miserable body. All for nothing. The firemage hadn't budged from his home, but he hadn't any visitors either. Maybe his plans changed, or maybe Elena's spies were misinformed, or maybe I was just wasting time. But instinct was screaming at me again, and I forced myself to stay one more night. Had I miscalculated the days? I tallied them in my head according to what Jules told me. No mistake.

Uneasy because nothing changed, I crawled to the nearest inn and slept for a full day and night before heading south to Port Alain, dazed and bewildered, still unsure of my friends.

Chapter Eight

"This squall isn't natural." My comment was directed at Jules as we watched the dark, distant cloudbank rapidly glide across the horizon and turn with distinct sharpness toward our ship.

"It's just a bay storm."

Didn't he notice the swift change in direction? "Out of season, from the wrong direction, and utterly controlled."

I still wasn't at ease with him. Well, he wasn't at ease with me either. Lauryn seemed surprised when I agreed to join them on this last family outing before the coolness of autumn put an end to marine activities. Practically part of the family at this point, Kerrie came along, too, as did Brendan. Rosanna, the only one absent, preferred to spend the afternoon on solid ground. From the looks of the oncoming storm, I wished I were with her.

Jules squinted into the distance, light brown hair tossed by the rising wind gusts, his tone hushed as he acknowledged the truth. "You're right." Turning to Lauryn, a little way behind us, he kept his voice calm, though his grip on the helm revealed whitened knuckles. "Get the boys below."

She managed to collar the twins and drag them, protesting loudly, in the direction of the cramped cabin.

Brendan, opposite me, held onto the railing as the ship rolled and pointed to the threatening cloudbank. "Ships."

The twins weren't quite through the tiny door when Brendan made his discovery. Lauryn struggled as they slid through her hands and ran directly into my path.

"Get below. Now."

Carey started to protest, but Hunter grabbed him by his tunic sleeve. After a hasty appraising glance at me, he dragged his brother past their mother and into the cabin.

As the door shut behind her, Lauryn smiled in appreciation, catching her balance with elegant grace as the ship lurched. "Trouble?"

"I think so." I looked ahead to where Khrista and Kerrie were helping Brendan with the sails as the swells rose to a dangerous height. "Jules, can you see any identifying sails on those ships?"

Jules squinted into the distance again, shaking his head. "No. Sorry." He met my gaze with a trace of anxiety in his own, quickly banished. "If they're marauders, do you think the storm is connected?"

I grabbed the wooden railing as the sleek ship lurched again. "The mage council in Belbridge Cliffs might be trying to fight them by storm. The direction of the squall and our presence here might just be coincidence."

"If that's true, I wish them luck," he muttered, wiping spray from his face as the ship slammed down against the rising sea, "though it's not doing us any good."

"Perhaps we should turn back to port?" I hugged my cloak closer as the air chilled. "We can always continue this adventure on dry land."

"What in hell do you think I'm trying to do?"

Lauryn raised an auburn brow in my direction at his sharp tone.

When I started to shrug, dismissing his attitude, my attention was caught by a sight that chilled my blood. "Brendan!" I pointed to the cabin hatch as Carey wiggled his tiny body through.

Muttering an outraged oath under his breath, Brendan flew past Jules. Grabbing for a sure handhold wherever he could find one as the ship rocked against the rough seas, he yelled something inaudible at Carey. I ran forward to help Brendan, though whether to drag Carey back to safety or throttle his slender neck I wasn't sure. Not until I heard the panicked scream and inevitable splash.

"Carey!" Lauryn screamed, running madly past me, her face white with fear.

By the time Lauryn and I reached the forward railing, we were soaked from sea spray. Brown hair plastered to his forehead, Kerrie dove in after the boy, both of them disappearing as the swells rose and fell. Jules was frantically trying to get some measure of control over the ship as we edged perilously close to the storm, unable to turn back.

"Jules, there..." Khrista pointed landward when she caught sight of the two bodies struggling to stay afloat.

I grabbed a coil of rope and threw one end overboard in Kerrie's direction. When it fell short, I pulled the rope back in to try again. Brendan grabbed it from me with a mumbled apology and cast the soaked hemp back into the bay. Brown eyes watching its graceful arc over the water, Kerrie caught the slick rope before it slipped through his fingers. Carey held in his arms, close to his chest, Kerrie wrapped the rope firmly around his hands and held on tight.

Brendan, Khrista, and I struggled to pull them back in, their weight doubled from being soaked in the frigid sea. Safely back on deck, Kerrie shivered violently, teeth chattering. Carey, sheltered in his embrace, lay still. Lauryn grabbed the limp body from Brendan's arms after the young man freed him from Kerrie's desperate hold. She rubbed his limbs with vigor to get the boy warm and start his blood flowing again.

"Let me have him."

"No, Alex." Lauryn stared wild-eyed at me and then at Jules. He was still fighting the surging waves, though green eyes darted anxiously at his son before turning back to the helm, Khrista at his side.

"Lauryn . . ." I struggled to keep my voice even. "I can help him."

Ignoring her maternal terror, I pried Carey's icy body from her shaking, resistant hands. When she finally released him, I placed Carey flat on the deck, and turned his small, curly head to the side, gently pressing on his chest. I squeezed the drowning waters from his body, over and over. He finally gagged and choked, the skinny little body jerking awkwardly as he coughed.

"Get him inside. Keep him warm and dry." I met Lauryn's relieved expression with one of my own. Behind his mother, huddled by the cabin door, Hunter stared, tears streaming down his reddened cheeks. When I crouched down, he ran into my embrace and put his arms around my neck, holding me tight. "It's okay," I whispered. "He's okay now."

While Hunter calmed, the storm vanished as suddenly as it appeared. Clear, seasonal skies and a steady breeze pushed the tendrils of wispy clouds far out to sea, waves flattening as the sea calmed.

"The ships are gone." Kerrie shivered under the heavy cloak Lauryn found for him. "Lost, or forced to retreat?"

"Forced to retreat," Jules said quietly, staring out to sea. "At least the mages in Belbridge Cliffs fight back."

I looked over Hunter's trembling head to where Jules controlled the sails, bitterness and cool anger in his eyes as he turned to face me. Instead of answering that challenge, I scooped Hunter into my arms as I stood unsteadily and went below in the cramped cabin to see about Carey.

* * * *

Harsh, furious knocking pounded at the cottage door not long after I'd started a blazing fire to chase the chill from my aching bones and from my heart. "If you don't open this door, Alex, I swear I'll tear it down with my bare hands."

Sighing heavily, dreading this confrontation, yet needing to see it through, I opened the door and turned my back on Jules.

"My son almost died out there."

I clenched my fists. Slowly, so very slowly, I forced myself to face Jules. Lords of the sea knew how I managed to keep my tone neutral. "Have you come to thank me for helping him?"

That stopped Jules for a mere second. "It should never have happened."

"Because I should have controlled the seas?"

Jules' eyes had a dangerous glint to them, making me more uneasy than I should have reason to feel. "Yes. The seas, Alex. And the wind." His accusation was more sullen than angry.

"And the wind?" I repeated, confused. What was he mumbling about? Wind? My mother was a seamage. If I were any kind of mage, chances were I'd be a seamage, according to mother's notes. I took a small step backward and leaned against the arm of the nearest chair.

"We were in danger." He ignored my blank look, though whether he was even aware of it, I couldn't tell. "Just as we were along the sea road . . ."

Something in the way he connected the two incidents made my stomach lurch as though I were back at the ship's railing, rolling with the storm-tossed waves. Something in my expression must have finally made an impression on Jules because he fell silent. Impossible. Wasn't it?

"Did Elena plan the attack on the sea road?" When he hesitated, I jumped up and inched closer, unsure where my thoughts were heading, though instinct was screaming so loud it was giving me a blinding headache. Trouble very close ahead. I was afraid to go on, more afraid to stop.

"Of course not! Don't be ridiculous. Why would Elena do something like that?"

But I'd caught the merest hint of hesitation. And Jules knew it. I edged closer, backing him against the cottage wall. "It would seem an opportune way to force your own personal mage to fight back, wouldn't it, Jules? And if Elena dreamed up today's little adventure—"

"She didn't." Jules was immediately defensive, as he flattened himself against the wall, trying hard to scramble away from me. "You know that. I'd never risk my son's life, and neither would Elena."

"You didn't know Carey would be so curious, though, did you? Besides, your mage would have controlled the seas and the wind." And the wind. All color drained from my face as I reached to grab onto something, anything but Jules, for support. He caught me in his arms as I stumbled. I blinked rapidly to clear my head. "You bastard." I snatched his tunic in my fist. "You and Elena think I'm the Crownmage, don't you?"

Jules looked in every possible direction but mine, then pried my fingers from his tunic and guided me toward the nearest armchair, keeping a firm grip on my arm. "Here, sit down."

I threw his protective arms from me in fury. "Don't patronize me! I want the truth, Jules. Now." I forced myself to a measure of calm and confronted Jules as he turned away. Staring into the fireplace, his wool cloak still damp from the storm, Jules looked pitiful, but I had no room for mercy or patience. And I didn't trust him. "If you value any bit of friendship between us—*any* bit," I said coldly, "you'd better speak the truth now."

Jules shivered lightly and squared his shoulders. "We had nothing to do with the squall today. That was coincidental, though we did plan the attack on the sea road, as well as the tale of my being under suspicion of treason," he admitted, still not facing me.

I sat in stony silence, waiting.

"But there is trouble with Meravan and the Crown Council. They don't trust Elena and despise her independence, particularly Firemage Ravess. They want to control the monarchy. Elena thought it best to push you to your potential since you've been avoiding it. She thought if only you'd try once more." He shook his head in dejection.

And who would I hurt this time, if she pushed me again? If I let her push me again? I forced the pain and fear aside. "But you didn't think so?"

His broad shoulders sagged. "I agreed with her. The Port Alain council has been watching you. Damn it, Alex, you saw how Brandt treated you weeks ago. He's been asking questions."

"Of whom?"

"The children, on their way home from the schoolroom. And so has that stranger at the Seaman's Berth."

"Because of my mother's reputation."

"And maybe what happened years ago."

"You believed I was the Crownmage because whatever perverted talent I'd manifested then was so very different," I whispered, unable to believe what I was hearing. "The two of you thought it best to grab my talent for the good of Elena's cause, and to hell with what I thought, or what I wanted. To hell with my friendship."

"That's not true."

"Isn't it? All you want is to pull my strings like a royal puppeteer for the supposed welfare of the people of Tuldamoran." I got up and strode over to the fireplace, forcing Jules to face me. "Did Lord Ravess meet secretly with the council heads?"

Jules blinked in confusion at my abrupt switch. "Yes."

"When?" Another blank stare until I prodded his chest sharply with my finger. "When, Jules?"

74

"One week ago."

"What night?"

He swallowed, knowing full well he was caught in another lie. "Alex, if you'd just listen—"

I grabbed his tunic and shook him. "What flameblasted night?"

Jules calculated in silence, then, "The third night of the week."

"Liar." I took a deep breath to control the urge to smash my fist into his face. "I was there. He didn't budge from the safety of his home. And he didn't have any visitors. I would've noticed a crowd of mages." I released his tunic and shoved him backward in disgust as scarlet crept from his neck to the roots of his hair. "I can't believe you still have the utter arrogance to lie to me even now." I pushed him again in the direction of the door. "Now get out."

"That isn't how it was, or how it is. You know us better than that." When he reached out a hand to touch my face, I slapped it away.

"I'm not sure I do." Turning my back on Jules, I walked toward the small sleeping chamber in the back of the cottage, and stopped. "Maybe I never knew either of you. Maybe you've both been lying to me all my life."

He took a step toward me, but stopped as I raised a threatening hand. "Get out."

And when he finally went, I huddled on my bed, wrapped in grief and heartache, weeping bitterly. And, as Rosanna would have said, very sorry for myself, very betrayed, and very lost. But determined, in the middle of the night, to leave and never come back.

Chapter Nine

It didn't take much time to pack a handful of personal items. Mother's half-pendant, her notes, some clothes, a book or two, and coins I had put aside. Very little else mattered. Though it was still two hours before dawn, I couldn't sleep. Instead, I spent time packing and brooding and writing a brief note for Rosanna, after crumpling four others. Not much to say, I suggested she speak to her son.

I left in the hushed darkness before dawn, still feeling betrayed, alone, and sorry for myself. The trouble was I didn't really know where I wanted to go. Ardenna was out of the question. I'd had quite enough to do with Elena. I knew her troops would watch Belbridge Cliffs to the east because of the recent troubles. So west seemed my only option. West to Bitterhill, and perhaps beyond to Edgecliff and the Bitteredge Mountains, skirting Glynnswood.

I'd never had any desire to find my father's people. Odd, but my thoughts stayed with Mother, maybe because the half-pendant kept her alive for me. Maybe because Rosanna barely spoke of him. Odd, but no matter. Glynnswood wasn't where I was headed. And even if I were, it would have been irrelevant. Three days later, after an uneventful journey halfway to Bitterhill, Elena's guards caught up with me.

It was my own fault, truly. Thinking Jules too ashamed to admit his part in my abrupt departure, and Elena too angry and proud to care, I was careless. All too soon, I found myself trapped under the intense, curious though polite, scrutiny of Elena's guards in a tiny, nondescript inn. Forced to wait for the captain to receive official orders as to what he should do with me, I fell asleep in a cramped, stuffy room, too numb to care.

* * * *

"Alex."

I jerked awake at the soft insistent voice and sat up against the headboard of the lumpy bed. Shutting my eyes against the lamplight, I hoped it was only a nightmare and I could return to sleep.

"Listen to me, please." Elena's tense, pale face stood out in sharp contrast to the dark sheen of her disheveled hair. For all her royal poise in the audience chamber in Ardenna, she huddled with uncertainty at the edge of the bed with Jules behind her.

"Why?" I drew my knees farther away from her, hugging them against my chest. "You've nothing to say I want to hear."

"You're wrong." Elena stretched a hand to my knee, flushing in pained embarrassment as I pulled out of reach. "I'm sorry, Alex, but you're so thick sometimes. All we wanted was for you to accept your talent."

"Accept my talent?" I repeated in a voice hoarse with lack of restful sleep. "Easy for you to say. You haven't the slightest idea what it feels like to have something wild and uncontrolled inside you, afraid of what it might mean, or what it might do." I took a ragged breath, striving desperately to stop my body from shaking.

"You were a child. Not hard to be scared."

"I wasn't scared, Elena. I was terrified. Lords of the sea, you should have been terrified, too. But it doesn't matter anymore. It's gone."

"Maybe. Listen, I know it wasn't easy for you."

Pathetic little orphan child. "Spare me your sympathy." I tried, but couldn't quite keep the contempt from my voice. It was easier to be bitter and mocking than to acknowledge honest affectionate compassion. I struggled to hold back the tears and took the offensive instead. "I should be sorry for you, forcing you to leave whoever's been keeping you warm at night to go chasing after—"

"Damn you, Alex!" Dark eyes lit with impatient frustration. "You're being so difficult. It's not so hard to understand, but you twist my words and refuse—"

"What? To understand how easily you forget friendship and trust? Or accepting me for what I am? Or what I'm not? Or what I want or don't want to be? Even if I were a Crownmage," I hissed, "you never asked if I wanted to be. You assumed I should be. You thought to push me again until I tired of fighting you, until I tried one more time, and maybe hurt some other poor innocent fool. But that was never your concern, Elena, not when you wanted something."

"Stop it."

But I couldn't stop, I was so hurt by their manipulation I couldn't see reason. "You've only worn the Tuldamoran crown a short while, but already you're plotting for power with the best of the treacherous council. I didn't think it'd be so easy for either of you to lie to me." I laughed with bitterness, shoving aside the grief as though they were strangers. "I was wrong."

"Please listen."

"It doesn't matter anymore. I can't help you, Elena. So do me a favor and leave me the hell alone."

Her blue eyes darkened, all hint of power and position replaced by overwhelming sadness. She didn't answer, but she didn't deny my words either.

Jules was silent through our argument, braced against the opposite wall in a battered old chair. "Just come home, Alex. Please. Mother's beside herself. I expect she'll probably disown me after this. Lauryn and Khrista will never forgive me if you don't come home. I know you won't come back for me, but at least for their sake . . ." Jules glanced at

Elena, who turned her anguished face away, though not before I caught a glimpse of wet cheeks. "We never meant to disregard your feelings, but we did push them aside when matters started getting complicated. We never meant to hurt you, Alex. You have to believe that."

"Why? To make your guilt disappear?"

"Because it's true."

"I'm not so gullible."

"But it's true, Alex. Just as it's true Elena needs the Crownmage allied with her against the Crown Council. A Crownmage who controls all four elements could easily balance the council's powers and neutralize their influence."

"About time you said something honest."

"Elena believed you might be the Crownmage." Jules faltered, gazing at her averted profile, half hidden behind strands of her hair. "She still does. And maybe I do, too. I don't know anymore. But that doesn't mean she thoughtlessly tossed aside your friendship."

I snorted in bitter amusement, hugging my knees to force the pain away.

Elena flushed scarlet and met my accusing stare. "You're so wrong, Alex."

"Am I? You didn't care about what I wanted the day Jules caught on fire, either. All you wanted was to see me use my mage talent."

"Will you never forgive me?" When I looked away, Elena pushed on, likely believing she had nothing more to lose. "Maybe if you'd learned to control it then—"

"You wouldn't have to force me years later to try to harm him again. I'd already be your puppet, just like Jules, who'll do anything you ask, and this conversation wouldn't be necessary. Sorry to ruin your plans."

"We lied because you were being difficult, unwilling to even consider you have potential. I pushed you again because I need your talent. I can't deny it. But damn you, Alex, I'd rather just be your friend."

I murmured something crude.

"I was wrong to do what I did. Don't you think I know that? But I've never thought so little of our affection as you believe. You dishonor our friendship, and you dishonor me, if you believe I'd be so cold-hearted. I may wear the crown, but I've always been your friend first."

I met the pain in her dark blue eyes evenly, forcing myself to ignore the dampness on her cheeks. "Maybe in your eyes, Elena, but not in mine."

Elena sighed, resigned to the stone wall I'd built between us. "Go home, Alex." She grabbed her cloak. "Neither Jules nor I will trouble you any further. I promise you."

Chapter Ten

"I've promised my grandsons you'll tell them all about the holiday adventure you decided to take without saying a word to anyone." Rosanna chatted as she fixed a pot of cinnamon tea in my cottage some days later. As though I hadn't sat there weeping from the moment she walked in, going on about gossip in Port Alain. She stopped only when she sat opposite me, leaving my cup on the low, wooden table to my side. Shaking out a lace handkerchief, she handed it to me. "I doubt you have one as fine as this."

"I wouldn't know what to do with it." I sniffed, wiping my eyes and blowing my nose.

"You're managing well enough." She took a sip from her cup, waving me to do the same. "I didn't prepare this tea so you could stare at it. Now drink it before it cools and loses its tastes."

I obeyed, took another sip. "What did you put in it?"

"A little Marain wine."

Another sip improved my mood. Rosanna settled back against the overstuffed cushions she'd embroidered, fixing me with an intolerant stare.

"Must we?"

"I'm afraid so. Where did you think you were going? To Glynnswood?"

"Glynnswood?" I twirled the cup in my hands, sitting back against my own chair. "Why?"

"I thought you might be looking for your father's family." Her tone very subtly changed, but I couldn't read it.

"I never wanted to before," I hedged, studying her expression.

"I thought it possible. After all, Jules and Elena lied to you, abused your trust. Jules confessed the entire travesty. Why not assume you'd leave your adopted family and find your father's kin?" She toyed with the Barlow signet ring that had graced her finger since the old duke passed away. "I would have understood."

Flameblast Jules. I wanted to rip out his heart. Clamping tight control over the tears that threatened to betray me again, I said quietly, "I wasn't rejecting you, Rosanna. I was angry at Jules and couldn't bear to be near him." I put my cup on the table. "It had nothing to do with you. I wasn't even headed for Glynnswood. If I wanted to find my father's family, I would've badgered you long ago. Even then, it wouldn't have anything to do with you. Lords of the sea, you would've let me go freely if I asked. I know that."

"Yes." Satisfied for the moment, Rosanna decided to return to the matter at hand. "Jules is hiding from me, as he should. They were both wrong, Alex, but they did it for the right reasons."

"Some of the right reasons. I just want them to leave me alone. Maybe someday I'll be able to speak to them with civility."

"Someday, you'll be gray like me, and still ignorant of your talent."

"What do you want me to do? If this supposed talent has disappeared, I can't very well bring it back," I said in frustration, tapping my fingers absently against the half-empty cup. She gave me a long appraising stare, the kind I didn't like. And the old seawitch knew just how to use it on me to best advantage. "What?"

"Speak to the mages in some other town since the Port Alain mages aren't very friendly."

"Absolutely not." I slammed my fist on the table, spilling several precious drops from my cup. "My mother despised the councils, and you'd have me run straight into their hateful arms? Don't you think word's gotten around about me?"

"They're the only ones who could help you unlock your talent if it's there." Rosanna sighed. "Why are you so stubborn all the time?"

"Cynicism, disbelief."

"Fear."

I refused to take the dangling bait. "Maybe. I don't care. I won't do it."

"One day you might have to."

"What do you mean?"

"Instinct, wisdom."

"What aren't you telling me?" I asked, pushing some strands of damp hair back behind my ear. "Is there something else I should know?"

"Perhaps." She drained her cup, smacked her lips with exaggerated delicacy, and stood.

I grabbed her silken tunic sleeve to hold her back before she made her escape. "What do you mean 'perhaps'?"

"Perhaps there's something else you should know. Perhaps a talk with a mage might jolt my memory of what that something else might be." She shrugged again. "Perhaps." Eyes wide in feigned innocence, she left me alone.

* * * *

I didn't think it possible, but Jules and Elena kept their word and their distance. Rosanna, on the other hand, remained her usual mischievous, affectionate self, though there were no further hints to intrigue me. As some peaceful weeks passed, the dreams faded. So did I, from the life outside my own private world. News of sporadic, vicious marauder attacks along Belbridge Cliffs and the Bitterhill coast, still linked by rumor to Meravan, didn't trouble me. That was Elena's problem, not mine. She had her retinue of diplomats and armed troops to keep the peace.

I ignored Rosanna's worried chatter about Elena's harassment by the council at every move she tried to make. They blatantly overstepped their advisory role, taking a far more active stand against her than ever before. Every small measure of improvement she tried to push through was twisted until it turned against her. Each of the four mages in the council now spoke out openly against the crown, distorting her words and policies until her every intention was suspect. The loudest voice of all, of course, was Charlton Ravess.

And Elena was powerless to stop them. Too new to the throne, she lacked the full confidence of her father's advisers, cowards, in my opinion, who should have supported her from sheer loyalty to the old king. Well, I suppose, with all that, if I were Elena, perhaps I'd want a Crownmage beside me, too.

Chapter Eleven

Lessons ended for the day, without, thankfully, any questions about the Crownmage. I sent the children scurrying off for adventure, and planned to enjoy a well-deserved lazy afternoon in the unseasonably warm sunshine behind my cottage. I started to tidy up the scattered chairs and books swept aside as the children escaped. If I didn't know better, I'd think they didn't enjoy their lessons.

"Mistress Keltie?"

Mistress Keltie? No one in all Port Alain except Seamage Neal Brandt dared be so formal with me. Glancing up, I studied what was obviously a well-traveled stranger, judging from the scuffs on his worn boots and his clean, though well-faded woolen cloak. Hard to tell what its original color had been.

"Yes?"

"Lady Barlow told me you'd be here." A polite bow accompanied his courteous, unruffled tone.

Why would Lauryn send a stranger to see me? Particularly one old enough to be my father. No, not Lauryn. It had to be Jules.

"You must mean Duke Barlow," I commented dryly, without offering an explanation as I continued to straighten the chairs.

He looked puzzled. "No." His reply was accompanied by a shake of his full head of black hair, liberally streaked with gray. "Lady Barlow. The duke's mother."

The old seawitch, of course. I returned the stranger's befuddled expression with suspicion as I narrowed my eyes to study him closer. Only then did I recognize his features, those sea-gray eyes that had studied my own face with interest over thick sausage and eggs in the Seaman's Berth.

"Have I done something to offend you?" His hasty question didn't mask the too-innocent gleam in his eyes.

I knew by the immediate warning of my instinct he was trouble. "Not yet." Though it was ill-mannered not to suggest he lower his bulging pack to the floor and make himself comfortable, I didn't suggest it anyway. The stranger hadn't budged from the doorway, except to shift the pack on his shoulder. He smiled uneasily, waiting with an expression of infinite patience. He may have been at a loss.

Maybe. Maybe not.

I didn't trust Rosanna, or understand why she'd send a stranger to my door, particularly one asking questions about me in town. Though maybe she was unaware of that fact.

"Why?" I asked curtly, walking toward the table and throwing a few books together into a smaller sack at my feet.

"Why am I here? Why did Lady Barlow send me to your school-room? Why," he paused, a twinkle in those sea-gray eyes, "are you being so inhospitable?" He smiled as I flushed in embarrassment, and held out a hand.

"My name is Anders Perrin," he said quietly, studying my face as though searching for something. "I was a friend of your mother's."

* * * *

I was silent on the walk down the Hill to my cottage. Anders Perrin, Mother's friend, trudged along behind me. I didn't stop him, nor did he ask permission. An amused tolerance in his cool eyes spoke volumes of what he and Rosanna probably discussed about me. I felt trapped, torn, wanting to know, wanting not to know, and desperate to escape.

It was the longest walk of my life.

At the door to my cottage, I stopped in mid-stride and spun to face him. I faced instead a dangling half copper seamage pendant swinging in the afternoon breeze as Anders held it out between us.

"I thought this might at least guarantee me a cup of tea."

None of the vicious oaths I wanted to hurl at him managed to get past the lump in my throat. Turning my back to hide the sudden tears, I left the door wide open behind me as I stormed inside. Anders was patient and tolerant as I prepared hot cinnamon tea. He tossed his faded cloak over a chair, busied himself starting a fire, and stayed out from under my feet as I slammed teakettle and cups from cupboard to table. When I brought everything into the cluttered sitting room by the fireplace, he sat in one of the armchairs, plumping pillows behind his back.

"I've been rather rude."

"I assumed it was a Port Alain custom." When I flushed, he added with unnecessary kindness, "Though you've rather a good reason to be rude."

What had Rosanna told him? What hadn't she told him? "That's no excuse. If any of my students behaved like that, I'd give them a proper tongue-lashing for hours."

"Are you giving me permission to do so?"

"No." I took a sip of tea, noting the quality tailoring of his somewhat faded tunic and trousers, which managed to still look presentable. "Of course not."

Following my lead, he sipped the tea, closing his eyes in contentment. "By the way, Lady Barlow suggested a good bottle of Marain wine might make you civil, so she sent one along." Opening his eyes, his grin impish, Anders pulled a bottle from his worn leather satchel.

"That woman is—"

"Many things," he interrupted, holding the bottle out as peace offering. "But above all, devoted, concerned, and protective of you."

I laughed without hostility. "She already has you on her side."

"I didn't know there were sides," he commented blandly, stretching long legs toward the fire's blazing warmth.

He was definitely trouble.

"Listen, Alex." He paused. "It is Alex?" When I nodded, he stayed quiet, a sad expression replacing the mischief. "Lords of the sea, but you have her blue eyes." Anders sighed with regret and old grief. "Sorry. It's been a long time."

"That's all right."

"I won't force you to listen. But if you're willing, I'll tell you what I remember about Emila. It's your choice. What would you like to know?"

I sighed deeply, running hands through my unruly hair. My choice. What would I like to know?

"Everything."

"That could take some time." He rearranged the embroidered pillows behind his back.

"Do you have the time?" I leaned forward, surprised to find myself afraid he would leave without telling me a flameblasted thing.

"That's why I'm here."

"Oh." Had Rosanna contacted him weeks ago? But no, she said she didn't know who Mother's friend was. But there were many things she said that troubled me. Or didn't say. "Why now?"

"Fair question." His tone was equable as he tugged at a loose strand at the frayed edge of his sleeve. "I felt it was time to make your acquaintance, though I've passed through Port Alain before."

"I told Rosanna you probably did, and left disappointed."

"She told me you were hasty in reaching conclusions."

I flushed at the truth of his comment but stayed silent. Anders was more than simple trouble. He was dangerous.

"As I was saying, I've passed through Port Alain without speaking to Lady Barlow. She didn't know who I was until this morning. When I did visit in the past, I observed you and the Barlows."

I blinked. "How?"

An impish grin lightened the deep gray of his eyes. "I can't tell you my secrets, but trust I never intruded on anyone's privacy."

"You were asking the innkeeper about me over the few weeks."

He didn't deny it. "Your friends are admirably protective of you. Chester, I presume, warned you. And the duke—" A grin took years from his face. "I caught on to his tail the day he sent the boy to watch me. The very next day after you had tea at the inn."

"Don't tell Jules."

"I wouldn't dare. I don't particularly wish to be at odds with him. Anyway, I didn't visit with you in the past because you seemed well and content with your life. No need to disturb calm waters. But lately," he shrugged, sitting back again, "I've felt those waters were troubled and getting a bit muddied."

Despite his collaboration with the old seawitch, I trusted Anders when I had no reason to do so. Maybe it was just I trusted my mother. "How did you know?"

"I'm a seamage, Alex. Your mother and I were very close friends. Her pendant . . ." Anders pulled the half pendant out of its pouch and gave it to me, shrugging again. "It might seem crazy, but somehow, I don't know, it felt different."

I took his half of the copper pendant and went to my bedchamber to get the matching half. Taking it lovingly from the small carved chest, I brought the two pieces back to the table and placed them side-by-side. Anders leaned over and pushed them together so that the tidal crest was complete within the etched circle.

"This might seem crazy, too, but I often feel some sense of my mother when I hold my half," I admitted, certain Anders wouldn't laugh.

He didn't, and his smile was kind. "So do I. It's peculiar. She never told me how she split it so evenly. When I felt the subtle change in my half, I knew it was time to come take another look and make sure you were all right. Maybe she was warning me somehow. Emila always had ways of keeping an eye on those she cared about."

As an unexpected flash of deep grief shadowed his expression, deepening the gray of his eyes, I wondered about his relationship to my mother. Was there only close friendship? Or had there been something more? "Why did she give the pendant to you and not my father?" I studied his face as he thought about my question.

"Well," he finally muttered. "Why don't I open this bottle?"

"I'll open it, and even see you have something to eat after you answer my question." I grabbed the bottle and kept it out of reach.

"Rosanna told me you were stubborn."

"And beastly difficult, I'm sure." I grinned. "Well?"

Anders sighed in resignation, pushing a hand through gray-streaked hair. His seamage token, worn on a bracelet around his wrist, jingled as it struck the arm of his chair. "Your father never trusted mages and their elemental talents. Sernyn avoided mages, though he was civil enough to me."

"But he married Mother—"

"Well, yes." Anders smiled in bemusement. "Your mother had a certain charm that could wrangle anything she wanted from anyone she wanted anytime she wanted. She promised your father never to use mage talent when she was with him."

"That wasn't very fair of him."

"Well, no, maybe not, but he did love her. And," he added solemnly, "she loved him very much, Alex. Never, ever, doubt it. Not using mage talent in front of him wasn't a hardship to her."

"Still not fair."

"No," he agreed, "but she knew he wouldn't be comfortable raising a mage-talented child, which is why she gave me the pendant should something happen to her."

"So you could train me if I showed any signs of talent?"

"Yes. The task became quite interesting when you first showed a hint of magery as a child. Poor Jules."

"You were in Port Alain when that happened?"

"Not long after. I was eavesdropping on the council, who'd become interested in you. But then your talent seemed to vanish, and I hesitated to come forward. Perhaps I shouldn't have hesitated."

He left me an opening should I wish to continue his train of thought. I chose not to and went on to a topic I was all too familiar with. I yanked the cork free of the wine bottle. Standing opposite him, I took a deep breath and tried to find the right words. Not an easy thing to do under the circumstances. "When my mother was giving birth, could she . . ." I stopped to blink back unwanted tears. "Could she have saved herself if she hadn't made that promise to my father?"

He stared at me for a long silent moment, utter compassion in his eyes. Finally, he shook his head. "No. I feared so myself when I first heard the news. Believe me, Alex, it was the first thought I had, and I would've made your father suffer had it been true. But he told me what happened and that she'd been troubled by odd pains, and, well, no," he faltered, "I don't think she could have."

"But would she have tried?" I whispered, hugging myself to stop the trembling as he rescued the bottle from my hands.

"Does it matter?"

"Yes. No." Crying, I shook my head fiercely, embarrassed. "Not really. It was still my fault."

"You are stubborn." Anders pursued me to the alcove where I kept food and drink and slammed the bottle onto the counter. "You had nothing to do with her death."

"If I hadn't been born—"

"Alex." He grabbed my shoulders, shaking me with gentleness. "There were some odd things about her pregnancy, but that could easily have come from her own physical condition or problems no one knew about. You were the only child she ever had, so we don't know. But there are matters I do know something about, and I want the truth." His eyes turned unexpectedly grave as he tightened his grip on my shoulders. "I owe it to your mother."

Wiping my cheeks with the back of my hand, I stared, confused. "Like what?"

"Well, for one, what kind of mage are you, Mistress Keltie?"

I stared at Anders in silence for several heartbeats, and then headed for his pack. I grabbed the leather satchel and handed it to him. "I suggest you leave now, Master Perrin, and leave me the hell alone. In fact, if I ever see your face again, I may not be able to stop myself from ripping out your heart."

"Alex—"

I flung open the door, held it wide until he recognized my utter seriousness. Without a word, Anders nodded, eyes narrowed in thought, and left my cottage; left me alone with the two halves of my mother's seamage pendant.

As divided as my own heart.

* * * *

92

"Who is he, anyway?" At my immediate snarl, Lauryn's eyes widened. "Nevermind."

I straightened the stools from the children's abrupt escape at the end of their geography lesson. "Don't mind me. I'm a little cranky." When I glanced up and caught Lauryn's worried expression I forced a smile to my lips. "I'm sorry. He just rattled me a bit."

"That's obvious."

"Does everyone on the Hill know I had a visitor?"

"Yes, but nothing more about him. Except . . ." Lauryn had the grace to look embarrassed.

"Go on."

"Kerrie finished meeting with Jules late in the day to go over the accounts. When Kerrie was leaving Jules' study, he met the gentleman." When I muttered a rude comment at her loose use of the term, Lauryn didn't blink. "Kerrie saw him leaving Rosanna's suite. It seems he's staying at the Seaman's Berth."

I stopped straightening the crude, colorful maps of Tuldamoran and sank onto a stool.

"Alex, what's wrong?"

"If he's still at the inn, that means he's got no intention of leaving."

"Still?"

"It's a long story, but he's been there for several weeks already."

"Who is he?"

I sighed, knowing I owed Lauryn an honest answer for all her years of genuine friendship.

"If you don't want to tell me—"

"I don't, but I should. I need someone on my side I trust to be objective."

"It has to do with Jules and Elena and the whole fiasco."

"In an odd sort of way, yes." I rubbed my eyes wearily, choosing my words with care. "I'd rather what I tell you stay secret with you. Is that a problem?"

"Why would it be? We've always confided in each other."

"I know, and I'm grateful. I'd just rather no one but Rosanna know anything more about Anders Perrin, except he was a friend of my mother's." When Lauryn's jaw dropped, I explained, "He showed up unexpected and went first to Rosanna."

"Who sent him to you."

"Precisely."

"Is that a bad thing?" Lauryn asked warily, sitting on one of the wooden stools.

"I didn't think so at first. I never knew my mother. If he could tell me about her, then, well, you understand." Lauryn nodded, having listened to my grief at odd moments over the years. "But he wanted something from me," I explained, staring hard at my hands, busy tracing the wood, scarred from seven years of tangling with adventurous children. "He asked me what kind of mage I am."

Lauryn's hand came to rest on my bowed head before dropping away. "Elena, Jules, Rosanna, and now this gentleman are pressuring you to recreate a mage gift you want nothing to do with."

I looked up. "You're implying I have it."

"You had it. You had something long before I arrived in Port Alain." Her smile was warm. "You can't deny that."

"I thought you'd be on my side."

"Hush and listen before throwing me into the enemy camp." When I obeyed the maternal scolding, she continued, "From what I understand about magic, either you have it or you don't. Which means you still have it, but you don't want it. And in that case, they don't have any right to pressure you."

"They seem to think so."

"They're wrong." She scowled at my cynical expression. "I'm not just saying that to convince you I'm on your side. I mean it."

Relieved someone was content not to pressure me, I said, "Elena and Jules have backed off for the moment, but Anders looks to be staying in town for awhile."

"With Rosanna's encouragement."

"From the comments she's made these past weeks, I assume that's true."

"Shall I talk to her? Convince her to leave you alone?"

"Waste of breath," I muttered. "No, Lauryn, but thanks. I'll handle Rosanna and Anders on my own."

"Just let me know if you need reinforcements."

"I will, thanks, but now I've got a handle on the gentleman, I'll be able to deal with him."

Chapter Twelve

"Mistress Keltie."

Only two peaceful weeks had passed since I asked Master Perrin with impeccable courtesy to take his flameblasted satchel and leave me alone. It was obvious he didn't take me seriously. Lauryn and I guessed it was only a matter of time before he reappeared at my doorstep. Knowing Master Perrin was still at the Seaman's Berth, I sent quiet word to Chester, through the Barlows' trustworthy steward, to forgive me for staying away until the troublesome gentleman left Port Alain.

Anders Perrin was trouble, and it would just get worse.

"Alex." Carey tugged at my tunic sleeve. "There's a gentleman calling you." He gave me an odd look as he scratched his curly head, bewildered. "I think he's calling you."

"Of course he is." Hunter nudged his twin. "That's Alex's real name."

"Let's see what the gentleman wants." I ushered my flock of innocent lambs in the direction of the crafty old beast who stood by the side of the road leading north, away from the ducal manor.

"Thank goodness, I'm not too late. I was afraid I'd missed you." He bowed first to me, and then to my students, who stared in wide-eyed curiosity.

"We're on our way to Jendlan Falls, Master Perrin," I said with all the sweetness I could muster, "and I do wish to move along before it gets much later in the morning. What did you want?"

"Yes, well . . ." He coughed as Carey absently kicked up dust from the roadway in Hunter's direction. "Lady Barlow, the, ah, delightful grandmother of these young lords, sent me."

I clenched my fists, though continued to smile docilely over the children's heads. "I thought that possible."

"She thought you might. And, indeed, she suggested you might allow me to join your little excursion. With your permission, of course," he added with an all-too-innocent tone, "and perhaps speak to the children about, well, seamage talent as we will be so close to all that rushing water."

"Seamage!" blurted Carey, eyes wide, tugging at my arm. "Alex, please? Oh, please?"

The smile never left my face though I had the distinct feeling Anders was adept at reading my bloodthirsty intent. "I'm afraid that's not quite what I'd planned today." As I turned toward the falls, my ten adoring charges gathered around, pleading, as though their hearts would break if I didn't allow Seamage Anders Perrin to join us. I took a hundred thousand deep breaths before grabbing Hunter's hand. "I suppose I couldn't very well refuse Lady Barlow's wishes. She does so care their education is all-encompassing."

"She certainly does, mistress. She's a marvelous grandmother," Anders answered in a neutral tone, hands tucked behind his back. "Her foresight is remarkable, thinking of the future of her community by educating its little ones so well. Lady Barlow even gave thought to joining us, but was afraid she might intimidate the children from asking all their questions."

"Thoughtful of her."

"She is that, yes," he agreed with bland good-nature.

"And wealthy. Tell me, Master Perrin, is she paying for your stay at the Seaman's Berth?"

"Of course not." His smile was wicked. "Though she did offer to help share the expense. I refused. It would hardly be seemly for Lady Barlow to extend such generosity to a stranger. Though she is kind."

"She's a beastly old seawitch," I muttered under my breath and turned away to start north on the road to Jendlan Falls.

"Pardon?" His eyes brimmed with cool amusement as I watched from the corner of my eye.

"I said we'd best be going."

"Yes, of course." He gathered the children to him. "It's getting late. Come along, children."

As he shepherded my flock, I stomped ahead, setting a brisk pace, fervently hoping the old troublemaker would have a heart attack and beg for mercy. How had my mother tolerated him? And why? Anders matched my pace, ignoring me as I ignored him, speaking only to the children so they soon lost their awe and began hammering him with questions. I paid scant attention to their conversation, allowing my mind to wander as the road curved northward, beginning the gentle incline leading to Jendlan Falls. On both sides the forest was dense, predominantly oak and elm, though other types were scattered at random. So I was told. I couldn't remember the difference and made very sure Rosanna taught that particular lesson.

It wasn't very far to the Falls. Long before Carey exhausted his endless questions, I heard the rushing surge of water and quickened my pace. I'd been here countless times. Yet I still gaped in wonder at the sweeping force of the Jendlan River thrusting itself over the cliffs to the churning maelstrom below. It came to rest in a quiet pool before heading south to Shad's Bay and, finally, the Skandar Sea.

"Humbling, isn't it?"

"I didn't think you knew the meaning of the word."

"If you'd rather I leave—"

"I'd rather you leap off the top of Jendlan Falls," I whispered, "but the children would never forgive me."

"Yes, they would." An odd expression deepened the gray of his eyes. "The children adore you. They'd find some reason to explain away your change of heart, in spite of their disappointment."

I blinked and looked away, my gaze caught by the drifting spray that blew in our direction with the chilled breeze. "But they'd still be disappointed. And I adore them right back and couldn't have that. So give your flameblasted lesson."

"Then I'll leap off the falls." When I didn't bother to respond, he said, "I'd leap from the bridge if it was high enough." He nodded at the old wooden bridge spanning the pool where the children were waiting.

"It's not high enough to guarantee your demise."

"Your mother would be appalled."

"My mother would never tolerate your attitude."

His smile turned suddenly engaging, and I could see, damn his beastly soul, how she could tolerate him. "There were times I found myself fleeing a hailstorm of books, dishes, and any other loose articles she could lay her hands on."

"I can understand why."

"Alex, I'm not trying to make your life miserable." When I stared him down, trying to ignore the flush creeping up my face, he sighed and glanced back at the bridge. "Why don't we take the children up there? I can teach just as well from that point, and they could have a better view."

My heart started hammering. "No."

"Why not?"

"I don't like bridges," I was forced to admit.

"All right." His expression was nonjudgmental, though I didn't trust him. "I certainly don't want to make you suffer more than you need to during the lesson." Smug and satisfied, he turned back to the children and guided them toward the edge of the calm, shallow pool where the falls turned gentle.

Hunter tugged at my cloak. "Master Perrin's going to start. You don't want to miss this lesson, do you?" Wide-eyed, he studied me, uncertain of my mood, as perceptive as his mother.

"Of course not." I ruffled his hair and went to sit behind Carey, Hunter nestled close beside me.

Anders dispatched an unreadable expression my way before giving the children his full attention. "You all know what a seamage can do. But how many of you have ever seen one use talent?"

Not one raised hand, including mine. I refused to answer. Besides, Seamage Brandt was right. I didn't make a habit of hanging around the council hall.

Anders cocked his head to the side as the breeze ruffled his thick hair, a hint of amusement in his eyes. "Well, then." With a disarming smile aimed in my direction, he gestured at the placid pool. Eyes locked on the gently swirling water, he held himself to utter stillness.

I waited for some melodramatic, theatrical chanting, but it wasn't necessary to impress this adoring audience. All ten of my sheep gasped simultaneously as the pool turned to steam, formed a dense cloud over the still flowing water, and rained. A gentle fall at first; then a fierce downpour, still over the pool, and then again, a light spring shower that drifted in our direction until it was over our heads, sprinkling us with mist.

"Interesting sort of talent," I murmured, distracted by an odd feeling I couldn't quite identify. Or maybe chose not to.

Anders held my gaze over Carey's head for a long moment. "And useful. Don't think for even a moment it's not. Suppose there was a fire nearby? Or a flood? One seamage could put out the fire or dry up the flood, saving lives and crops."

"Is that how seamages contribute to society?"

With a smile at the children, his tone shifted with delicate subtleness as he looked at me. "Any mage, whether master or mistress of water, air, fire, or earth, is bound by all the laws of decency to contribute to the welfare of his fellow citizens."

"Is the Crownmage bound, too, Master Perrin?" Carey gazed wide-eyed at Anders, as though he'd discovered a new hero.

"Yes, of course." Though Anders answered the boy, his eyes never left mine. "Even more so because the Crownmage is master, or mistress, of all elements. The more power a mage has, the more responsible he or she must be."

"Like father?" Hunter asked.

"Yes. The Duke of Port Alain is a powerful man who must guard the livelihood of his people. Now go beyond him. To whom does he answer?"

"Grandmother," Carey blurted with a grin as I tweaked his ear affectionately.

"Yes, of course." Anders smiled, enjoying his jest. "But beyond your grandmother, your father must answer to the queen, who's responsible for the livelihood and welfare of all the people in Tuldamoran."

"Father says she worries about keeping us safe from raiders," Hunter said quietly, at my side.

"Not only raiders, but fires and floods, poor crops, anything that can harm you. She understands her responsibility and does everything she can to fulfill her duty. Something we should all do, whether we're bakers or sailors or even schoolmistresses." Anders' eyes met mine in a silent challenge.

"Why don't you show the children what other wonders you can perform," I suggested in an icy voice, tucking a clenched fist under my cloak so the children wouldn't see, wonder, and ask questions.

With a bland nod, Anders Perrin went on talking, answering questions, and demonstrating his talent. After quite some time, he explained constant use of his talent was wearying, and so they thanked him without my nudging them forward. The children then turned to thank me, wrapping their skinny arms around my waist. After returning their hugs with no less affection, I took a deep breath to confront Anders flameblasted Perrin one final time. But he'd vanished.

"Turned into sea mist and blown out to sea," I murmured, uneasy at the thought. "I hope."

* * * *

"If you ever do something so vile, deceitful, and underhanded again—"

"What have I done now?" Wide-eyed innocence met my gaze across the waist-high shrubbery.

"What have you done?" I snarled, edging closer to the bush Rosanna was busy pruning.

"I'm sorry you're troubled."

"Troubled?" I shouted, grateful for once Rosanna kept so few groundskeepers. "I'm not troubled at this moment, old lady. I'm furious."

She clipped dead leaves from the shrub as a chill wind rustled the overhanging branches nearly bereft of leaves. "I hadn't noticed."

I leaned over the bush and snatched the clippers from her hands. "What are you trying to do to me?" I shook the clippers at her tranquil expression. "It was horrid enough to send that—that—that old fool after me the first time, but worse now with the children. How could you?"

"Oh dear." She frowned, tugging worriedly at her garden gloves. "The children didn't find him helpful, did they?"

"The children loved him. And you knew I hadn't a seahag's chance in hell to deny them his far-too-entertaining lesson on what a civilized, well-mannered, responsible seamage could do for queen and country."

"Now, Alex, really. Besides, you could have refused." Rosanna retrieved the clippers with care. "You are their schoolmistress. I'm only the duke's mother."

"Only the duke's mother." I snorted. "I could sooner have shown some mage talent than refused." Hands resting in resignation on my hips, I stared her down, but her arched eyebrow was eloquent. I started to respond, thought better of it, and decided it wasn't worth the trouble.

"Alex?" Rosanna called sweetly from her side of the shrubbery as I turned to leave. "Did you at least learn anything?"

Muttering a long string of imaginative oaths, I nearly bowled Lauryn over in my blind fury.

She took one look at my face and sighed. "The children told me about the lesson."

"I was ambushed."

"No doubt about it."

"I'll rip out his heart if he comes within sneezing distance of my cottage."

"I'll hold him down while you do." Lauryn's expression was so determined I couldn't help myself and started to laugh. "Just when you think you're safe, he comes out of the woodwork again."

"I'll never be safe until he's gone." I sagged against the fence. "Sitting there today, watching his tricks," I chose my words with care, only then recognizing a truth I'd been hiding from all day, "I felt—"

"Angry."

"No. Jealous." When her blue eyes widened in surprise, I explained, "The old beast made it seem so effortless, so harmless. I know I'm being naïve, but I'd be lying if I didn't admit a tiny part of me wished I could do it, too."

Her voice was gentle, nonjudgmental. "That's a far cry from what you've been saying all along. If the feeling doesn't disappear maybe you should have a private little chat with Master Perrin."

Reality reared its ugly head. "I'm too afraid."

"Alex, listen to me." Lauryn grabbed my sleeve as I pushed away from the fence. "I can't imagine your fear, but I respect it. If you test your power . . ." She clutched my wrist to keep me still. "You have the chance to do it safely with a man who was trusted by your mother."

"I've only his word on that."

"He had the pendant."

"He could have stolen it."

Her expression was eloquent.

"Still . . ."

"I know you're angry with Rosanna, but you know she'd never let him near you if she didn't trust him, either."

"That's supposed to make me feel better?"

"Sometimes, Mistress Keltie," Lauryn's eyes held me motionless, "you even try my patience."

Chapter Thirteen

Lessons shoved aside until the next day, my thoughts were jumbled; my heart divided; my mood contentious. Distracted, I bumped into the table where I had set a light supper. The two halves of Mother's seamage pendant lay beside the plate and I wondered how she split the metal so perfectly.

"Now that was clumsy."

The jug sloshed, sending water down the side of the table, my motion knocking over the small loaf of brushed oats. As the bread sailed to the floor, it dragged the two pieces of copper with it.

"Damnation."

I bent to snatch the loaf before it became waterlogged. The pendant lay on a dry spot where the trickle of water sought to engulf it. Odd, both halves fell together so neatly keeping the circular shape intact. I suppose there was some truth to Mother's watchful eye.

"Now," I mused, kneeling on one knee, "if I were truly a seamage, I'd be able to focus inwardly and concentrate as Master Perrin explained to my lambs today. And divert that trickle of water around mother's pendant." Grinning at my foolishness, I gestured with excess drama and pretended to focus as Anders demonstrated to the children earlier. "Ah, well. See. I'm not a seamage."

I groaned as the floor chafed through my light wool trousers. Grabbing onto the chair to drag myself up, I lost my balance and yelped as ice slivers and flaming hot pain tore through my head. Flames of fire went running the length of the trickling water, heading straight for Mother's pendant. I snatched up the pieces and looked wildly about for a cloth to smother the flames. Grabbing the water jug instead, I poured the remaining contents over the fire, extinguishing the flames.

Breathing heavily, I sat back on my haunches, refusing to even consider what happened, or recognize the sensations I felt all those years
ago. I stood on shaky legs, leaning on the chair for support, and placed
the two halves of the copper pendant on the table. I caught my breath in
a painful gasp and dropped woodenly to the chair, uttering every single
vile oath I ever heard in all my years.

The pendant; Mother's seamage pendant, was intact. One piece. Not
a flameblasted scar or seam visible.

I picked up the empty water jug and flung it across the room, wincing as it shattered into a hundred thousand pieces.

* * * *

I woke, echoing Mother's scream. It was her scream, I knew it now.
Knew the fire and ice haunting my dreams were signs of my raw talent
lashing out. The untrained talent drove agonizing pain through every
inch of my mother's body as she struggled to release me. I knew it in my
heart as I lay weeping in my bed, but still needed to hear the truth, to be
judged and found guilty.

I flung back the wool covers, shivering in the cold. Grabbing clothes
blindly, I shrugged them on and made my way up the dark and lonely
road to the turret on the Hill. No servants were about to see me fumble
my way to Rosanna's suite and shove past her bewildered expression.
Still weeping, hand still clutching the pendant I wouldn't let from my
sight, I shivered without control.

"Alex." Rosanna followed me to the window where I leaned my
throbbing head against the windowpane. "Child, what's wrong?" Voice
gentle, there was deep, abiding, and unconditional love in the touch of
her hand on my shoulder. "Tell me."

I wiped my eyes free of tears with the sleeve of my rumpled tunic. "Did my mother scream as she lay dying?"

Rosanna paled. "What's brought this on?"

"Did she?" I grabbed the older woman's arms and gripped them tight, unwilling to release her until she answered me with the truth.

Rosanna nodded, eyes brimming with old grief and heartache. "She was in terrible pain."

"Did she . . ." I paused, throat on fire from weeping. "Did she say anything about fire and ice?"

"What are you talking about?" Tears came to her own eyes as she caressed my cheek. "What's happened? Is it the dreams again?"

"Please." I sobbed, leaning in exhaustion against the window ledge. "I need to know. Fire and ice, Rosanna. Tell me. Please."

"Right before the end, as she struggled to birth you, she was burning with fever, muttering in delirium. She cried ice and flames were devouring her. She pleaded for help. We didn't know what she meant, Alex. We thought she was talking about the fever. We thought—"

The rest of her words were lost as I felt the remnants of fire and ice and unforgivable guilt devouring me.

* * * *

I pried one eyelid open.

"Thank the lords of the sea for watching over you," Rosanna muttered in open relief, coming to my side, tucking me back under the woolen covers of her huge bed.

My throat was hoarse and dry, as though I hadn't used it for a time. "How long have I been here?"

"Two days."

"Two days!" I sat up, immediately dizzy, and fell back against the pillows, appalled at the weakness in my limbs.

"Easy," she soothed, resettling the soft pillows behind my head. "You were burning with fever. I couldn't very well send you back to your cottage now, could I? What would the neighbors think?"

"Rosanna—"

She stopped her maternal fidgeting at the tension in my voice.

"I'm sorry," I whispered, unable to meet the old grief in her eyes.

"For what? Something troubled you deeply, and you came for help. When you're quite ready, you'll tell me. And not before."

Listening to her calm assessment of the facts, I remembered the pendant. Pulling my hand out from beneath the heavy blankets, I caught back a gasp when I saw the pendant was gone. In my blind rush to get to her rooms, I must have lost it along the way, though I remembered clutching it tightly.

"It's on your neck," Rosanna said softly.

I fumbled at my throat and pulled the copper pendant to where I could see it. Rosanna had placed it on a delicate leather thong around my neck. Seamless, unscarred. I met her compassionate look with an anguished look of my own.

"When you're ready to tell me, Alex. And not before."

* * * *

"I had an entire party of very promising, eligible young men and wealthy older gentlemen rounded up to visit you, but Mother found out, and wasn't impressed." Jules lounged in the doorway to his mother's suite, a trace of uncertainty in his voice despite the lightness of his words.

"I wish I could say I missed you, Jules, but truly—" I shrugged, tucking bare feet under me on the soft armchair Rosanna had snuggled me into beneath a pile of wool blankets.

"I was worried about you." Exhibiting a wariness in his movements, he edged into the spacious sitting room, inch by inch.

"I'm sure," I said dryly, though caught off guard by the honest hurt in his clear green eyes. "I know. I'm teasing."

Taking a relieved breath, he sat in the other tapestried armchair. "Lauryn and the twins have been frantic with worry. Mother said you were burning with fever, delirious. I told the boys they could see you later if you were strong enough."

"If I could tolerate their father's presence." I shrugged.

Jules' answering smile was warm and affectionate. "Well, Alex, I have missed you. But I've been afraid you'd cut off my toes if I came anywhere near the schoolroom or cottage."

"I'd probably have cut off more," I said with a grin, "but then Lauryn would suffer, and I'm terribly fond of her."

"Is this a formal end to hostilities?"

"Consider it a tentative truce."

I was still confused, weary, and not a little terrified from all that happened. Before we could explore the end to our fighting, the door opened as Rosanna came in, Anders Perrin close behind her.

"Is he bothering you?" She glared at her son, one hand perched with authority on her hip, looking more the stern schoolmistress than I ever could.

"He's been quite civil. Probably up to mischief." I threw a cautious, noncommittal glance in Anders' direction as he nodded a polite greeting.

"No doubt. Jules." She turned back to her son, mistress of the manor again. "Aren't you needed somewhere else?"

"I was just on my way to somewhere else." Jules met my gaze with ease now. "Shall I send the captain or one of those wealthy old gents to visit after lunch?" With a hasty bow to Anders and a jaunty kiss on the cheek for his mother, he fled.

Rosanna looked after him, sighing deeply.

"It's all right. He really was civil. But what does he know about Master Perrin?" I tucked the blankets back around my toes.

"Only that I'm a friend of your mother. Nothing more," Anders said quietly. "May I stay a moment without causing you undue temptation to rip out my heart?"

"You promised to leap off the falls."

"I'd forgotten."

Rosanna cocked her head, decided not to comment, and started to leave, but I called her back. "You may as well hear my story so I don't have to repeat it."

"You're sure?"

"Yes." As they settled near the fireplace, Rosanna in her ancient rocking chair and Anders opposite me. I related what happened the night after we'd gone up to Jendlan Falls. Rosanna's eyes widened as I spun my tale, but Anders, well, Anders was his calm, infuriating self. Nothing of his thoughts betrayed themselves in those cool sea-gray eyes. Nothing.

"May I see the pendant?" He examined it after I tugged it over my head, holding it up to catch the late afternoon sunshine, peering at it from every possible angle. "Useful talent."

I rolled my eyes.

"I knew there was something odd about you, but I'll be damned if I know what it means. Although it might just be explained by the fact your father was from Glynnswood."

"I don't understand."

110

"Mage power is different there, so I've been told. I've been trying to find out what that means, but they're a very closemouthed people."

"And you couldn't charm them?"

"Not yet. However," he added, as I started to answer, distracting me by returning the pendant, "I'd like to see if I can help you find out just what sort of talent you have. If you'll allow me, of course."

I stopped with the pendant half over my head and looked at Rosanna with an accusing stare. "I don't know how, old lady, but you planned this."

"If I could have planned it without your pain and grief," she said, hands fisted in the folds of her gown, "I would have, believe me."

I settled the pendant on my neck. It always came back to trust, good intentions, deep love, and affection here on the Hill. I was surrounded by all this care but refused to accept it without a fight, without feeling burdened or suffocated, without feeling I didn't really belong. Lauryn was right. It was easier to stay away, on my terms, regardless of how anyone else felt about it.

Rosanna watched the subtle shift in my expression as though she knew precisely the pattern of my confused, defensive thoughts. "If Master Perrin can help you, please let him try. He's not a member of the councils. He's a renegade like your mother. And if you're both discreet, the council won't suspect." She added as an afterthought, "Besides, Anders knows the difference between ferns and weeds, and I could use help in my gardens."

"As partial payment for his lodgings at the Seaman's Berth?"

"Anders Perrin is a gentleman. He refused payment. However," Rosanna held my gaze, her own mischievous, "would you rather he stay here on the Hill?"

"Absolutely not."

"Then don't protest if he's helping me in the gardens. He, at least, knows how to use his gifts, gardening being one of them. So, Alex, will you let him help you?"

"I don't have a choice," I complained like a petulant child, knowing this was untrue. No one needed to force me. I was well hooked and snagged. And the old beast knew it.

Chapter Fourteen

"I forced Rosanna to tell me the truth." Lauryn stepped aside as I tucked my breeches into well-worn boots before heading back to the cottage.

"It's a hell of a tale, isn't it?"

"Yes." Lauryn touched my arm, seeming to instinctively know there were some bits of the tale I didn't want to discuss. "It's not your fault."

I shut my eyes. "How can you say that?"

"Because I'm a mother. I've borne twins. No one could have guessed what happened to your mother."

"It doesn't erase the simple fact her body couldn't handle the wild magic I was releasing." I opened my eyes and met her compassionate gaze. "I killed her, Lauryn. It's as simple as that."

"Some things aren't so simple."

"This is."

"You're wrong." Lauryn didn't flinch as my anger flared and died.

"I killed my mother. I almost killed Jules years ago. Who else am I going to hurt? Sure, I've no choice but to see what talent I have, but I'm scared half out of my mind."

"Then learn to control it."

"It won't bring my mother back."

"No, but it will give you peace of mind."

"I doubt it."

"Stop being cynical."

"Stop sounding like Rosanna."

* * * *

"If it weren't for Rosanna, and Lauryn, I might add, I wouldn't even be talking to you," I complained to Anders.

"Is Lauryn on my side, too? I hadn't known that."

"You stay away from her."

"What exactly did you do that night in your cottage?" Anders asked, ignoring my rude words.

"If I knew I wouldn't be having this problem, would I?" I dropped to the cluttered floor of my parlor, absently shoving aside a pile of books.

Anders rolled his eyes, sighed with melodrama, and poured himself a full glass of cool Marain wine.

"That might help me," I suggested, holding out an empty glass.

"Absolutely not." He took a sip from his glass and sighed in contentment before taking the empty glass from my outstretched hand. "It'll ruin your easily distracted concentration. Now think back, Alex. One more time."

When I tugged off my boots and flung them in a far corner, he chuckled. "What's so humorous?"

"You've your mother's impatience."

"I thought you said she was lovely and charming."

"And incredibly impatient," he finished, a warm smile lighting his face. He tucked his legs beneath him with a grunt as he joined me on the cramped floor, knees barely inches from mine. "Did I forget to tell you that?"

"Apparently. Though you did mention she'd lose her temper with you."

"Not often, young lady. Anyway, when Emila wanted to learn something, or get to the bottom of whatever matter was intriguing her, sooner or later, she'd lose all patience. Then she'd start throwing things as though those particular flying objects might somehow resolve the missing piece of whatever eluded her."

"Did they?"

"Every so often, yes." Chuckling again, he sighed, lost in thought, and took another sip of wine.

"So if I inherited part of her, ah, temperament, you'd be wise to hide behind a chair? Or maybe the old seawitch?"

"Precisely. Now back to your problem." He cocked his head to the side. "And don't call Lady Barlow an old seawitch."

"She is. All right, here's what I remember. I was mocking you and found myself putting out a blaze that threatened to burn down my humble cottage."

"I can't have you calling up your mage talent by mocking me, but let that go for the moment. What fascinates me is you were able to touch on three elements." He stared off into the air above my head, muttering to himself.

"Two," I said. "Fire and water."

"Three." Scratching his head, he frowned, narrowing his eyes. "Earth. Remember when you changed Jules' chair all those years ago?"

"Oh, right. Well, I haven't touched the wind."

"Not yet," he muttered. "Intriguing though. The Crownmage—"

I scrambled to my feet. "Don't ever say that name in front of me. If you do, the truce is ended, and I'll rip your heart to bloody shreds."

"It seems I may have to bind and gag you before we get anywhere."

"Try it."

"Just listen for one brief moment."

"No."

"For your mother's sake."

"That's unfair."

"That's how I've been told to deal with you if I'm to make any headway."

"If the old seawitch would mind her own business—"

Anders rapped my knuckles. "Pay attention. All I was about to say was the legendary figure . . ." He paused. "Is it quite all right, to use those words instead?" When I didn't bother to answer, Anders sailed along. "That legendary figure had control over all four elements."

"That legendary figure is simply legend." I crossed my arms in defiance, on certain ground now.

"That legendary figure is quite real. I can assure you."

"Mother's notes—"

"Were incomplete. I have the rest of them."

I sank down in defeat. "He's real?" I asked in a small voice.

"He was. About five hundred years ago. She was. About five hundred years earlier." Pouring a bit of Marain wine for me, he said dryly, "On second thought, maybe a glass will improve your concentration. Listen, neither Crownmage could do what you've done."

"What do you mean?"

"According to your mother's detailed notes, they both could control all four elements on their own. You, on the other hand, are altogether different."

"That's a relief."

"You try to call on one element, and end up calling another. Except for that bit about the pendant. I'll consider your mother somehow responsible. She always had a way to drive me mad."

"I don't blame her."

"Anyway, your talent is uncontrollable." He raised his glass solemnly to me. "So far."

"How can I possibly do what I did? It makes no sense."

"Mage talent rarely makes sense to ignorant apprentices."

How did Mother tolerate him? A better question, really, is why? And another thing... "Why do you have Mother's notes on Crownmages?"

His neutral expression was eloquent. "I was collecting information for her."

"I see." Not really. "Why was my father so against mages?"

Anders stared at me. "Are all your students this curious?"

"Not half as much."

His eyes were unreadable as he looked away and then back at me. "Your father was from Glynnswood. There's not much known about his people because they've kept somewhat to themselves. As you would know," he added reprovingly, "if you paid attention to what you teach the children."

"I'll continue mocking you to use my talent."

"Maybe something happened to your father that shaded his thinking." Anders shrugged. "I don't know. But your mother respected his feelings about magic because she loved him."

Instinct tugged at my heart. I felt as though half this conversation was missing. "It still wasn't fair of him to impose his fears or dislikes on what she was."

"No, it wasn't." Anders twirled his glass between his hands. "But your mother went along with it. And I respected her feelings." A tinge of regret colored his words.

I wondered again about their friendship, but couldn't bring myself to ask. Not yet. "Was he afraid?"

"Like you?" When I flushed, thinking evil thoughts, Anders leaned over to ruffle my hair with affection. "I'd be afraid, too, if I had half your potential. In fact," he graced me with a disarming smile again, "I'd be terrified."

* * * *

Some days later, I leaned against the low garden wall, watching Rosanna dig around the roots of her beloved shrubs, Anders working amiably beside her, neither of them mindful of the chilly gusts of wind. Ample time for them to plot nasty intrigues. Dusty and covered with dirt and loose weeds, they were intent on their work, necessary before winter cloaked her gardens with snow.

"Are you sure he knows the precise difference between ferns and weeds?" I asked when I was sure they hadn't heard me approach.

Rosanna's head came up sharply to peer over her shoulder. "He's already proven he does. Just as clearly as you've proven you don't."

"Well, perhaps if you had the patience to teach me," I suggested, one eyebrow raised in a failed attempt at innocence.

Anders stopped digging and laughed aloud, brushing specks of dirt from his face. "Whoever teaches you needs more than simple patience."

"I never made any promises, Master Perrin," I grumped, taking a seat on the rough wall. "At least I've made progress. Or haven't you admitted that to Lady Barlow in between your nasty plotting?"

"Of course Anders told me." She gave me a smug smile when she added, "I told you so."

I snorted in disgust. "It doesn't matter. I can't do a thing with it."

"Not yet. But you will. I know you, Alex. You're very determined to put me in my place and exact your just vengeance."

I couldn't argue with her logic. "You've become more obnoxious since Master Perrin arrived." I shifted on the wall to counter the rough surface. "I didn't think it possible."

Rosanna threw me a careless grin before turning back to her relentless weeds.

"You haven't told Jules anything, have you?"

She shook her head, tugging at a stubborn clump of tangled dirt and weeds. "I told you I wouldn't."

"You tell me many things."

She sat back on her heels, studying my face, her expression serious. "I didn't tell him, Alex. My son knows Anders was a friend of your mother's, so he may be curious. Lauryn promised she wouldn't say a thing to him."

"I can trust Lauryn."

Rosanna frowned at the implied insult but chose to sidestep it. "Jules hasn't asked me anything he shouldn't have, or anything to make me suspicious." She brushed a spider's web from her pudgy hand, frowning. "Has he been pestering you?"

"Not really," I admitted with a grudge. "It's just he keeps telling me the latest news from Ardenna, and how troubled Elena's been. And how he wants to help her, but doesn't know how."

"Elena is his friend," she said quietly. "And yours, too."

I looked away.

"You've made your peace with Jules, but not Elena. Why not?" Her tone was mild but insistent, keeping a careful balance between pressing me and leaving me alone. Under her scrutiny, I stayed silent for a long, tense moment. "I don't understand, Alex."

"If anything should come of this abominable talent of mine, I expect Elena to hound me again. And she won't care who gets hurt, just so I'll do as she wishes. I wouldn't be surprised if she sent her own spies to hustle me north to Ardenna the very moment I do anything near miraculous."

"You're wrong, Alex."

"No, you are. Elena's the one who needs the help. She's the one who wants to use my mage talent for her own power-hungry reasons. Not Jules," I said fiercely. "He just wants to help Elena for all she means—" I stopped in mid-sentence, aware of Anders' curious glance as I flushed in embarrassment.

Rosanna skirted my careless words. "Elena won't easily come to you. She gave her word not to trouble you." Rosanna stood with a muttered oath as she rubbed her knees. "And she'll keep her promise, despite her need. When you build a wall around yourself, you're very persuasive at keeping people away."

"You think I'm selfish," I said in an injured tone, uncomfortable beneath Anders' quiet scrutiny.

"No." Rosanna shook her head. "But I do think you're doing Elena an injustice by not accepting her apology or believing her sincerity. And I think you're afraid because you've no idea where all this will end. I know you well enough to know you wouldn't hesitate to help Elena if she were desperate. You'd complain and protest loud enough she'd hear you in her fortress," Rosanna said wryly, "but in the end, you'd help her, because Elena wouldn't ask lightly. You love Elena too much to see her hurt, particularly when you could aid her in your own way."

"That's your interpretation."

Stubborn, Rosanna rolled right over my denial. "And despite your supreme indifference to what Jules is telling you, I can't believe the distance between you and Elena doesn't cause you grief."

I met Rosanna's gentle eyes without flinching, refusing to acknowledge the truth of her words. "Maybe you don't know me as well as you think. Maybe you don't know me at all."

* * * *

"Since you're the keeper of the juicier remnants of mother's notes, I suppose I should ask you," I said moodily as Anders and I ambled down the path to my cottage. He'd trailed along in companionable silence when I left the garden, still smarting.

"Go ahead." He sighed in mock resignation.

From the corner of my eye, I watched him. "If you'd rather I didn't ask questions, I won't." When Anders growled, shaking stubborn, clinging dirt from his patched tunic sleeve, I asked a question that had been troubling me. "Why are you so sure it's time for another Crownmage to appear? There have only been those two."

"Actually, there've been more. Though they're somewhat hidden in time, they seem to have appeared at about the same rough approximate time interval. Don't ask me why, because I haven't a clue." He fended off my questioning look with a shrug. "Neither, it seems, did your mother. The records of their appearances are more tangled with legend than the two most recent Crownmages, and details have been lost over the years. To be honest, I'm not sure the time interval means anything. It could be simple coincidence."

"Here's another question. Why was my mother so interested in the Crownmage?" He stopped walking and stared, bewildering me. "That was a reasonable question, wasn't it?"

He shook his full head of dark hair, streaks of gray ruffled by the light breeze, and continued down the path. I quickened my pace to catch up with him, restraining my impatience as he started to answer. "Emila was interested in anything new and different. The Crownmage was that if anything. She wanted to see one in her lifetime," he said wistfully, old grief surfacing again.

"But she didn't."

He didn't answer. I didn't press him. We were silent until we reached the cottage door.

"Is it hard to be with me? Am I a constant reminder?"

He shook his head. "Yes, you're a constant reminder. No, it's not hard to be with you. Your mother wanted to know everything she could possibly know about everything that possibly existed. You ask no less questions than she ever did." His smile was affectionate, though sad, as he touched my cheek. "I'm certain you have plenty more."

"Sure. But I won't ask until I rummage through my cupboards and feed you."

"No need." He pulled a wedge of cheese, some apples, and a loaf of brushed oats from his pack.

"That old witch," I muttered, grabbing an apple from his hands as he struggled to balance the food in his arms without dropping it.

Once everything was placed on the table, Anders cut a bit of cheese and bread, and made himself comfortable on the cluttered floor. "Now then."

"Shouldn't you be sitting in the chair? It might be easier on your old bones."

"I'm not as old as you think," he grumbled, trying not to look insulted. "Now ask your questions."

Settling myself opposite him, I bit into the apple, savoring its sweet juices. "Does the Crown Council of Mages really believe in the Crownmage?"

Anders blew out his breath with a loud noise. "Yes. Unfortunate that. It's the one thing Jules didn't lie about. The council's giving Elena a difficult time."

"She deserves it."

His expression was eloquent. "They want the Crownmage on their side to control Elena, and Elena wants the Crownmage on her side to control the council, or at least neutralize their influence. The ridiculous fact is the council thinks it *can* control the Crownmage."

"Is it ridiculous?"

"Absolutely. They should be thinking the way Elena is. She wants an alliance with the Crownmage, or so Jules tells me." Anders ignored my deepening frown, as he'd ignored my careless words about Jules and

Elena back in the garden. "The council's causing her endless grief by making her lords doubt her ability to hold Tuldamoran together. With Charlton Ravess leading the wolves, they want to dictate how Elena should deal with the Crownmage and themselves. The Firemage is more ambitious than past council heads. And Elena, by the way, strikes me as exceedingly stubborn."

"She is."

"You should know. If they crush her influence, they'll pay dearly."

"Do you think the council's behind the trouble with the Meravan raiders along the Belbridge coast?"

"Unproven as yet that they're from Meravan," he reminded me, bringing to mind my own words to Carey the day he came shouting into the schoolroom about pirates. "But, yes, I do. Still, it troubles me because I can't think why the Meravan monarch would risk Elena's displeasure. They've too much to lose."

"Maybe the monarch's a victim of his own political intrigues."

Anders looked thoughtful. "Maybe."

"Why doesn't the Crownmage make an appearance if trouble's brewing?"

Anders shrugged, swallowing a bite of mild cheese. "Maybe the Crownmage isn't sure yet which side would offer the better alliance."

"An opportunist."

"Perhaps." Anders' sea-gray eyes were amused. "Perhaps he, or she, doesn't think the time is right. No crisis yet, simply trouble brewing."

I ate in silence for some long moments, thinking unwillingly about Elena, until Anders interrupted my thoughts.

"Do the dreams still come?"

"No."

"That means we're making progress," he said with a satisfied smile, draining his glass of Marain wine.

"Please explain, wise master."

"Well, if you were still fighting the talent within you, I should think the dreams would still trouble you. Since you're not, well then—"

"Anders," I said with a trace of impatience. "I'm not fighting the talent. It's fighting me."

* * * *

"Is it fighting you?" Lauryn asked some days later, after listening to my grumbled complaint.

"Easier than blaming myself, isn't it?" I grinned, prompting my friend to toss a cushion at my head.

"You're impossible. Alex," Lauryn looked thoughtful. "I spoke with Anders yesterday while you were in the schoolroom."

"He's the impossible one."

"I'm sure he's a match for you."

"I thought you were on my side."

"I am, though he thinks I'm on his. That's why . . ." Lauryn shook her head, bemused. "Nevermind."

"Oh no, you don't." I threatened to return the pillow. "Finish the thought."

"It's nothing." She fiddled with a lock of unbound auburn hair.

"You expect me to believe that?" I tossed the pillow anyway, catching her in the head. "Finish your thought."

"He knows you told me why he's here, so he was pleased to have a willing ear. Alex, he really believes in your potential."

"That's his ego talking."

"I don't think so. Alex, he . . ." She stopped, unusually flustered. "Listen, it's just a hunch."

"You're a mother. Your hunches are usually sound."

"Stop flattering me." Lauryn hugged her knees close to her chest before daring to answer. "I think you've taken him by surprise."

"In what way?"

"Hard to say. I just get a vague impression he enjoys teaching you."

"I hope so."

"No, I mean really enjoys teaching you." When I stared blankly at her, Lauryn shook her head. "I think he enjoys teaching you because of you, Alex, because he enjoys your company."

"I insult him half the time."

"It's part of your charm." When I frowned at the affectionate insult, she shrugged. "I told you it's just a hunch."

"He's twice my age. Be realistic."

"I don't think he's as old as you think he is."

"That's his opinion, too. But it doesn't matter. This particular hunch is one of your incorrect ones. He's not interested in me, not that way. And I'm certainly not attracted to him. Anders is here to help me uncover my mage talent. And then he'll be on his way. Besides," I said matter-of-factly, as though it explained everything, "he can't stay at the Seaman's Berth forever now, can he?"

"I'm afraid if he has financial trouble, Rosanna will be only too willing to lend a hand."

"Then I'd better focus on my talent so he's not tempted to stay."

"Not a bad idea. And the sooner he's gone, the sooner Jules will stop sniffing around with questions he daren't ask."

"Is he driving you mad?"

"More for the very fact he's not brave enough to ask. At least he'll be out from under our feet for a few days."

I eyed Lauryn warily. "Why is that?"

"Elena's called the dukes together. When she calls—" The moment I started to protest, she waved away my concern. "She's besieged, and I don't begrudge her needing him."

Judging the sincerity of her words, I nodded, suddenly caught by an idea. "Would it make it easier if you knew I was going north, too?"

"Jules didn't tell me."

"Jules doesn't know." Lauryn eyed me with matching wariness, so I added, "I need to find out a few things."

"I suppose you'll want me to take over your lessons."

"Only if I'm late coming back."

"What things? Nevermind. I don't want to know."

"Yes, you do, but you're polite enough not to ask."

"One of these days, old friend, I won't be so polite."

Chapter Fifteen

Politeness and good manners never entered my dreams, but Elena Dunneal did, pestering me when I should have enjoyed a peaceful sleep. I woke with her image holding a sword to my heart, commanding use of my mage talent. If not for the tears running down her flushed cheeks, I would've ripped out her throat. In my dream, anyway. Disturbed, I fumbled my way out of bed and made my plans. Knowing Jules was heading north that afternoon, I contrived to reach Ardenna first and commit the unforgivable.

By tacking a note to the accustomed crack in the cottage door, I evaded Anders' questions. Besides, I didn't owe him any explanations.

Several weeks later than my previous trip north, I felt a distinct chill in the air, accompanied by the constant sight of drifting leaves and bare branches the closer I got to Ardenna. Unfortunate the Marain Valley vintners had started to shelter their delicate vines against the encroaching frost. No matter. Maybe I'd borrow a bottle or two from the Dunneal wine cellar.

Unable to find an available shipmaster to ferry me north along the Kieren River, I traded stories to a farmer's small children for a ride in his cart as far as the city outskirts and the tunnel entrance. Once safely inside, I found my way to the old storage rooms, stifling a sneeze from the dust. I shed my trousers and tunic, tugging on the careworn dress I'd pirated from Rosanna's cook. Neither Jules nor Elena would expect me in the city in a servant's dress.

Nor would they expect me to do what we'd vowed as children never to do. Eavesdropping on each other was unforgivable. Bad enough to spy on Elena in her throne room, but to eavesdrop on her private conversation with Jules was truly unforgivable. But they'd both betrayed my trust by lying, though it didn't make me feel any better to betray them. Shoving aside the guilt, I decided to go ahead anyway.

Taking a deep, steadying breath, I made my way with caution between aisles of stacked crates and released the latch on the panel leading to a little-used corridor. I timed my entry to coincide with Jules' probable arrival, and walked through the empty corridor as though I belonged there. I spied a forgotten basket tossed aside in a corner and snatched it up as an excuse should anyone question me.

Walking through the halls at a steady pace, I neared Elena's suite of rooms without incident. Unwilling to press my luck further, I edged along the corridors until I found the side entrance into her private garden. I knew she'd walk with Jules here if he'd arrived, from old habit. If not, I was prepared to wait.

Luck was with me. Jules appeared scant moments later. I held my breath, kneeling in a shadowed corner; far enough to be out of sight, near enough to hear, fervently hoping I wouldn't overhear anything I'd regret. Which made me think of Rosanna's accusation. Yes, of course, it hurt to keep Elena at arm's length. But I wasn't ready to forgive her or acknowledge her side of this ridiculous situation.

But then why else was I here?

Waiting in the garden, I started to worry when they were both so silent, thinking of Lauryn back in Port Alain, until I heard the distinct rustle of paper. I breathed a sigh of relief as I realized Elena had handed Jules a letter.

"Charlton Ravess is becoming intolerable, his accusations worse." Elena took the paper back from Jules' outstretched hand.

I peered through unfamiliar shrubbery, poisonous for all I knew to keep intruders out.

Jules frowned. "Can't we do anything to stop him?"

"Short of murdering him? He criticizes every measure I propose in the assembly, twisting my intent to serve his purpose. Even lords who supported my father distance themselves from my policies. I don't know how to reach them."

Jules slapped leather gloves against his thigh. "They look ridiculous."

"They don't care. Believe me. I've talked myself hoarse trying to convince them they're making a mistake. The problem isn't they don't support me. It's that they're afraid to cross him."

"Maybe they should fear you."

"If I threatened them, I'd be no better than the Firemage."

Jules tossed his gloves to the stone bench and paced. I ducked swiftly as he came close to my hiding place. "Cowards."

"I don't disagree." Elena sounded weary and disheartened.

"You need to draw the Crownmage out into the open."

In the tense silence, Elena shook her head fiercely. "No."

"I'm not implying what you think. I know Alex isn't the Crownmage. I've accepted that. But something's going on with Anders Perrin, and no one, including my mother and my wife, is willing to tell me."

"Can you blame them?" Elena's dark blue eyes flashed. "We've brought Alex enough pain. Leave her be." As Jules started to protest, her tone sharpened. "I mean it, Jules. Promise me." Her expression was vulnerable, and Rosanna's words came to mind again, shaming me. "If I'd known the high price I'd pay, I'd never have troubled her," Elena said quietly. "She'll never forgive me, and I'll never forgive myself for that."

I wanted to cover my ears like a child, but I'd brought this on myself, and forced myself to listen.

"She's made her peace with me, surely—"

"No." Elena shook her head, running slender fingers through tangled black hair. Sapphires and diamonds on the Dunneal ring glittered in the late afternoon sunlight. "I'm the one she's judged guilty. I need the Crownmage for selfishly political reasons."

"Not selfish."

She laughed with bitterness at his loyal defense. "To Alex, it's selfish. And maybe, just maybe, she's right. But I'll tell you one thing. She was right when she accused us of never asking what she wanted." Elena's smile was sad. "And somehow, Jules, I think that pains her even more than our lies. Even if by some farfetched chance she turns out to be the Crownmage, or any kind of mage, it's her choice to accept or reject that power, not my right to command her."

"I know, but—"

"Alex has never forgiven me for pushing her to use her talent when we were children. I've done precisely the same thing years later. Only this time, she dug in her heels and refused to let me win. In some perverse way, I'm glad. I respect her for that." Standing suddenly, she picked up Jules' gloves. "Alex is out of reach for the moment. But I have to do something about Charlton Ravess before he destroys what little influence I have left. And Jules, keep an eye on Alex. If the council starts badgering her, let me know. I'd sleep better if I knew she wasn't in danger."

* * * *

Fire and ice entwined in my head some days later with exquisite pain. I tried to concentrate as Anders taught me to ease the discomfort and diffuse it smoothly through the rest of my body. But Elena kept running through my thoughts. Maybe Rosanna was right. Maybe I was doing Elena a grave injustice. But she knew what she was doing, admitted as much to Jules, and then to me the day her guards held me captive. But it wasn't enough. Why not? What was the point? Did I need to watch Elena suffer my own brand of lunatic insecurity before I'd be satisfied? That didn't say very much for me, did it?

So hard to concentrate. Finally, the heat turned to warmth, the ice to a blessed coolness, for one brief moment.

"Alex?"

My eyes flew open to find Jules peering at me with an anxious expression. I lost my focus, and my balance, as the warmth veered back to blazing heat and the soothing coolness to icy slivers. Intense pain centered in my head. I barely caught myself before falling face down on the hard floor. But not before the flame on the candle I'd been using for practice sizzled with steam as it was extinguished.

"Are you all right?" Jules whispered, helping me regain my balance.

"Why can't you knock like everyone else?"

"I did," he said earnestly. "Several times. There was no answer, and I was concerned."

"I might have been enjoying a pleasurable afternoon in bed with one of your eligible young men."

"Oh." At least he had the grace to blush.

"What do you want?" I tried to distract his attention from what I'd been doing.

"Someone tried to murder Elena."

Tried. Didn't succeed. "Is she hurt?"

"No." Jules brushed light brown hair back from his forehead and sat in one of my armchairs near the fireplace. "More shaken and furious than hurt. You know Elena. The assassins escaped, and she wants blood."

"Meravan?"

Jules tapped a finger against his boot heel. "No proof. At least not yet. But if so, they had inside help. There's no other explanation."

"Thank the lords of the sea she's not hurt," I said quietly, disregarding Jules' wide-eyed expression at my sincerity. Did he truly think I didn't care?

"She's concerned about Brendan. He was ready to saddle a horse and travel north to Ardenna, but Elena forbade him to leave Port Alain. I caught him just in time."

"I don't blame her. He's safer here, though I can understand his wanting to be at her side."

"Could you speak with him? I'm afraid he'll ignore her orders and sneak away when no one's watching. He's furious with the world right now. But he listens to you."

"Why? No one else does."

"That's not true, and you know it. Will you?"

"Of course." I grabbed my wool cloak from its peg on the wall. My quarrel with Elena had nothing in the world to do with Brendan.

"Thanks." Jules' green eyes were dangerously curious as he held the door open for me. "Then you can tell me as we walk back up the Hill what you were doing when I barged in."

For reasons unknown even to me, I admitted the truth. "I don't understand," I complained some moments later, tugging at the edge of Jules' cloak.

"What don't you understand?" His eyes were neutral, as he lounged against the carved gate to his mother's precious gardens.

"Why you're not being smug."

"I saw how ill you were. I was honestly worried. Do you think I'd be so crass?"

"Well, yes."

Jules grinned and lightly smacked my shoulder. "Under ordinary circumstances, I might have been."

I crossed my arms and stared him down, watching the breeze wreak havoc to the top layers of his light hair. "I suppose you'll tell Elena."

"Not if you don't want me to," he said evenly, hands tucked in the folds of his cloak against the chill breeze.

"As though I'd believe you."

He gripped my arm, oddly sincere. "I'm serious."

I shrugged. "Not that it matters. My talent is useless."

"I saw the flame and the water that put it out."

I started to laugh and pushed past him through the well-oiled gate and into the garden. When he called my name, I stopped, chuckling to myself.

"What's so funny?"

I brushed tears from my eyes, still laughing. "I was trying to change the flame to a gust of wind. Wind, Jules. Not water. Now do you understand?"

* * * *

"Don't you understand, Alex? Besides, they can't stop me."

"No, of course not," I said, keeping my tone reasonable and taking a seat on the hard bench opposite Brendan. I'd cornered him by the stables, just in time.

Dark blue eyes watched with suspicion at my unexpected agreement. I waited, swinging my legs slowly back and forth. "Elena needs my help. But she only wants to protect me. I'm not a child," Brendan sulked, reaching for the heavy pack of provisions.

"That's why she thought you'd understand." I was rewarded with a blank expression. "You're Elena's only heir. She's not married and has

133

no immediate plans to be married or produce heirs. If something were to happen to you, or if they held you for ransom, they'd use you against her without mercy."

"But—"

"They'd force your sister to give in to their demands because she'd never risk you. Never. And you know that because you'd do the same for her."

Shamefaced, his cheeks turned bright red. "I didn't think of that."

I removed the pack from his hand and set it down. "You would have eventually. But by then, you would've been halfway home. Elena needs to know you're safe so she can go on plotting her vengeful plots. Trust me, she has enough to fret about without worrying you'll scurry all over Tuldamoran, charging to her rescue."

"Jules must think me a fool." Brendan turned embarrassed eyes away from me and kicked the pack.

"Jules would've reacted just the same if Khrista were in trouble," I said gently, fighting back the barest hint of envy, pushing it aside to simmer with all those other pathetic yearnings my merciless heart used to snipe at me. Besides, if I had a brother, I wouldn't have a clue what to do with him.

* * * *

I didn't need a brother or sister. I had Lauryn, who argued with me all the way from my cottage to the Seaman's Berth, where I'd eventually dragged her.

"Anders isn't here."

"That's why we are." I pushed open the swinging doors and waved to Chester, guilty as his eyes lit up.

"I thought you ladies despised my establishment."

"Didn't Kerrie tell you what was going on?"

"Yes, of course. If he didn't, Khrista would never forgive him." Chester scowled at me as he brought us both foaming mugs of ale, though he smiled for Lauryn. "Lady Barlow, it's been a long time."

"Too long. But that's Alex's fault."

"It usually is."

"I'll take my business elsewhere," I grumbled, glad his daughter was nowhere in sight, presumably at the mage council hall.

"I thought you had."

"I was avoiding your guest."

"He's still here. Alex, who is he?" The inn was quiet as we'd chosen an off hour, and Chester took a seat at our table.

"At the moment, he's not the enemy."

"An odd way of saying he's a friend."

"He was my mother's friend."

Chester digested this bit of information. "Then he's all right for the moment? Can I trust him?"

"He's driving me mad, but, yes, you can trust him."

"And answer his questions about the mage council?"

I nodded. "Just don't get yourself in trouble."

"I'm not afraid of Neal Brandt."

"He'll turn your daughter against you if you're not careful," Lauryn intervened, lightly touching the innkeeper's arm.

"I'll be careful. But so should you," he warned, looking pointedly at me. "I'm serious. Neal Brandt is still asking my daughter about you. He's also asking the children questions when they leave your school-room, wanting to know what you teach them, and how."

Lauryn and I thought the same ugly thought. "Then he knows about Anders," I murmured.

"He's a mage?"

"A seamage. A rogue seamage."

"One of the good ones, then. As for Brandt, I wouldn't be surprised if he's keeping an eye on your comings and goings."

"Then he can tell us where Alex disappears to, every so often." Anders strolled into the common room, an innocent grin on his face.

"It should be obvious I'm trying to get away from you." I caught the innkeeper's puzzled expression and diverted his attention. "An ale for the gentleman, Chester, if you don't mind. I suppose I'll have to pay as he spends all his coins for lodging."

"Now, Alex, that's unfair."

"Hush and sit."

Anders nodded to Lauryn, leaving me with the distinct impression the two of them were trying hard not to laugh. Chester returned, a mug of ale for Anders and himself, uncertain of his welcome until I waved him to join us.

"You should heed the innkeeper's warning." Anders sipped at his ale, wiping a spot of foam from his upper lip. "Neal Brandt may appear civilized, but he's vicious."

"Like you?"

Chester nearly choked on his ale.

"What will our host think?" Anders demanded.

"He's already warned me about you."

Chester's face flamed scarlet, though he managed to control his voice. "Alex tells me you knew Emila."

"I did." His gaze turned serious. "And it was an honor. No less to have finally met her daughter." His expression was unreadable as he glanced at me, then away. "I owe a debt to Emila to keep Alex safe, and I'd appreciate a warning if Seamage Brandt makes any threatening moves."

"You've my word on that, Master Perrin. I knew Emila Daine Keltie a lifetime ago, and the woman was special. No different than her daughter," Chester said quietly, surprising me. "Now, I'll let you chat in private. And maybe," he grinned, "give you a better rate on your lodging, seeing as you're friendly with the Barlows."

"I'd raise his rate, if I were you," I grumbled, "so he'll leave."

But Chester only laughed and busied himself behind the bar.

"Lady Barlow," Anders began.

"Don't you think 'Lauryn' is better? It isn't as though we're very formal here in Port Alain."

"I didn't want to be presumptuous."

I rolled my eyes.

Anders twirled his glass slowly. "Lauryn, you might want to impress upon your friend Chester is entirely correct in his warning. I've been spying and eavesdropping on Seamage Brandt. I didn't like him years ago, and I despise him now."

"Alex has no intention of crossing him."

"No, but every time she disappears, I wonder if he has someone unwholesome dogging her trail."

"Do you?' I drained my mug of ale and set it aside. "Unwholesomely dog my trail, that is?"

"Much as I'd like to," he answered, eyes on mine, causing me the slightest bit of uneasiness, "only to keep you safe, mind, I don't."

"Why not?"

"I may be an insufferable, annoying fool, but I do respect your privacy."

My eyes darted to Lauryn's face, caught by her puzzled query.

"That shouldn't surprise you, Alex. You have a life apart from the small role I play in it." Anders met Lauryn's gaze across the table, exchanged some private, unspoken thought I couldn't interpret, and drained his glass. "I'll leave you ladies to your conversation." Without another word, but thanks for the ale, Anders grabbed his pack and headed up to his room.

* * * *

Some days later, I found Khrista with Lauryn, talking quietly in the huge sunroom adjacent to the ducal suite on the far side of the manor, away from Rosanna's turret. The chamber was airy and pleasant, brightened by freshly cut blooms. Or ferns. I'd no idea, nor any interest in learning the difference.

Lauryn handed me a dainty cup nearly overflowing with cinnamon tea. "Kerrie brought word from Port Alain earlier."

I sipped at the tea, studying the wisps of steam curling around the rim. Swirls of fire and ice. Lords of the sea, it haunted me at every turn. "An excuse to gaze with undying adoration on his beloved?" I arched a brow in Khrista's direction.

Khrista flushed scarlet, which immediately started us laughing, though Lauryn was a bit more discreet. "Do you want to hear the news or not?"

"Any news our loyal steward brings is apt to be significant."

"I can't wait until you're in a position to be embarrassed," Khrista grumbled, with a look so like Jules I laughed again.

"Neither can I."

"I'll have to remind my brother to introduce you to that sea captain."

"Don't you dare," I warned, glancing at Lauryn, surprised to see an appraising look on her face I chose not to pursue. "Now what's the news?"

"Charlton Ravess arrested a false Crownmage."

"On what grounds? Jealousy?"

"They claim he's responsible for the attempt on Elena's life."

"Absurd," I muttered, trying to figure out the implication.

"What is?" Lauryn's face was grim. "That they arrested him? Or that he's a fraud? I know you now believe in a Crownmage, but surely there are mages who would claim Crownmage talent."

"Why bother?" I said impatiently. "If a mage doesn't have talent to control all four elements, it's easy to expose him. Why risk it? It doesn't make sense, unless he's protecting someone else."

"The Firemage claimed Meravan's behind the fraud Crownmage," added Khrista.

"Now that makes more sense," I said, conjuring an image in my mind of the arrogant, white-haired, treacherous mage. "But maybe the Crown Council just wants to provoke the real Crownmage into coming out of hiding."

"I think you're right," Khrista agreed. "Kerrie thought so, too."

"Well, I guess that settles it," I teased, turning serious again. "If they can prove Meravan support, or fake the evidence, that's going to place Elena in a rather slippery situation. If Ravess is blaming the Meravan monarchy, and they've no real part in his intrigue, Ravess is risking outright war with Meravan. With the Crownmage to oppose Elena, Ravess could step in, force her from the throne, and negotiate a peace." I crossed my legs and tapped my fingers against the worn leather of my boot. "It'll be interesting to see what she does."

"What can she do?" Lauryn asked quietly.

I gave Lauryn a wicked smile. "Knowing Elena, something nasty."

Chapter Sixteen

My thoughts were far from Elena and her troubles two days later as I wandered through the ground floor corridors of the manor toward the schoolroom. The quiet was a blessing I fully appreciated, knowing from frequent experience how noisy the children could be when they had a mind to take an interest in the lesson. Muted voices came from the direction of the large parlor to my right. As I passed by, I glanced in the open doorway, curious, and stopped in embarrassment when a rotund gentleman in bright green silk caught my rude stare.

Jules, who'd been hidden from sight opposite the gentleman, rescued me. "Henry Raynard, ambassador from Meravan." With a wave in my direction, he added, "Alexandra Keltie, Schoolmistress of Port Alain."

A deep bow accompanied the ambassador's courteous smile, along with curiosity that flickered briefly in his eyes. As I acknowledged his greeting, my thoughts were scurrying freely, wondering what the ambassador was doing here. With Jules, who no doubt recognized the hundred thousand questions that flashed across my face. But Jules hadn't a chance to answer even one of those questions before the ambassador bowed once again, deeper, and with far more genuine respect, his eyes looking beyond me.

My stomach clenched in a knot the size of my fist when I caught the distressed look in Jules' eyes. Very slowly, keeping all emotion from my face, I turned, knowing Elena would be there. Her dark blue eyes betrayed nothing as I presented her with a formal bow to match the ambassador's.

"Your majesty. Forgive me. I didn't mean to interrupt your business." I walked past her, half expecting Elena to grab my arm, though she made no move to stop my flight.

* * * *

"She hinted what?" I shouted later that afternoon, shattering the quiet of Jules' book-lined study.

"I can hear you quite clearly," Jules commented, head hidden behind the document he was reading. "Elena hinted to the Ardenna Crown Council of Mages she had been approached in secret by the Crownmage," he repeated with exaggerated patience, as though speaking to the boys.

"She'll get herself killed if she keeps this up," I muttered. "They tried once, and they'll try again until they get it right."

"She is taking a bit of a risk."

"Empty-headed royal seahag."

"She's keeping the Crown Council on their toes, not knowing what she's plotting or with whom."

"If Ravess has the Crownmage tucked in his backpocket—"

"He wouldn't be so easily rattled by Elena's cruel hints. The attempt on Elena's life annoyed her quite a bit. She's thirsty for blood."

"Can't blame her."

Glancing over the top of the document, Jules added, "That's why she met the Meravan ambassador away from the city. She wanted to give him fair warning of what's been going on. I think he's the only one she's inclined to trust. Despite what you believe," he added, "Elena is handling the whole situation with a fair amount of efficiency."

"She can be diplomatic and charming when she wants to be."

"Yes. She can."

His cool, clipped words expressed his lingering disapproval that I continued to spurn her apology, particularly in light of my chilly greeting earlier in the day. But she'd made no attempt to hunt me down after her clandestine meeting. Not that I'd wanted her to, though it grieved me she hadn't. I ignored Jules' frown and studied the assortment of books scattered on his desk.

"She told the ambassador there were unfounded claims of Meravan support for the fraudulent Crownmage, and that she didn't believe them."

"Did she mention the raider attacks?"

"No. She's holding that back until she's forced to use it. Elena's depending on the ambassador's intelligence to send the right message back across the Skandar Sea. There's something else, Alex."

"There always is." I met his cool green eyes without flinching.

"She's sending a small troop of elite guards here, out of uniform, to keep an eye on Brendan. She said to make sure you know she's grateful for persuading him to stay in Port Alain after the attempt on her life."

"Couldn't she have told me herself?"

"You didn't give her a chance."

"She could have come after me."

"You made it very clear you wanted nothing to do with her."

I swung a leg over the arm of the chair I was nestled in and shrugged as though it didn't bother me.

His green eyes narrowed to slits. "How are your mage studies coming along?"

"As inconsequential as ever."

Jules drummed his fingers lazily on the carved desk in no recognizable rhythm, and I grew suspicious.

"How many guards?"

"An inconsequential number."

I leaned across the desk until our noses were scant inches apart. "In your next letter to our monarch, tell her to keep the royal guards far from my cottage," I warned, "or I'll send them back to her fortress without fingers or toes."

"She had no such intention. She has no reason to—"

"Liar." I sniffed in disgust, cutting across his hasty protest. "If Elena's sending troops, then she thinks I'm valuable to her intrigues. Not because I'm her friend who might be in danger."

Jules winced at my sharp words. "That's not true. But even if it were," he said evenly, "the mage council here in Port Alain has been snooping around, asking questions about you. I should think you'd feel safer knowing someone was keeping an eye out for you."

"And grateful? Is that what you want, Jules? To see me crawl all the way to Ardenna and thank Elena?" When he didn't answer, I shook my head in disgust and left.

* * * *

"At least he told me Elena was coming this time." Lauryn caught up with me as I was heading for the safety of my cottage.

"Did you see her?"

"Yes, for a bit. Alex—"

"Don't start."

"She asked how you were." When I didn't answer, inching toward the gate, Lauryn added, "She came close to coming after you."

"I doubt it."

"I wouldn't lie to you. Jules might, but not me."

Without turning back, I nodded. "Fine. She came close. Didn't think it important enough."

"Didn't have the courage."

I glanced up, read the truth in Lauryn's eyes. "It's the same end result."

"You could have waited for her." Lauryn tested the limits of my patience. "You didn't have the courage either."

Guilty, I didn't answer, couldn't find the courage to admit the truth to Lauryn. I pushed through the gate and away from the reminder of ice flowing through my veins. Though that was a desperate lie because the ice burned with the fire of a heart grieving for a lost friend.

Chapter Seventeen

Ice melted into soothing warmth that flowed through my body until I was blanketed from head to toe with an old familiar and very welcome mage talent. Not that I'd ever admit it to the old seawitch. I sighed with deep contentment despite the fact the talent was still wild and uncontrolled. As wild and uncontrolled as when I was born.

Lords of the sea, would that pain ever leave?

"Good," Anders whispered, cutting into my thoughts. "Now focus on that tree branch. That's it. Feel the flames. See them burn. Burn the branch, Alex," he encouraged, laughing softly when the wood turned to a puddle of water I'd pulled from some invisible corner of my useless, inconsistent talent.

"Maybe I should focus on the opposite of what I'm trying to touch." Sitting on a tree stump behind the cottage, I shook my head in bemusement.

Anders reached over and took my hand, squeezing it. "I can sense you're finally, finally, comfortable with the talent as it wakens inside you. It'll take some time, but at least you're not resisting it. That's what I was afraid of. Your control is better. And," he shook my arm for emphasis, "you're doing something with the talent. Not quite what you plan to do, but you're using it."

"So, what you're telling me, Master Perrin, is not to despair, keep trying, and sooner or later, I'll succeed."

"Precisely."

"It's a bit seductive," I admitted, "once you tap into it."

"It is that."

"Were you counting on that to sucker me in?"

"I'm horrified you would think me so contemptible."

"I'll bet." I narrowed my eyes to slits, studying the lying old wretch. "All right, let's go on. But only because I want to catch Elena's guards sneaking around my cottage and teach them a nasty lesson."

"Mage talent is not to be used for frivolous vengeance."

"Yes, Master Perrin."

"I'll tell Lady Barlow you're developing a vicious attitude."

"She'll only say I already have one. Besides, you tell her everything anyway."

"The pouting student look does not become you," he chided. "You're a mage apprenticed to me. Now act like one." He crossed his arms. "Try again."

I threw Anders a most disrespectful look, settled more comfortably on the tree stump, and turned my attention back to the uncooperative puddle. Focus. Cool warmth. The puddle turned to flame. "Damn."

"Excellent." Anders smiled, rubbing his hands together in triumph.

"Don't be so delighted," I grumbled, sitting on my hands to keep them warm against the chill air. "I was trying to touch the wind."

"Oh. Perhaps there's something to the theory of thinking about another element. Try again."

"Anders—"

"Try again."

"This is the last time for today."

"Try again."

Cool warmth still flowing through me, I focused on drenching the flames with buckets of seawater. Hoping for water in any form, I envisioned wind.

"Interesting," he said in a neutral tone, eyes fixed on the mound of dirt that appeared in place of the flames. "Were you, ah, perhaps, focusing on earth?"

"Not at all." Clearing my throat, I ventured an opinion. "There's nothing to this theory of envisioning another element when a very different element unrelated to the other two elements shows up."

"It would appear not," he agreed, steepling his fingers beneath his chin and trying hard not to laugh.

"And we don't quite know what will happen when I focus."

"It would appear so. For now."

"Is Elena paying you to teach me?"

"Of course not! That's not a very honorable accusation."

"Elena's not very honorable," I shot back without thinking. Lords of the sea, he'd repeat that comment straight back to Rosanna, who'd be fretting even more.

"From what I hear, that's not the least bit true."

Ah well, if she'll fret about one comment, why not two? "How do you know? You haven't met her."

"Well, no. But you've met me. And I hope you'd consider me honorable." The inscrutable look in his eyes gave me pause to wonder about him again. And my mother, along with what Lauryn seemed to imply about me. None of which made the least bit of sense.

* * * *

"This is a waste of time."

Cool, patient sea-gray eyes studied me. "Will you ever allow me to attempt anything without resistance?"

"That would make your role as master mage far too easy." I grinned, leaning back against the ancient oak behind the cottage the very next afternoon. If anything, Anders was persistent. Once he had me cornered back in Port Alain, the old beast pressed me every day to practice. Probably vengeance for sneaking away without telling him when I was going, where I was going, and with whom I was going. Despite his noble words about respecting my privacy.

"I'd settle for easier. Now pay attention."

"Yes, Master Perrin."

"Don't mock me, Alex. Focus. I want you to touch the wind. You haven't been able to yet, and I'm not sure why." He stood over me and pointed at the pile of dead leaves he'd scooped into a neat pile. "Focus!"

"Don't yell."

"Call the talent. Feel the wind. Envision it blowing through your unruly hair, making it more disheveled than usual. Change the leaves to nothing but insubstantial air." He paused dramatically, arms outstretched. "And do it now."

"Yes, Master Perrin."

Anders started to say something, and then decided against it. Turning his back, he stomped to another old weather-beaten tree stump and sat down.

"Shall I hold mother's seamage pendant for good luck?"

"I don't give a damn what you hold in your hand, Alex," he bellowed across the clearing. "Just do it."

I grinned, pulled out the copper pendant, and clasped it tight between my hands, thinking of my mother. Eyes closed, I coaxed the mage talent awake, felt the fire and ice entangle and swirl, felt the wind in my hair, envisioned it in my mind as leaves vanished, and focused with such fierce intent I thought for certain I'd faint.

"Lords of the sea!"

I was afraid to open my eyes. What had I done now?

"Alex."

Something in Anders' tone gave me courage and tugged at my curiosity. I pried one eyelid open a sliver. The leaves were gone, changed to a miniature whirlwind churning over a small patch of ground between

148

us. Anders looked a little windblown himself as he stepped around the tiny whirlwind, took my hand in his, and raised it to his lips.

"If it takes Emila's pendant to give you confidence, then use it. But, by the lords of the sea, Alex, you finally did it."

"I'm not sure what I did," I said faintly, releasing the whirlwind and the breath I'd been holding.

"A favor?"

"Try again?"

"Please. Fire this time." Hastily, he brushed together another pile of leaves before I changed my mind.

Pendant clasped in my hand, I focused, envisioning the flames blazing on the ground between us. I opened my eyes to see Anders clapping his hands together in childish delight at the small blaze I'd created.

He danced over to where I sat and crouched beside me. "One more small test, please?"

Still in rather a bit of shock and confusion, I asked, "What would you like this time?"

"Wait here." Anders ran into the cottage and came back with a cup full of water. Calling on his own seamage talent, he closed his eyes, changed the water to a cloud of steam, and back again. "Try that."

I nodded with unbridled eagerness, wondering at the guarded look on his face. Clutching the pendant again, I held the cup. Nothing happened. Not at first. As my frustration grew, I dropped the cup with a shout and a vicious curse as flames danced inside, singeing my fingers. Anders caught the cup and extinguished the flames. I was shaking and didn't bother to hide it.

"I suspected you'd fail."

Puzzled, I stared at his sympathetic expression as he took my singed fingers and cooled them with water. "I don't understand."

"I think you can use your mage talent to control all four elements. Fire, water, earth. Even air now." He smiled in open delight. "But not like the Crownmage, who can control all four elements within themselves. You, it seems, dear Alex, can use your mage talent to change elements. Thus, water becomes wind; fire becomes wind or earth, or whatever you choose."

"I'm still not sure I understand," I whispered, uncertain whether to laugh or cry.

"The Crownmage can take the water from a stream, divert it, turn it to steam here, send it as rain there." An amused expression lightened his eyes, taking years from his face. "You, on the other hand, can take the same stream and turn it into roaring flame or take the raging fire and turn it into a windstorm. You change elements from one to another. The Crownmage changes the form of the element within itself."

I was doomed, had known Anders was trouble from the very moment I laid eyes on him. I tried to ignore the rising panic in my head. "But what about Mother's pendant? How did I manage to unite the pieces?"

"That's still a mystery. It may have something to do with your father's bloodline, or perhaps it was simply Emila's way of touching you." He took the copper pendant from my trembling fingers and held it in his own palm. "She never admitted how she split the pendant. Knowing that devious woman, she had a trick or two hidden away." Anders returned the piece to me, lifting my hair to settle it on my neck. "Maybe she just wanted you to use it the way you just did. Alex—" He touched my cheek, tracing the lines of my face, his expression a mix of emotions I couldn't quite read. I wondered what Lauryn would make of it. "She would have been very proud of you."

My voice shook as I tried to laugh away my tears. "What would she have done with such a monster?"

He never even hesitated. "She would have loved you. Taught you all she knew, and more." Hand still resting on my cheek, he kept his eyes fixed on mine.

"I was frightened before. But now," I swallowed with deep uneasiness. "I'm absolutely terrified."

"I don't blame you." His voice was calm, soothing, and I neatly fell into his little trap.

"There's a question in your eyes."

"Just wondering if you were going to tell anyone about your talent."

Chapter Eighteen

"Are you going to tell Jules?"

Expecting that question, I turned from the window overlooking the gardens to face Rosanna. "You mean am I going to tell Elena?"

Rosanna sat in the old, carved rocking chair by the fireplace in her parlor, teacup poised in mid-air. "I can see maturity, wisdom, and tact don't accompany mage talent." When I laughed aloud and turned back to stare out the huge window, she said, "If you're trying to decide whether to turn my blossoms into mud-splattered weeds, I can breathe a sigh of relief. I know they're safe because you can't tell the difference."

"It'd serve you right," I muttered, tracing a random pattern on the frost-covered pane.

"I'll be frightened when you pose a real threat to my garden. And we both know that won't be in my lifetime. Besides, my aging heart couldn't survive the shock."

"Are you quite finished?"

"I suppose. Alex—"

"You're not finished."

"I suppose not. In theory, your talent makes you just as valuable to Elena as though you were Crownmage. It would ease her mind to know she has a uniquely talented ally." She paused a long moment after that word, ally, not friend, but I chose not to comment. And so she pressed on, "It would ease her heart more to know she has a loyal friend. I've known Elena from the moment she was born and disciplined her with the rest of you ill-behaved beastly children over those long, hot summers. So I know she values the friend far more than the ally." When I still didn't respond, she added, "You know it, too."

I continued to trace my finger along the smooth glass, leaving a smudge. "I won't be a pawn in one of her vicious political games."

"This vicious political game isn't a game. Elena's struggling to hold her monarchy together. And you're denying—"

I spun around to face Rosanna's blatant disapproval and accusation. My stomach tightened at the disappointment in her eyes. It wasn't fair. "Make me feel guilty for not offering my unique talent to our devoted monarch, and sitting by, doing nothing, while the kingdom crumbles. You're very good at this, Rosanna, but it won't work."

"I do it when I need to." She fidgeted with the teacup. "Only when I think you're wrong."

"I'm not the one who's wrong. She tried to deceive me into using my talent with no regard for how I felt about it. She's the one who's always pushing. I won't be used as her weapon. All I want is to be left alone. Is that so much to ask?"

"When you deny her your help because of pride? Yes."

"Pride? She betrayed my trust." Pushing aside the memory of my last visit to Ardenna when I eavesdropped on Elena and Jules, I added, "If there's an ache in her heart, she has only herself and your son to blame."

"I'm relieved to see there's no ache in your heart."

"Because I don't have one?"

She watched me in silence for a few tense moments. "You haven't answered my question."

"Which one?"

"Well," she sidestepped my bitter words, "since you insist they're one and the same. Are you going to tell Jules and Elena?"

I shrugged and headed for the door. "I haven't decided."

* * * *

"I've been trying to solve this riddle of your unconventional talent," Anders said later that afternoon after another exhausting session of experiments.

"You're really trying to find out why a selfish, immature, ungrateful, disloyal woman is graced with such magnificent talent." I knocked aside a pile of books.

When I didn't bother to pick them up, one black brow rose eloquently. Anders settled back against the huge pillows on the floor of my small, cluttered parlor that always seemed smaller when he was there. "You've been to see Lady Barlow."

"You noticed? Has she convinced you I should tell Elena?"

"No."

"Preserve me from the wrath of the lords of the sea," I muttered. "How on this wondrous earth is that possible?"

"Simple, Alex. It's your decision. When you're forced to act," he held up a hand to forestall my indignant reply, "if you're forced to act, you'll still do whatever you think is right. Despite her anxiety and your stubbornness, you have a very powerful sense of right and wrong. She trusts you." I muttered a crude oath, which he ignored. "Now, back to your unconventional, magnificent talent."

"Any ideas?"

Anders steepled his fingers under his chin and narrowed his eyes to slits. "There has to be a connection to your father somehow, but there's so little known about his people. Not even your mother was able to pry many secrets from your father." He tapped his fingers against his chin. "But that's got to be the key."

"How can we find out?"

"We could journey to the forests of Glynnswood."

"I can't leave the children now," I said, rubbing nonexistent dirt from my scuffed boot. Even to my own ears, my reaction seemed peculiar. But I could only explain it away as instinct. "Perhaps—"

"Perhaps means you've no intention of ever making the journey. Besides, you've left the children before."

"This is different."

"I'm not entirely sure how, Alex. Why don't you explain it to me?"

"I don't want to go, all right?"

Anders eyed me with wariness. "It might be worthwhile to find out just what you're capable of doing. In case you're needed."

"I won't be needed."

"Perhaps not," he said mildly, a twinkle in his sea-gray eyes made me want to strangle him, "but your talent might be."

* * * *

"Have you been avoiding me?" Jules' deep voice thundered across the length of the schoolroom, quiet now the children had escaped for the afternoon. Honestly, one would think I punished them.

"Would I even consider such a thing as avoiding you?" I continued to sort through the children's art drawings, humming to myself.

"It's been weeks."

I looked up in surprise at his pouting tone. "I should think you'd feel easier knowing we weren't at each other's throat all the time. It's not good for the children to be around such bloodletting."

Expression serious, Jules strode into the room and propped a muscular leg on one of the low wooden benches. He leaned over, chin in hand, arm on knee. "Whenever you avoid me, you're either angry or secretive."

"I'm neither. I just thought it wise to avoid confrontation."

"So your lessons are progressing."

"I said no such thing." Annoyed, I reached over and shoved his leg from its precarious position.

"Ow." Catching his balance, he smiled, staring me down with those huge green eyes. "Come on, Alex. Tell me the truth."

"Jules," I sighed with unfeigned weariness, "there's nothing to tell. Go away."

"I will. But not yet." I grabbed a massive book and aimed it at his head, but he persisted. "Don't you want to hear the latest news from Ardenna?"

"No." I slammed the book on the table, scattering some of the drawings, and started sorting through them again, putting them into meaningless piles.

"You're just saying that to be difficult. Elena's found an eyewitness to disprove the charges against the alleged assassin. Seems the poor gentleman—"

"I'm not interested."

"Had a reputable witness to provide an alibi. The Crown Council's furious. The Meravan ambassador's relieved. And—"

I slammed another book on the table, making Jules jump. "Elena's happy as a seawhale frolicking in the Skandar Sea with a mate in heat."

"Well, yes." Jules looked surprised. "Shouldn't she be?"

"Don't you see how self-sufficient she is? Elena doesn't need you or me. And she certainly doesn't need my insignificant talent."

"Just how insignificant?"

"Very. And very useless."

"Then I'll tell Elena," he said in a silky smooth voice that made me want to leap across the desk, rip out his heart, and stuff it down his throat, "not to bother you over insignificant and useless talent."

Chapter Nineteen

"You can't seem to change the magnitude of what you're doing."

"Would you rather I tried to set the entire woods ablaze?"

The same argument had gone on for some days, though now it seemed to have lost its subtle tone as we both reached a breaking point.

"Alex, be reasonable," Anders tried the diplomatic approach, "for a change."

Well, not quite diplomatic.

"I should be reasonable?" I shouted, grateful for my lack of neighbors in the forest. "You want me to risk the woods, my cottage, your worthless body, and me, by trying to force my uncontrollable talent to its potential?" I stamped around the clearing, muttering and swearing viciously. "Are you mad? Or just an idiot?"

Anders stood in the center of the glade, arms crossed against his broad chest, legs slightly apart, balanced. The man was persistent as a hungry seahag with delicious, tempting, and cornered prey within reach. Engaging, in an odd sort of way I wasn't quite able to put my finger on.

"I don't want to push your talent to its limit, Alex, particularly since we don't know what those limits are. These puny manifestations you've been showing may be all you can do."

"Puny? How dare you?"

"It wouldn't surprise me."

I should have scratched out his eyes the first time I saw him. He was nothing but trouble. Suddenly, he didn't appear quite so engaging.

"All I want is for you to give me a bonfire, perhaps, instead of a candle flame. Not a forest ablaze with crackling flames. A small hill of dirt rather than a pile no bigger than I'd find in Lady Barlow's gardens. Not a mountain. A pool of water bigger than a bucket. Not the Skandar Sea."

"I quite get your insulting point."

"Then do it." Anders stood motionless, taunting me with a cool stance. "Stop muttering, and do it before I grow old and die."

"I wish you would."

"I'm not quite ready."

"That's too bad."

Furious at his nagging, I coaxed the fire and ice and tamed them until they merged with scant effort, copper pendant clutched so tight in one hand I thought the imprint of the tidal crest would burn into my palm. Not a candle, or a hill, or a bucket for this flameblasted old beast. I kept an eye on the fallen, decayed log to Anders' side and envisioned a gust of wind stronger than my first attempt those weeks ago. Not a tempest, of course. The old man wouldn't approve, but a gust strong enough to make him pay close and careful attention.

Envisioned it. Felt it.

Opened my eyes to watch in spiteful joy Anders' dark hair tossing wildly in the wind I'd created. Stubborn, he stood in the same spot, cloak snapping from the force of the wind. I coaxed the talent further, seduced it, pushed it. Felt the gust increase a hundred-thousand fold in strength. Watched as small pieces of deadwood and leaves were swept away. Watched tree limbs bend and sway, fighting the gale.

Watched in horror as the wind snatched Anders up as though he weighed nothing more than a fallen leaf and slammed his body against the oak tree.

I panicked.

Losing control of the cool warmth, I felt the sharp pain of ice and flame rip through my head, blinding me. Shaken, I waited only a heart-beat before running across the clearing to Anders. He lay unconscious, slumped against the tree trunk, just like Jules all those years ago. Frantic,

I felt Anders' neck for a pulse in the loud silence of the banished windstorm.

* * * *

"You're reacting like a frightened child."

Refusing to listen or watch Anders limp painfully to my side, I turned my back on him. "I won't use the talent ever again, Anders. I could have killed you."

"But you didn't." He eased the weight from his bandaged knee with careful movements. "Besides, I provoked you. I wouldn't leave you be."

"That doesn't excuse what happened." Bitterness and shame nearly choked me. "I risked hurting you to spite you," I admitted, studiously avoiding his eyes. "I was careless and arrogant."

"Yes, you were." Anders put a hand under my chin and forced me to look into his calm gaze. "So you learned a lesson."

"At your expense."

"You would have been well rid of me if the wind was any stronger. That should be a comfort to you should you ever be angry with me again. Or are you so accustomed to my engaging personality you would have missed me?"

"You know I would." My voice was subdued, instinct telling my heart a truth my head wasn't quite ready to accept. "That's not funny."

He restrained a laugh, hand still resting under my chin. "I'm all right."

"You were lucky." I sat back, forcing his hand to fall away.

Anders straightened, groaning involuntary as he leaned on his injured knee. "At the risk of making me aware of my aging, decrepit bones, you will, at least, admit we made some progress?"

"It doesn't matter. I'll not use it again. Not ever. Not for you or Elena. Most of all not for me."

"Then you'll have wasted everything I've taught you."

"I'll make it up to you somehow; pay you for the time you wasted."

"Don't be sorry, Alex!" he snapped, grabbing his woolen cloak and heading for the door. "And don't insult me. I'm not doing this for money. I'm here because of your mother. And because I believe in you."

"Even now?"

"Learn from this mistake and put it behind you. You're not a coward, but you're acting like one. You'll withdraw where it's safe just so you won't risk making another mistake. And another lifetime will pass."

"My choice."

"A wrong one. You'll throw away your talent when you could be doing something useful with it. How can we ever learn or better ourselves without making mistakes or taking risks?" I didn't bother to answer, didn't move, fighting back tears of grief and humiliation, of which he took unfair advantage. "Your mother would have been disappointed."

"Bastard." I snarled, spinning to face him. "Get out."

Anders shuffled to the door of the cottage. "When you've come to your senses, you know where to find me."

* * * *

"You've let the little beasts out early?"

Without much enthusiasm, I waved Lauryn into the empty schoolroom. "They were unusually smart today."

"And you were unusually sad," Lauryn shoved aside a pile of books to perch on the edge of the table, "according to Hunter."

"That child is as bad as you."

160

"Thank the lords of the sea I have one son with my temperament. Anything I can do to cheer you up?" When I shrugged, she changed tactics. "Anders is taking it all pretty hard."

"He should. He almost died."

"I'm not talking about his aches and pains, Alex, but his heart."

I glanced up and away. "He's lost his star pupil."

"He's lost a companion."

"You're crazy. Look, he's got no reason to stay in Port Alain."

"You are one stubborn woman. And beastly blind, though I can't quite determine if it's on purpose, or you're just a little dense."

So many insults coming from Lauryn in one breath was a little unsettling. "You're the one with the imagination." I growled, standing to leave.

Lauryn grabbed my sleeve. "The man's attracted to you, and it's got nothing to do with your mage talent. You've pushed him away, and he's not very happy at the moment. In fact," she stared me down, "he's as pathetic and mopey as you."

"I am not pathetic and mopey," I said in self-defense, trying to snatch my sleeve from her deathlike grip.

"Nor are you attracted to him, are you?" Lauryn dropped my sleeve, an odd expression in her eyes. "I didn't think so. Come see me when you open your eyes, Alex."

* * * *

I don't know how the old seawitch managed to restrain herself for two weeks. But two weeks and one day was too much.

"Self-pity isn't very attractive."

I didn't bother to look up from reading Carey's illegible lesson. In addition to his father's temperament, he inherited his poor handwriting. "Is that what I've been doing? Pitying myself?"

Rosanna strode across the schoolroom and leaned against the wall nearest me, arms crossed in an attitude of blatant disapproval. I still didn't bother to look up, noting her movements from the corner of my eye as I continued reading, adding an occasional comment on Carey's work.

"Poor dear." Rosanna's tone was cool. "I felt sorry for you when I heard the same fearful demon that confronted you as a child is back to haunt you. Not surprising, I thought, your response is the very same. You hurt poor Jules then and Anders now, and ran away both times."

It took immense effort not to flee.

"What a magnificent role model for my grandsons. You're given this marvelous gift and find it's just a bit too demanding. You're expected to be responsible for all that mage talent. Imagine."

Knowing full well I was acting like a child, I couldn't resist throwing my pen clear across the length of the room. "I'm not feeling sorry for myself."

An arched brow over a steady eye appraised me and found me severely wanting. "You've been self-absorbed then, not caring a bit about the rest of us. Did you know Anders was questioned by Seamage Brandt?" My stomach dropped to the floor, and Rosanna correctly interpreted my expression. "You didn't know, did you? Well, then, let me tell you all about it. Seamage Brandt forced Anders from the Seaman's Berth and had him brought to the council hall. Chester sent word as soon as it happened. Brandt kept Anders there for a few hours, asking all sorts of questions about you."

"Why Anders?"

"Brandt has a long memory. He recognized Anders in Port Alain as your mother's very good friend."

I turned away, sick at heart. "Is he all right?"

"Do you care? Or are you asking to be polite?"

"Damn you, Rosanna!" I stood up, glaring at her confident, smug expression. "Is he all right?"

"Brandt only questioned him this time around. You might thank Anders for being discreet."

I slammed my fists against the wooden table, leaning forward in anger, barely able to restrain myself from leaping over the wood. "I'm tired of people telling me what to feel, how to act, what to do with my life, and what to think! Every one of you hides behind well-meaning intentions and sweet-sounding words that accuse me and judge me and tell me in precise detail what I'm doing wrong. And I'm tired of it." Refusing to acknowledge the stricken look on her face, I went on, "Jules wants me to help Elena. Elena wants me to help Tuldamoran. Anders wants to make me useful. Lauryn wants to bind me into this wretched family. And you," I said, concentrating all my fierce anger at Rosanna, "you're the worst of the lot! You act like my conscience, always hovering, always waiting to pounce the moment I slip."

Rosanna's face had grown pale.

"You're so frightened I won't be the mature, loving, responsible woman you raised me to be. You judge me every moment of my life," I accused. "That's why I stay away. I don't need any of you. I'm sorry I ever came back to Port Alain. It's not home anymore. It's a flameblasted prison." I turned away, leaning my head against the wall to soothe the unbearable heartache. The silence was so heavy after that outburst, my heart pounded in my ears. But I wouldn't budge. If I conceded now, I'd never be free of her loving interference. From the corner of my eye, I saw Rosanna edge closer to me, hesitate, and place a shaking hand on my shoulder.

"I'm sorry, Alex," she whispered, voice heavy with unfeigned grief. "I've never meant for you to feel that way. If I'd known how much you resented me . . ." Her words faltered as she choked back a sob and walked from the room.

Chapter Twenty

That little scene forced me north again.

As the steward pounded the staff against the dais once in his usual ritual, I cringed against the lingering echo in the cramped alcove behind the tapestry. I set my teeth until the sound and vibration dissipated, replaced by the rustling of Elena's heavy silk robes of state. I'd arrived just in time for the formal assembly of counselors, with Jules tucked somewhere in the crowd.

Further rustling above indicated Elena's restlessness. "My lords and ladies." Her voice carried a tinge of irony maybe only Jules and I recognized. "You've all heard by now there's been a raid along the Bitterhill Coast."

This was news to me.

Elena paused, giving the murmurs a chance to subside. "Two days ago."

"And Meravan behind it."

Utter and complete silence descended over the assembly at the rude, disrespectful interruption. The tone's contempt brought the speaker's face to mind. Long, thick white hair, with deep brown eyes too rich for the sour expressions one was accustomed to seeing on the face of Firemage Charlton Ravess. I strained for any clue of Elena's reaction, but her robes were still, hands probably clenched out of sight.

"Lord Ravess, we've all heard this cry from you before."

"It's not a cry." His voice was louder, approaching the throne. "It is, instead, a formal accusation."

Silk rustled in warning, at least to me. If given the opportunity, Elena would probably like nothing better than to leap from the dais and rip out his tongue before he uttered another word. But she was raised on diplomacy and courtesy and far more civilized expressions of hostility and aggression.

Betrayal, for one.

Manipulation, for another.

And let's not forget deceit.

Shoving those thoughts aside, I listened. Vengeance wasn't my reason for eavesdropping.

"With proof?"

"There were wounded survivors from the raiding ship who admitted the truth of their government's aggression before the Bitterhill Seamage." Ravess' tone was polite, calm, and brimming with confidence.

"Then you'll have no objection to having them appear before the assembly."

"Unfortunately, that would be impossible."

Elena's icy tone left no room in my imagination of the hatred in those dark blue eyes. "Why is that?"

"Their wounds were fatal."

And if they weren't, he made very sure they were. Elena knew this as well as I did, and knew the Bitterhill Seamage would lie through her teeth to support the traitor. My mother had reason to turn rogue, not that I'd ever doubted her decision. Perhaps my father had reason, too, when he spurned any talent at all. Maybe I should follow in his footsteps rather than hers.

"Who inflicted the killing thrusts, my lord?"

I stifled a gasp. Lords of the sea, but she'd gotten feisty.

"How dare you imply I would ever—"

"Dirty your hands? No," Elena cut in. "I was wondering who did it for you." From the loud rustling overhead, I assumed Elena had gotten to her feet. "How dare you," she snarled, voice pitched to carry throughout the audience chamber, "presume to act so bold and discourteous to me, with utter disregard and contempt for my counselors? How dare you risk Tuldamoran's very life in war by accusing the government of Meravan without real proof any judge in any court of law would demand but the purity and credibility of your word?" Her voice dropped to a low, menacing tone which gave me pause to wonder. "Guards!" Elena's unexpected shout startled me back to attention. "Escort Lord Ravess from the hall. Now."

"You wouldn't dare," he challenged, raising his voice above the shocked murmurs running like wildfire around the hall.

"I would. And I will."

"Then take care, lady, for this is one mistake too many you've made."

"Push me a little further, Firemage, and you'll find I enjoy every one of my mistakes. Now get out." Silence descended once again as Ravess was escorted from the hall, broken when Elena, her voice tight with restraint, informed the court, "I think it best to reconvene the assembly tomorrow." The rustle of her robes moved farther away as she left the hall, her counselors following in shocked obedience.

I waited for some long moments, thinking hard. Compelled by an idiocy I couldn't quite identify, I left my pack in the far corner of the alcove and wedged through the narrow opening into the audience chamber. Certain no one was about; I slipped out the side entrance. Instinct screaming I should turn back, I made my way instead toward the central courtyard. The corridors were empty, as though word of Elena's temper had swept through the fortress, warning everyone to find safety out of sight. Careless, I rounded a corner without watching my step and smacked hard into a cloaked and hooded man.

"Idiot." He shoved me aside, out of his way.

"Sorry." My apology died in my throat when I recognized the shock of white hair sticking out from the hood.

Charlton Ravess started to walk past, and then stopped, narrowing his eyes to peer at me. "Orphan child. I remember you." His laugh overflowed with malice and contempt. "Elena always pitied you, but you were too desperate for her friendship to see it, tagging along behind like a pathetic little puppy."

I started to speak, but his eyes held me silent.

"She kept you dangling because she thought you had mage talent. An orphan child with no blood ties could be very useful to a future monarch. Even I kept my eye on you for awhile, hoping for a sign after those odd rumors. I would've snatched you from her grasp so fast she wouldn't have noticed. Or, for that matter," he sneered, "missed you."

I kept silent, heart full of grief.

He pointed a jeweled finger at me. "Your friend," he said the word as though it were a curse, "has made one mistake too many this time."

If he'd said those words to Elena earlier with the same malevolent loathing in those deep brown eyes, I admired her restraint in not strangling him. I pushed him and his hateful words away from me in disgust, forcing him toward the wall.

"Back, orphan child."

With no effort, he switched our position so my back was to the wall, snatched the cover from a wall lamp over my head, and directed the flames through his talent toward the edge of my cloak. As I struggled against his superior strength, he chanted, "orphan child," over and over, taunting me as the flames crept closer. With one burst of strength, fueled by anger and heartache, I shoved him away, barely escaping the flame that turned about with an abrupt motion to trail upward toward the lamp.

Chuckling to himself, Firemage Ravess turned his back on me and walked away, though not before one last remark. "If Elena depends on help from the likes of you, orphan child, then I've nothing to fear, do I?"

* * * *

The cool breeze from Shad's Bay was soothing against my skin, ruffling my tangled hair as I sat along the seawall east of Port Alain. Waves rolled unceasing against the slick, seaweed-covered rocks below as sea hawks flew in lazy spirals, swooping and hunting for prey. Fishing vessels made their way back to shore, evading the larger, colorful merchants sailing in and out of the harbor. I closed my eyes, enjoying the warmth of the afternoon sun on my face, enjoying the deceptive serenity, grateful to be home again.

"Raiders landed at Bitterhill five days ago."

I jumped, almost falling from the seawall. "Lords of the sea, Jules," I said, my voice shaky, "must you be so stealthy?"

"I'm sorry." He perched beside me on the seawall. "I thought you heard me and decided to ignore me."

"Not a bad idea," I grumbled, replying to his news. "I'd heard raiders landed, looted, and vanished back to sea. Are we next?"

Jules shifted to get more comfortable, hugging his knees against his chest. "I've alerted the Port Alain troops, just in case, but I don't think they'll bother us. At least not yet. We're larger than Bitterhill and wouldn't be such easy prey."

"Is Meravan blamed again?" I asked with feigned innocence, looking out to sea, shivering as the sun slid behind a passing cloud.

"I'm afraid so."

"Who pointed a finger?"

"Ravess."

"No surprise."

"No. I was in Ardenna two days ago. He accused the Meravan monarch of responsibility for the raid at a formal assembly. He didn't have any proof that would stand up to scrutiny. Elena was so outraged she

169

threw him out." Jules rested his chin on his knees, light brown hair lifting in the bay's breeze. "Is it so very much to ask that you help her?" I started to jump down from the seawall, but Jules' firm grasp held me back. "Please just listen. Please, Alex."

I didn't answer, sat back down at his uncharacteristic plea, and stared moodily out across the bay.

"Thank you." Jules released his grip. "I don't know how far you've progressed with your mage talent or what you can or can't do. But if there's any talent you could offer Elena as counterbalance to the Ardenna Council until the Crownmage appears, if the Crownmage ever does appear, is it really so very much to ask?"

I stared across the bay, seeing nothing.

"Suppose the Crownmage appears and decides to ally with the Crown Council, what then? Or, suppose the Crownmage never appears? Alex, don't you see?" he asked, taking complete advantage of the fact I was at least listening.

"See what?"

"Maybe I'm naïve, but even if you can't offer Elena any mage talent that's reliable or potent, at least you can offer your friendship back. Elena needs every bit of confidence and trust we can give her. She's left you alone as she promised," Jules reminded me, "but it's hurting her deeply. She needs you. You, Alex. Her friend."

How I'd needed to hear those words as a child. Yet if I were honest, when ever did Elena turn me away or deny me genuine affection? Not ever. I was the one rejecting her now, though I shared the heartache. "Isn't your support enough?"

Jules chose to ignore my needless cruelty. "I could tell you it's our duty as royal subjects, and I'd be right. But not you and me, Alex. That's not a good enough reason. We're her friends. We've always been her friends, despite all your doubts. And that's far more important, and more demanding." When I turned away, Jules reached out to touch my hand. "At least think about it. That's all I ask."

I watched him leave, guiding his horse in the direction of the manor. That's all any of them asked.

Anders. Whom I hadn't seen in a month's time.

Rosanna. Who avoided me for the past two weeks.

Jules. Elena. Lauryn.

If I gave in, what would it cost me? If I didn't, would it cost me more?

The heart of the matter was I didn't need to think. I'd decided a long time ago. I just hadn't bothered to accept the decision, or face it honestly.

Flameblast all of them. I hoped they'd rot in hell.

* * * *

I stopped at the door to Jules' study, hearing a murmur of deep voices within. "Who's in there?" I whispered to Brendan who came down the hall from the twins' connecting rooms, Kerrie beside him.

"Master Perrin, I think," he whispered back, dark blue eyes, identical to his older sister's, wide with curiosity.

Kerrie cocked his head to the side, listening. "Sounds like him."

I nodded with a conspiratorial smile and lifted a finger to my lips. Both young men grinned and left me to my tricks. Closing my eyes, I slipped the copper pendant from my neck and coaxed the fire and ice to life. It'd been so long, and I so missed their presence.

Damn Anders Perrin to flaming hell.

I merged the fire and ice to their familiar cool warmth, took a deep, calming breath, and flung open the heavy door, slamming it against the inner wall.

"Alex?" Jules peered at me as I leaned against the doorframe. Unable to read my neutral expression, he stole a sidelong glance at Anders, who kept silent, a raised brow the only hint of reaction.

Good. Even better, Jules was sitting just where I wanted him, in the huge carved, wooden chair behind his desk. I ignored Anders and stared at Jules, keeping my inscrutable facade in place. Controlling the cool warmth until I envisioned the precise image I wanted, I concentrated on Jules' chair. And almost bit my tongue to keep from laughing as Jules landed with a thud and a splash in the huge pool of water that replaced his wooden chair, a stunned expression on his face.

"Alex?" His voice came out a harsh croak. "How—"

I ignored Jules and turned to Anders, who arched the other brow. "You tell him. If you haven't already done so."

Anders steepled his fingers beneath his chin, cautiously amused, but held his tongue. I turned to go and then paused, staring at Jules, still sprawled on the floor.

"I'll tell Elena myself."

Chapter Twenty-One

Telling Rosanna fell to me, too.

I watched her from the doorway to her sitting room. Busy writing some correspondence, she hadn't heard me come in. Given our last conversation, I knew she wouldn't ignore my presence. "I'm taking my demons with me to Ardenna. Elena needs all the help she can get, even if it's offered by an unreliable, third-rate apprentice mage."

Her pen froze in mid-stroke as she looked up, brushing a gray-streaked strand of hair from her face. She waited, letting my words sink in.

"Well," I said with forced lightness, "I can't very well leave them with you, can I?"

Rosanna put the pen down, eyes sad with old grief and failure. I was poised to flee, but scrounged around for every bit of courage and stayed.

"Rosanna, I'm sorry."

Jules' mother pushed back her chair and stood shakily behind the neat desk. "There's no reason for you to apologize."

"You're wrong." I crossed my arms, still leaning against the door-frame, still poised to flee. "What I said had the same effect as though I grabbed a dagger and plunged it into the heart of the one woman who spent countless years caring for me. I haven't been very grateful. I'm the one who should be sorry."

"No. No, Alex, please don't. You had every right to say what you did. I wish I'd known how you felt." Her voice faltered, though she didn't look away.

I stepped away from the doorway. "I don't feel that way, Rosanna. I never did. It's just my life's turned into complete chaos, and I don't know what to think anymore. What I really wanted to tell you is you raised a loving, responsible woman."

Orphan child.

"It's just she's a little reluctant and has to be nudged from time to time to remember what she was taught."

"Oh, Alex," Rosanna cried, coming around to embrace me, "I knew what kind of woman I raised. I know it hasn't always been easy for you. When you stay away, I don't begrudge you that distance."

I hugged her tight and stepped back, a sly expression on my face. "Did Jules tell you of his, ah, mishap?"

Wiping tears from her eyes, she chuckled with open wickedness. "That was well done, very well done. Actually, Lauryn came running with the news before Jules arrived. I wasn't very sympathetic when Jules complained. He expressed a very strong opinion of my lack of tact."

"I can well imagine."

"Are you really going to Ardenna?"

"I'd rather not. I've been there too often."

She arched one brow with practiced ease. "Recently?"

"Very."

Rosanna appraised me again, thoughtful. "May I ask why?"

"I was gathering information," I said dryly, refusing to explain my visits. It was good to keep the old seawitch on her toes from time to time. "Lauryn said she'd keep the children busy for me until I return. She's already used to it," I added, before Rosanna could sneak in her own nasty comment.

She laughed, appreciating my tactic. "Is Anders going with you?"

"I haven't decided."

"I forgot. Just because you're a loving, responsible woman doesn't mean you're sensible."

"Don't you think your expectations are a bit high?"

"I suppose they are. But then I forget the monster I raised."

"You shouldn't speak of Jules like that," I scolded, turning to leave. "He's not here to defend himself."

* * * *

"I just thought I'd tell you if you don't let me travel with you to Ardenna, I'll just tag along anyway." Anders led his horse into the clearing behind the cottage, saddled, packed, and ready to leave.

It was the first real conversation we'd had since the day I'd slammed him unconscious against the oak. I studied him before saddling my own horse, a sturdy animal Jules let me borrow. To get to the city all the faster, he'd said with an infuriating grin, before I changed my mind. With a final, resigned glance at the cottage, I mounted my horse, and steadied the restless beast beneath me.

"Rosanna told me about Seamage Brandt."

"We had a pleasant conversation."

"Did—"

"Of course I didn't tell him about you."

"That wasn't what I was going to ask." I flushed scarlet. "I wanted to know if he hurt you."

Anders shook his head. "Just warned me to stay out of trouble and wanted to know why I was back in Port Alain."

"What'd you tell him?"

Anders' grin was impish. "I was determined to bed you."

"There goes my reputation."

"I believe it was already somewhat muddied."

"Did you disapprove of Jules' mishap? Or was that justified vengeance?"

Anders laughed openly, sea-gray eyes changing to a lighter hue. "I'd say Jules had it coming."

"Then watch yourself, old man." I gathered the reins loosely in my hands. "If you misbehave just once on this journey, just once, I'll find something nasty for you, too."

"Rosanna warned me to be cautious."

Chapter Twenty-Two

Apparently, Rosanna didn't warn him about everything.

"You're going where?" he asked, mouth open in utter disbelief. "In the middle of the night, you intend to knock on Elena's bedchamber door?" Sitting on the lumpy mattress in his adjoining room, Anders stared at me as though I were mad.

"Sure."

"I think the fire and ice in your head has destroyed what little common sense you had."

"Trust me." I laughed from my comfortable position leaning against the wall. "Elena will absolutely appreciate the gesture."

"Not if she's, ah, entertaining a gentleman."

"It won't be as amusing if she's not."

Anders refused to let me go alone, even though he still believed me a little crazy. "I'm impressed," he whispered, amazed at the ease with which we passed from guard to guard with the sealed message bearing Jules' Port Alain crest.

Elena's guard was reluctant to disturb his monarch at such a horrendous hour and present her with a bottle of Marain wine as I requested, despite Jules' influence. Eventually, he ushered us into the queen's modest, though tasteful, private parlor.

"I didn't realize Jules had so much clout."

"He doesn't deserve it."

"Jealous?" Cool eyes, very much alert and curious despite the lateness of the hour, twinkled with undisguised wickedness.

"Not in the least." I stopped the rest of my comment as the guard returned.

With a bemused air, the guard bowed with deep respect. "Her majesty will see you now."

Anders shot me an appreciative glance as we passed through the carved door into a larger, empty chamber that reflected Elena's simple, elegant taste.

"I should have known it was you."

I jumped, having thought the room was empty. But Elena, black hair a bit disheveled, was standing in a shadowed corner of the chamber, a curious expression on her face. She kept her tone light, cautious, probably fearing, as Rosanna had, I'd run away.

"Did we interrupt anything?" I asked with suitable blandness and a suggestive nod in the direction of her bedchamber.

Elena laughed, blue eyes flashing in appreciation. "Vengeance?"

"Sure. And a bribe to go with it." I pointed to the wine bottle she held.

"Not to mention a rather interesting companion." She appraised Anders from the top of his gray-streaked hair to his well-worn boots. "Indeed."

"Her royal majesty, Elena Dunneal, beloved monarch of Tuldamoran, gracious and compassionate ruler of all that is wise and noble—"

"Alex—"

"Anders Perrin, majesty." The old seamage cut in with the barest hint of amusement in his eyes as he knelt.

"The infamous Master Perrin." Elena coaxed Anders to his feet, eying him with renewed interest. "Well, it doesn't matter Alex has no manners and comes barging into my private quarters in the middle of the night. I'd never do such a thing." She laughed, though I saw the hint of doubt that flashed in her eyes. "But since you're here, the least I can do is be gracious and accept the bribe." She uncorked the bottle and pointed me in the direction of some clean glasses.

"You see how controlled she is, Anders? She hasn't asked why we're here."

"Not yet." Elena handed me a glass of the rich Marain wine. "By the way, how much of this wine did you bring?"

"If I confess, you'll raid my gear. I don't trust you. Besides, you have your own wine steward." I raised my glass, all banter gone, fighting the compelling urge to flee. "To old friends."

Elena exchanged a long, questioning glance with me and nodded, apparently satisfied at what she read in my eyes. "To old friends, Alex. And," she added, with a warm smile for Anders, "to new friends." Taking a generous sip, she grabbed embroidered pillows and tossed them onto the sculptured carpets.

"Well, old man." I turned to Anders. "You're free to sit in that armchair if it's better for your creaking bones."

Anders put his cloak aside, threw me a disgusted look, and proceeded to sit opposite Elena on the floor, biting his lower lip to stifle a groan.

"Don't complain to me about your injured knee."

"It's your fault."

"You provoked me—and admitted it."

"If you hadn't been so damn stubborn—" He stopped, embarrassed, at Elena's thoughtful expression. "Forgive me, majesty, but she has a distinct skill at sticking a knife under one's skin and hitting the most sensitive nerve with exquisite precision."

Elena composed her face to avoid insulting Anders, but a hint of amusement crept through and she started to laugh. "So I've noticed. Well, then, Alex, to use your own words, why are you here? Not that I'm not glad to see you, of course."

"Of course," I said, remembering her visit a lifetime ago. "It's rather a long story."

Elena looked over her shoulder in the direction of her bedchamber. "I don't exactly have a reason to run back to bed."

"Sorry."

"Me, too, but I do have a large supply of Marain wine, should we find the need." She fixed me with curious dark blue eyes, resting her chin on one slender hand. "I know how much you despise coming here. And worse, how angry you were at me."

"Was I angry?" Matching her shy smile, I pushed aside the memory of Elena's grief, even now alive between us, and settled down for a long tale. "Do you remember when we were children, and I changed the chair poor Jules was sitting on to a puddle of water?"

* * * *

Not only did we finish the bottle of Marain wine I'd brought, but we drained two more with practiced ease. Talking was thirsty work. So was listening.

Elena leaned back against the pillows when I reached the end of my tale. "What you're offering me is a rather unique Crownmage-like talent, significantly different, incompletely trained, thoroughly unreliable without the pendant clasped in your hand for luck, and utterly unknown as far as limitations?" Blue eyes danced in a face that had been desperate for comforting news.

"More or less."

"That's so typical of you."

I didn't take the slightest insult. "I didn't want to disappoint you."

Her expression subtly changed, somber as she looked away, and then back again, hearing the old grief-stricken words in a different tone. "You didn't. I know how difficult it was for you to come here. I know how much I hurt you. I promised to stay away, and I did. But it wasn't easy for me either, knowing how you felt." Elena toyed with the Dunneal ring on her finger. "I meant what I said about our friendship, with or without mage talent. To think you believed—" She shut her eyes, sighing.

I tugged at the sleeve of her silk robe until she looked at me. "I only believed it when I was angry. I knew better, but I resisted for a long time."

"You are stubborn."

Shrugging, I stifled a yawn. "If you had to listen to Jules and Rosanna and this old cranky beast, you'd give in sooner or later, too."

"If they yelled and screamed and threatened until the seas boiled over," she countered, "you wouldn't be here if you didn't want to be."

"Which is why you didn't force me to practice on Jules all those years ago." That point caught her attention. "And you didn't force me now. I could have refused."

"But you didn't. Why not?"

Orphan child reared her lonely head again. "I didn't want to disappoint you."

Elena blinked. "Didn't you say that moments ago?"

"When we were children, I practiced on Jules because I was afraid you wouldn't be my friend," I admitted, surprising her. "But now, well, I'm here because I know it's where I should be. If you keep talking about it, I might change my mind."

"That's why Jules let us borrow horses," Anders chimed in. "The faster to speed Alex on her way north should she reconsider."

"I don't blame him."

"You wouldn't." I squinted at the early dawn light coming in through the window. "Elena, I'm exhausted and witless, and you're drunk."

"Queens are never drunk," Anders interrupted with a semi-courteous bow in Elena's direction, as he staggered to his feet. "They're weary and overwhelmed by an abundance of good food and drink, perhaps, but never, ever drunk."

Elena studied him with a bemused expression. "I think Anders and I are going to get along rather well."

"Then please take him off my hands. I've been trying to get rid of him for months."

She laughed as she caught sight of Anders' indignant expression. As Elena rose to her feet with an uncharacteristic lack of grace, Anders hastened to assist her. "You know, there's something to be said for older men. Not that you're old," she apologized, "but Jules would've reached out and shoved me right over."

Anders laughed and stepped back as I slapped away his proffered hand.

"Will you stay in Ardenna awhile?"

"Absolutely not. Besides, I have more freedom and privacy in Port Alain to experiment. If I try anything here, I'm afraid I'll have Firemage Ravess and his three companions breathing down my neck. But you know where to find me."

She placed a hand on my arm and squeezed. "I am grateful, Alex. Despite being whatever it is Anders said meant drunk. But never forget I'm grateful." Elena hugged me tight for a brief moment. I didn't fight her, but embraced her back. Turning to Anders, she said with an impish tone, "I trust you to keep her out of trouble. And make sure she doesn't dream anything nasty to try on me for vengeance. You wouldn't teach her anything like that, but I know Alex."

"I wouldn't let her near you, majesty, if she had any mischief in mind."

Elena, disheveled and exhausted, and quite drunk, despite Anders' courteous words to the contrary, still managed to look every bit the monarch. "Be nice to him, Alex. I like him."

"You're sure you don't need an extra seamage?"

"No." She shook her head, an unreadable expression in her dark blue eyes that reminded me of Lauryn. "I think he's better suited to Port Alain."

* * * *

"Whatever has put you in such a snit?" Anders asked as we made our way south through the Marain Valley the next afternoon.

"You, Master Perrin, have a very poor and annoying habit." I guided my horse back toward the center of the road.

"If I only have one poor and annoying habit, I consider myself fortunate."

"You manage to weasel yourself into the good graces of everyone who makes my life difficult."

"You mean I charm your friends into liking me?"

"Charm? Friends?" With a muttered curse, I pushed my horse into a gallop and slowed when my instinct suspected he wasn't following. I brought my horse to a standstill and turned around, shading my eyes against the bright sun. He'd stopped a ways behind me at the crossroads I'd just ridden past. Vexed, I rode back the way I had come. "What is the problem? We go south. You can't possibly be lost."

"Wouldn't a side trip west be a good idea?" he suggested in a neutral voice, inclining his gray-streaked head in the direction the sun was following.

"West? Why? Oh—" As I sputtered he grabbed the reins as I started to edge my horse away. "Absolutely not."

"You've offered Elena your talent. Don't you think it wise to try to find your father's people and see if they can provide any clues? At least, you owe it to my aching knees to find out anything you can and save me from any more of your damaging wind gusts."

"For that very reason, I'd avoid Glynnswood altogether."

"Admit it makes a fair amount of sense."

"Maybe. But I don't have to like it."

"I don't care if you like it or not. But you do have to come with me."

"Beastly old man," I grumbled, turning my horse around and snatching the reins from his hands.

"At least Elena likes me," he said with an irritating smirk before taking off in the direction of Glynnswood, not bothering to see if I followed.

Chapter Twenty-Three

"Waste of time to follow you," I grumbled as we cantered down a quiet, well-traveled back road in the foothills of the Bitteredge Mountains. Due west and halfway between Ardenna and Port Alain lay Glynnswood. It was somewhat independent in a peaceful sort of way, a duchy of her royal majesty Elena, Queen of the World. In keeping with her royal predecessors, however, Elena chose to leave it somewhat independent in its peaceful sort of way. Glynnswood preferred to resolve its own troubles, and the Crown obliged.

"You may think we're wasting time," Anders said, scratching his chin, "but I've the distinct feeling we've been watched all day."

I spun in my saddle to face him. "You felt it, too?" I kept my own counsel as we first entered the deep forests of Glynnswood, convinced it was only my imagination, though instinct was fast persuading me otherwise.

"I think we can't find the people of Glynnswood because they don't want to be found."

"It doesn't make you uneasy to know we're being watched?" I asked in amazement, shifting to a more comfortable position as my horse sidestepped a fallen branch. My gaze darted left and right, seeking any hint of watchers through the dense foliage.

"I don't sense any danger, do you?"

My gaze darted around again, searching the intimidating forest lining both sides of the dirt road. Instinct warned me we were being watched, but it didn't screech of danger. "Not yet, anyway. It's just that we've left the inn behind."

"Afraid of sleeping on hard ground?"

"Listen, old man," I grumbled, "how often did you sleep under the night sky in your travels gathering information for my mother?"

"More often than you'd think these old bones could manage." He grinned. "Unlike you, I haven't spent my entire life coddled by Lady Barlow."

"Coddled." I brought my horse to an abrupt halt.

"Have you ever wanted for anything?" At the peculiar expression in my eye, he held up his hand and forestalled my answer. "Anything Rosanna could have given you, but denied you?"

"No," I mumbled, feeling sheepish, "of course not." I pushed aside memories of a very well-loved, though ill-at-ease orphan child. The girl had been ill-at-ease for no reason except her own ridiculous insecurity.

With a stern look, he held his mount in check and studied the small clearing just ahead of us at the side of the road. "Perhaps we should stop here for the night before the sun sinks altogether. I don't know what we'll find ahead."

I jumped down with a muffled groan and led my weary mount toward the clearing. "I thought you knew everything there was to know about everything."

"Almost everything. Now, be useful and transform that pile of dead leaves into a roaring campfire while I tend the horses."

"Wretched old beast," I muttered, coaxing the fire and ice to life. I presented him with a respectable campfire, welcome for its immediate blaze of warmth. As the sky darkened, the temperature chilled considerably and swiftly. My breath frosted and the air grew cold enough to make me shiver from head to toe.

"That's a bit bright, isn't it?" Anders tossed my gear to the ground at my feet, just missing my toes.

"Do it yourself next time," I snapped, rummaging through my pack for our travel rations. Elena sent us home with enough provisions for twice the journey, including two extra bottles of vintage Marain wine. As though she knew we'd take a side trip to this lords' forsaken part of her realm.

"I'd have to use considerable human energy to do it the usual way, after gathering twigs and branches. I'm only a crusty old seamage, remember? Far better for my apprentice to practice."

"I wish Elena needed another seamage in Ardenna. I wish—" Stunned, I sat back on my heels, one hand still caught in my old leather pack. I kept both eyes fixed on the man who appeared, with no warning or sound, in the midst of our makeshift camp.

Anders, on the other hand, showed surprise, though no alarm, and held both hands before him to show they were weaponless. "Alex," he said quietly, exchanging a significant glance with me, "I suggest you remove your hand, with no rush, mind, from your pack and show our visitor you're harmless."

I held back a sharp answer and did as he suggested. My eyes still locked on the man standing between us, lean, supple, and poised to react. In turn, he studied us with calm interest, waiting. Dressed from head to foot in dark shades of leather to match the natural tones of the forest and foothills, he blended into the land surrounding us. Easy enough to see how we could be watched by invisible eyes.

"You are strangers to Glynnswood." His rich voice, surprising in its gentleness, startled me into standing. The woodsman stepped back, alert for any false or threatening movement.

"The young woman is here searching for her father's family," Anders said with unusual courtesy when I didn't answer. "Her father was Sernyn Keltie, dead these past twenty-five years."

Caught off guard, the woodsman turned his gaze back to me and studied my face, muttering some words I couldn't hear or understand. With an abrupt, yet graceful movement he confronted Anders. "Do not leave this place. I will find them." Stepping back to the fringe of our camp, he spoke in the same placid tone that had so startled me. His intent was quite different this time. "If you mean them harm, you will not leave Glynnswood alive."

* * * *

"Try it again." Anders sat beside me on a fallen tree we'd dragged closer to the campfire.

"Don't mages apprenticed to you have any days where they can just laze about without being nagged?"

"Of course not. All you want to do is waste precious time. Now, try—" In his desperate haste to stand, Anders barely missed knocking me from my perch on the fallen tree.

"Flameblast it, Anders," I snapped, trying to regain my balance without falling on my face. "What's wrong with you?" I watched all color drain from his face as he stood rigid at my side, hands balled into fists. "What is it?"

He didn't move, didn't answer, but stared across the crackling campfire like a man who saw a ghost. Following his gaze, I stood as well. My eyes held fast by the intense, unsettling stare of a tall, lean woodsman standing near the horses. Damn them all, didn't they make any noise? Backing up until I bumped into Anders, I felt his fingers grip my shoulders, holding me against him in an odd protective gesture. Thoughts of Lauryn and her insinuations drifted through my head, but I didn't have time to reconsider her instinctive opinion. I was only aware of Anders' hands and the fact I didn't feel the urge to push them away.

"Anders Perrin." The Glynnwoodsman was dressed in the same fashion as the man who found us the previous day. He met Anders' stare with a grave expression before bowing in polite greeting. "I never thought to see you again in this lifetime."

Anders' grip tightened on my shoulders, fingers digging into flesh, as the woodsman turned appraising eyes to me, and I studied him in turn. He appeared a bit older than Anders, though that comparison stemmed from the exhausting emotion I read in his deep, rich brown eyes.

"There is so much of Emila in you, child. The blueness of your eyes." His voice, gentle like his kinsman, faltered. Haunted grief shone clear and bright in the eyes staring with open hunger at my face. He exchanged a peculiar look with Anders and approached me with caution.

I wanted to escape without knowing what I was running from. "Did you know my mother?" I managed to stammer as he stopped, mere inches from me.

His gentle laugh rang with heartache and self-mockery. Behind me, Anders caught his breath, muttering something I couldn't quite hear, gripping me so hard my shoulders ached.

"Yes. Oh, yes." The woodsman edged closer to me. "I knew your mother."

"Who are you?"

Seeming reluctant to answer, he shut his eyes.

"Who are you?" I demanded, sounding rude against his courtesy.

Fear was the most visible emotion when he opened his eyes. "Your father, Alex. I am Sernyn Keltie."

Rosanna lied. That was my first thought. The second was what escaped my lips before I could think. "You ran away because I killed her."

Anders supported my weight as I sagged against him. "Damnation, Alex." He shook me hard, rattling my teeth. "You didn't kill her."

"Then why—" I choked on the words as I started to cry, shamed I'd destroyed my mother, guilty I'd survived.

"If anyone is responsible, it is me. I killed her." Sernyn Keltie's voice was soft, distressed by my reaction. "If I told her the truth, she might have been better prepared for a mage child. Emila might still be alive."

"What truth?" I shouted, breaking free of Anders' protective hands as I faced my father. My father! "Tell me."

"Your mother married a Glynnswood mage, but never knew it. I never told her the truth of what I was. I never told her my power terrified me, Alex. Never, ever, dreaming I would father a daughter with such raw talent. When Emila—" He stepped back as I clenched my fists, striking them against my legs in impotent grief and anger. "When she cried out fire and ice was destroying her from within, I recognized the truth. But by then, it was too late." He blinked rapidly against unshed tears. "So you see, it was my failure that killed her."

"So you ran away, abandoned your responsibility, and me," I whispered hoarsely. My throat was raw when I continued, "Threw me aside because you hated me for surviving. You forced Rosanna to raise me all these years. How much did you pay her?"

"Child—"

"Lords of the sea, was I worth it?" I cried out, frantic and overwhelmed with grief and pain. I was desperate to flee.

Orphan child.

Sernyn Keltie tried to caress my cheek, but I shoved him away. Shuddering at his touch, I stumbled against Anders in my haste to put distance between us.

"Rosanna returned every coin I sent her, refusing any part of it. When she promised to keep my secret, at my request, Alex, she did not know how difficult it would be. If she had known how she would grow to love you . . ." He took a deep breath, steadying his voice, compelling me to look at him by his feverish plea. "Hate me, if you must hate someone. But do not lay the blame where it does not belong. I did not throw you aside. I did not leave you because I did not, or could not, love you. I fled because I was ashamed and feared you would hate me. As you do now." He held out a hand in a desperate gesture to make me understand. "I loved your mother, and I failed her. And in failing her, I failed you."

"Bastard!" I slapped Sernyn Keltie with the force of a lifetime of grief, and stormed past him, avoiding the haunted expression in the depths of his eyes. Untying my horse, I mounted, trying to find my way through blurred vision. I fled into the twilight shadows of the Glynns-wood forest without Anders.

Chapter Twenty-Four

"Anders?"

"Here."

I heard the sound of a match being struck. Shielding my eyes from the lamp's glare, I squinted. Anders was sitting in a very uncomfortable-looking rigid chair opposite the bed in a very small, though neat, room. "Where are we?"

He rubbed bloodshot eyes, peeking between his fingers to study me. "Back at the inn we passed on the fringe of Glynnswood."

I glanced down at my underclothes beneath the heavy wool blankets, and shivered. "I don't remember coming here."

"I'm not surprised." His voice was gentle. "When you rode off like that, I . . ." Anders studied the floor, face hidden in the shadows cast by the lamp. "You frightened the breath from me. I was terrified something would happen to you."

Tears welled up in my eyes again. Impatient at my emotional response, I brushed them away.

"I'm so sorry, Alex." When he glanced up again, guilt was clear in his eyes. "I didn't know your father was still alive. I thought he died when you were an infant. If I'd known the truth—"

"I know," I whispered, pulling the threadbare blankets close around my shivering body. I took a deep, calming breath to still my grieving heart. "Anders?"

Anders watched me, his face full of uncertainty and misery.

"Hold me for just a little? Please."

He didn't bother to answer, but came at once to sit beside me on the narrow bed. The seamage rocked me as I wept uncontrollably, without shame. The shock, the guilt, and the plea in dark eyes that begged forgiveness and understanding haunted me. Whispering soothing words to calm me, Anders held me close. A long while later I stopped trembling and listened with childlike wonder to instinct's clear voice. Lauryn was right all along.

In the light of the inn's meager lamp, I held Anders' gaze, sad and grieving, so I imagined, for me, mother, and even, lords of the sea bless him, for my father. His eyes filled with helpless compassion and guilt, and something more. The emotion had been there before, though until this quiet moment I didn't recognize it. In spite of Lauryn's hints and my own denial, I knew it now for what it truly was, and realized he recognized it in my eyes, too.

I traced the beard-rough lines of his cheek as he cradled me in his arms. Cautiously, so very cautiously, he took my fingers and kissed them one by one with infinite tenderness. Far more cautiously, lords of the sea how could I blame him, he leaned closer to kiss me on the lips. With not a thought for hesitation, I recognized with utter clarity what I had and what I wanted. I returned his kiss with warmth and deep affection and fierce need.

* * * *

I squinted against the intrusive sunshine and huddled with a groan beneath the threadbare blankets. I pulled them over my head to shut out any hint of morning.

"Was the night so devastating and horrid you have to hide from me?" Anders yanked the blankets back to expose my rumpled head and bare shoulders.

"As a matter of fact," I shivered, resigned to the bright sunlight, "it wasn't horrid at all, considering what a bone-rattled old man you are."

"Not so old when it matters."

I looked away, studying the repetitive pattern of the faded blanket, tracing it with my finger. "Anders," I began as he twisted a strand of my hair around his fingers. "Were you . . ." Embarrassed, I turned my back. "Listen, this isn't easy for me," I whispered into the lumpy pillow. "I need to know if you and mother—"

"Never. Though it took you long enough to ask me." He grinned with obvious self-satisfaction, pulling me around to face him. "With all the hundred thousand questions you've pestered me with, that was never one of them. I did wonder why not."

"Not one I ever said aloud." I ran a finger through the hair on his chest, gray-streaked to match his head.

He laughed with genuine amusement. "It wasn't like that with us. Your mother treated me like a younger brother. Which, by the way, means I'm not really as old as you think."

"I could tell."

"Good. I was trying hard to make you notice. Anyway, we were never lovers. Only good friends, like you and Jules."

"Please."

"Stop that."

"Well, here's a good thing about Jules," I said. "If there's a man in my bed, he won't try to find me a husband." I trailed my fingers along his stomach. "You never told me how you and mother first met."

"Another of those hundred thousand questions you never got around to asking."

"Stop being an idiot."

He gathered my fingers in his hand and pulled me close for a deep, teasing kiss. "It will cost you dearly."

"I may not be able to tolerate the price."

"You owe me." He plumped the meager pillows behind his head, trying without success to coax them into a semblance of comfort as I leaned

194

on one elbow waiting. "Your mother was privileged to witness my physical eviction from the Belbridge Cliffs Mage Council."

"Belbridge Cliffs?"

"That's where I was born."

"Oh. You never said."

"You never asked." He traced a lingering finger on my shoulder.

"Go on. You were thrown out in disgrace."

"I never said that. I was thrown out in a rude fashion." Sea-gray eyes flashed with an unpleasant memory, though a tiny smile tugged at his lips. "They did have cause, however, as I'd just told them what I thought of their bureaucratic, whining, pompous council of idiots."

"I knew you were a natural diplomat the moment I saw you. Perhaps Elena can use your smooth-talking skills."

"I can use them when necessary." His fingers traveled a bit farther down my shoulder.

I slapped his hand away. "You'll get your fee later."

With a long-suffering sigh, Anders stared at me with soulful longing. As I started to laugh and reach for a ticklish spot, he grabbed my arms and held me fast. "You win. At the very point where they tossed me out the door into the middle of the muddy street, I heard a very loud, distinct sound of someone clapping."

"Mother?"

"None other." His smile was genuine now, lost in memory. "The first thing I noticed was her eyes, bright clear blue to match yours. And they were trying so hard not to laugh. Young idiot that I was, no older than Brendan, I was indignant. My pride was sorely wounded, and then to be laughed at by an old woman—"

"How old?"

"About as old as you."

"Young then, you mean."

"Not if you ask Brendan." He laughed, dodging my groping hands. "She had the grace of a dancer, always appeared tall, though she was a tiny slip of a thing. When Emila was sure she had my full attention, she put her papers and pack aside and pulled me to my feet."

"I would've pushed you over."

"Your mother had better manners, most of the time, anyway. She told me her name and how she traveled up and down Tuldamoran. Watching the councils and looking for rebellious young idiots like me. Not that she called me so, mind you." He laughed to himself, hand tracing the line of my jaw, roaming with a gentle touch to my neck. "She had my friendship and loyalty from that day, Alex. I was intrigued at the notes she kept and studies she compiled, convinced her mages didn't need the councils to guide them."

"What made her think that way? Didn't the council here in Port Alain train her to be a seamage?"

"Your grandmother sent her to the council the moment your mother showed the slightest indication of talent. Emila lasted one month before clashing heads with the master seamage." He grinned at the irony. "Who was none other than the esteemed and beloved Neal Brandt. She was only fourteen and refused to go back and apologize when the master sent her scurrying home for conduct unbecoming a mage apprentice."

"Grandmother didn't force her back?"

Anders steepled his fingers beneath his chin. "Your grandmother told me she went to the council with every intention of dragging your mother back to apologize. But Brandt was so overbearing, pompous, and arrogant, your grandmother slapped him soundly and walked out. Then she trained Emila on her own, with a fair amount of intention to spite the mage council."

"Rosanna never told me. Probably so I wouldn't get it into my head to behave worse than I do." I chuckled, and then had a serious thought. "Why would Rosanna suggest I go to a council mage, if that was true?"

"I asked her that myself." At my raised brow, he admitted, "Well, I was curious. But she told me she always believed you had potential, and there was no one else to turn to for help. She'd no idea who I was or where to contact me."

"And when I didn't show any more talent, you never declared yourself."

"Precisely."

"But if you were friends with Mother, didn't you visit here? Didn't Rosanna ever see you?"

"Your mother lived in the cottage."

"My cottage? No one ever said a word."

"It must have slipped Rosanna's mind." At the murderous look in my eye, Anders changed the topic, though it was no less controversial. "Your mother met your father very soon after." When the murderous look turned violent, he added with quiet force, "It's part of the answer to your question, so listen. When she met your father in Edgecliff, over on the border of Glynnswood, she fell wildly in love. Sernyn agreed to live in Port Alain if she'd agree not to use her mage talent in front of him."

Thinking evil thoughts about the man, I tugged the threadbare blankets upward as the room chilled. Anders pulled them up to my chin, tucking me in.

"Emila settled down to put her studies in order, and I traveled in her place. I returned from time to time, behind Seamage Brandt's back. I brought her my observations and, frankly, Alex, just to be with her. Emila was my friend and mentor, and I adored her. But I never stayed for very long."

"Sernyn Keltie was jealous."

197

"Yes, but not of her affection for me. It was obvious we were very much like siblings, truly. No, he was jealous and uneasy of my mage talent."

"He was afraid you'd influence her to rebel against her agreement with him not to use her magic in his presence."

"Well, yes."

"Did you try?"

"Of course." Anders' expression darkened with shadows of painful memories. "It was the only time your mother was truly angry at me. She told me in irrevocable, unmistakable terms if I ever brought up the subject again she'd sever our friendship."

I resisted the urge to snuggle against his warmth, needing instead to watch him and listen.

"Like you," he continued, "I didn't really know my family. What was left of them after an illness swept Belbridge Cliffs; my two brothers who I didn't want to know. They were worlds apart from me, and I wanted it to stay that way. Emila was the only family I had. She trained me, as did your grandmother for a time." His eyes darkened as he brushed wayward strands of hair from my face. "I didn't want to damage our friendship, so I kept my visits to a tolerable limit. If I'd known years later her daughter would mean as much to me as you do, I don't think I would've stayed away from Port Alain."

I cupped his cheek in the palm of my hand and leaned up to kiss him, still bemused by what happened between us. Lauryn would have smacked me soundly for being surprised.

Anders tugged at my hair, playful again. "Would it have mattered if your mother and I were lovers?"

"Yes."

"Why?"

"I don't want to be a replacement for her in your affections."

His smile was equal parts affection, mischief, and open lust. "You're very much an individual with a very different place in my heart than your mother."

"Just how different?"

"I suppose I'll have to show you," he said, pulling me back into his arms. "Though it isn't part of my fee, you still owe me."

Chapter Twenty-Five

"I know you don't want to talk about it." Anders hesitated as we rode south past Tucker's Meadow at an easy pace, a day's ride from Port Alain.

"Then don't press me."

"Just listen."

"I don't want anything to do with him."

"Your father said he'd send word through Rosanna." I urged my horse ahead of Anders so I didn't have to listen. "Damnation, but you are stubborn!" Anders shouted after my retreating back. "If we're to understand your talent, we need to know something of his talent." He lunged for the reins of my horse as he caught up to me, missing them as I pulled away. "All right. Be thick-skulled."

My horse stopped abruptly as I held his reins in check. I turned in frustration to confront Anders' exasperated expression, pushing aside painful memories. "Don't you see how difficult this is for me? He wanted no part of me all these years, but you want me to learn from him? Can't you understand?"

"Of course I can." His expression softened, cool sea-gray eyes remaining wary. "But we need to know, for Elena's sake at least, if there's any chance you'll need to represent her in a Mage Challenge."

"I'll think about it."

"Then think about this, too." He reached out a hand to reason with me as he changed the topic. "If I have any amount of influence over you, please don't grieve Rosanna. It wasn't her decision to make, or her choice to tell you the truth about your father."

"She lied to me," I said coldly, biting my lip. "For twenty-five years, she lied to me. How can I ever trust her again?"

"Give her a chance to explain. You owe her that at least."

"One chance." I looked away. "Only one."

* * * *

"Alex!" Rosanna rushed across the length of her parlor to greet me. She stepped back, holding me at arm's length. "What's wrong?"

"I promised Anders I'd give you one chance to explain. He convinced me I at least owe you that much."

Her eyes were puzzled. She seemed not certain whether to be alarmed. "Explain what?"

"Why you didn't tell me Sernyn Keltie was still alive."

Rosanna paled, hands falling limply at her sides in defeat.

I walked away to lean against the window ledge overlooking her frost-covered gardens and left her standing like a lost child in the middle of the room, eyes burdened with old grief and heartache.

"When you were a day old," she spoke with such softness I strained to hear, "your father begged me to care for you. He was sick with grief and burdened with guilt. He wanted you to have no part in his guilt, Alex, wanted only you to have a chance at happiness without his misery shaping your life. Neither Sernyn nor I ever thought you'd take the guilt on yourself."

"Wasn't it logical?"

"Not to us. Not then, not now. And when you did blame yourself, nothing I said ever eased your pain. I found it unbearable for you to hold yourself responsible, knowing Sernyn was still alive." With a resigned sigh, she sank into the rocking chair by the fireplace, fidgeting with the sleeve of her woolen tunic. "We were so wrong about you. I promised the day he left Port Alain to care for you and protect his secret because I loved your mother. I raised you as my own, because I loved you, too."

Rosanna raised a tear-streaked face to meet the challenge in my eyes, waiting for my judgment, which she expected to be harsh.

"Did you know he was a mage?"

She nodded.

Hell, at least she was honest. "Is there anything else you've kept hidden from me, other than the fact Mother lived in my cottage?"

Her eyes widened, though she chose to sidestep the comment. I didn't let her.

"Why didn't you tell me?"

"I didn't want you to leave the manor. If you knew, it would only have encouraged you more. My husband didn't agree with me, called me selfish."

"I'm not surprised. What else?"

"Your father asked me to write and tell him what I could about you. I did, faithfully, telling him everything. I knew from his letters he was hungry for every last piece of the puzzle that made you who you are." She stared at me in quiet defiance.

I pushed away from the ledge and walked over to Rosanna. She watched anxiously, tears glittering in her eyes, and then in open surprise, as I bent to kiss the top of her graying head.

"One thing more," I tossed over my shoulder, as I walked toward the door, "Anders is leaving the Seaman's Berth."

"Is he coming to live here?"

"He's coming to live with me." I grinned with utter satisfaction as delayed realization flashed in her eyes.

* * * *

"Your father's people seem to be the only ones in Tuldamoran who have a mage talent somewhat like yours, though still far removed. No one seems to know why." I stiffened beneath Anders' sheltering arm as we lounged on overstuffed pillows in front of my fireplace. "Just listen," he coaxed, knowing better than to wait for a reply. "It's different, restricted. Your father, for example, can change matter between water and fire, but that's all. Other Glynnswood mages can do the same with two elements, but only two, and there's no rhyme or reason to what those two elements may be."

"Being from Glynnswood is reason enough."

He ignored me. "Your talent is rather unique." When I stayed silent, Anders added, with a subtle nudge in the ribs, "I found out why your father was so against magic."

"I'm not interested."

"You should be. Seems he almost killed his closest friend when he was practicing his talent, long before he met your mother."

Oh, hell. "And then he killed her." I freed myself from Anders' arm to sit up and defy his words.

A cool expression hid his thoughts, "He was responsible for the circumstances that allowed her to die without any help. He's suffered all your life for his error."

"Error? He killed her, Anders, and he hasn't suffered near enough. I don't want to talk about him."

"All right." He touched my cheek in apology. "But at least we know there's some basis for your talent in his bloodline. But you're still a mystery." Tugging at my hair, he inched his arm around my shoulders and drew me closer.

"What about the Crownmage? What bloodline produces talent like that?"

Anders stared into the blazing fire, thinking. "There's never been any solid evidence to prove a specific combination of talents would produce a Crownmage. Your mother had some wild theories, though no proof.

Otherwise, there'd be countless couples jumping into bed trying to do just that. Remember, there haven't been too many of them."

"And probably none like me."

"Most assuredly, none like you." Eyes wide, he wrestled me to the floor until I persuaded him it was time to go to bed.

Chapter Twenty-Six

Loud, persistent knocking in the middle of the night some days later brought us both awake.

Anders fumbled for a lamp. "Wait here. I'll see who's bothering us at this uncivilized hour." He grabbed wrinkled tunic and trousers and climbed into them, almost tripping in his haste.

I took my time hunting for my own clothes, prepared to find the Duke of Port Alain at my front door.

"Who's there?" Anders' voice was scratchy with too little sleep as he pulled the cottage door open a tiny crack to peer outside. Beneath a barely visible moon, Anders hadn't a chance to see who was out there.

No answer, but a low, rich, amused chuckle. Flameblasted hells. I pulled my tunic over my head and stumbled into the sitting room.

"Let the royal seawitch inside, Anders, only if she has a bottle of vintage Marain wine in her hand."

A dark clad arm thrust a bottle through the narrow crack in the door as Anders opened it. Throwing back the hood of her dark woolen cloak, Elena sauntered inside the cottage. She eyed Anders' disheveled form with open interest until he blushed crimson to the roots of his gray-streaked hair.

"No one bothered to tell me about this, um, recent development."

Jules followed close behind, cloak tossed over his arm, trying to hide a grin at Anders' obvious distress.

"Be a dear, and open this, please, Master Perrin," Elena purred, handing Anders the wine bottle.

"Majesty." He bowed with awkward stiffness and started to walk away, but Elena grabbed him with a light, firm grip by the sleeve of his wrinkled tunic.

"'Elena' will do, since you're such a, well, close friend of Alex."

I rolled my eyes at Anders in disgust as he managed to turn an even brighter shade of scarlet and then shoved him in the direction of the inner alcove. "Lords of the sea, but you deserve it."

Anders relaxed enough to laugh and fled to open the bottle. I rummaged for glasses as my visitors settled themselves. Jules fanned the flames back to life in the fireplace before dropping to the floor at Elena's feet. When Anders returned, the old wretch poured Elena a glass first.

"Do any of you ever visit each other during the day?"

Elena laughed in appreciation, accepting the wine.

"Elena travels by night," Jules answered with a smug grin, "because she's plotting something nasty. Alex travels by night for vengeance."

"True enough," I muttered, raising the glass Anders shoved into my hand as he sat in the armchair opposite Elena. "To old friends."

"And new," Elena added, with an eloquent, suggestive arched brow in Anders' direction. When he flushed again, she reached over to squeeze his hand. "It's quite all right, Anders. In fact, I would've been disappointed if it hadn't happened. Though I didn't expect it to happen quite so fast, knowing how stubborn Alex could be."

I eyed Elena after that peculiar comment and sat at Anders' feet, leaning back against his knees. "Lauryn did."

"Lauryn knew?" Jules practically squeaked.

"She started giving me hints weeks ago. I told her she was crazy."

Anders nudged me. "Should I be insulted?"

"Probably. Now, my glorious and revered monarch, what are you plotting this time? Or did you hear the rumor I took pity on Master Perrin and you couldn't resist finding out for yourself, even though you claim no one told you he was here?"

"I'd never do such a thing."

"You're a pathetic liar."

"Hmm, but I do have a serious reason for being here. I've been approached, with absolute discretion, by the Meravan monarch. His ambassador gave me substantiated evidence the Crown Council is paying Meravan mercenaries to create problems between our two nations."

"That's credible."

"Yes. Their crown offered open support if I choose to expose the Crown Council. If I don't, or until I do, they'll still support me in secret. Meravan doesn't want war any more than we do."

"Their support in exchange for what? Wanting peace is all very honorable, but I'm sure they want something more."

"Better trade terms which would hurt us only for a short while until our merchants have a chance to adjust. In the long run, Tuldamoran would feel only a minimal pinch, though I believe we stand to gain. If I can convince our merchants to accept these terms, without too much grumbling, we should be able to expand our trade in the future. At a slow pace, naturally, but we'd still benefit." She shrugged her slender shoulders. "It makes sense to me."

"What do you think the Council will do?" My heart sank to my toes, already knowing the answer.

Elena hesitated and drained her glass.

"They'd feel justified in asking for Mage Challenge," Anders slipped his hands onto my shoulders. "Charlton Ravess will do everything in his power to disrupt Elena's influence. With no Crownmage in sight, I'm sure he won't be able to resist creating havoc."

Elena studied him with interest and nodded, avoiding my eyes.

"I told you I'd help you." I kicked her boot with my bare foot. "Though I can't promise how it will end."

Elena's dark blue eyes caught the firelight's glint, black hair framing troubled features as she stayed silent.

"It's all right."

Her expression held heartbreaking vulnerability I'd only witnessed twice before. When she had no choice but to hurt Jules and turn away his affections all those years ago. The second time when she had me arrested in the inn outside Bitterhill, forced to confront my accusation of betrayal. "I still hope it won't be necessary, Alex. I'm frightened for you."

"So am I. And worse, I'm afraid you'll lose your crown because of me. I couldn't live with that."

"If I lose, the crown goes to Brendan. Despite what you believe," she grinned, "I don't need the crown. As long as I know it's in good hands, I don't need it on my head. If you believe I do," her tone shifted with a subtleness that caught me unprepared, "then you and I haven't made much progress, have we?"

I stared at Elena for a long, long moment, uncertain whether to rip out her heart or acknowledge her challenge. "Sometimes, you're an utter and complete idiot."

"Speaking of idiots," Anders cut in, "I wonder if we can rattle the Crown Council a bit."

Elena looked intrigued and nodded encouragement, an undisguised smug expression still lingering on her face.

"I was thinking maybe we can spread subtle rumors they're sure to hear," Anders explained. "Something to suggest one of the four Crown Council members is, in fact, the true Crownmage and plotting to make a bid for control of the Council? If we assume they don't have a Crownmage at hand, then they don't know who this legendary Crownmage really is."

"Wait a minute. There's a flaw in your thinking. Why would they believe that? How could one of them have hidden it all these years?" I countered. "It seems like an impossible task."

"Not if the person's determined." His answer held a trace of something I couldn't quite read, but he continued before I could think any further about it. "Look, Alex, I'll admit there is a chance they won't believe the rumor. And a risk, too, that a genuine Crownmage will appear. But I think it's worth it."

"Who would be the alleged Crownmage?" Elena sipped her wine, the question directed at Anders, but her eyes on mine.

"Since Ravess already controls the Crown Council, I think he should be our main target. And if successful, it will rattle him, as well as the others at the same time."

"Yes." There was a predatory gleam in Elena's eyes. "I think the idea will work." She laughed softly. "Not only is Anders a gentleman, he's devious."

"That's why I knew you'd like him."

"Alex, play nice." Jules stirred from his comfortable spot at Elena's feet. "It all makes sense, but how should we spread the rumor? Who can we trust to see word gets to Firemage Ravess?"

"I think we can find a way for him to hear the rumor." I leaned forward, chin cupped in my hand. "But once he does, I'd like a closer look at Ravess. I think I can rattle him on my own, without revealing my mage talent."

"How?"

When I didn't answer right away, Anders pulled me back toward his knees. "What are you planning?"

"I'm not sure yet."

He poked his head around to stare at me, sea-gray eyes wide with suspicion. "Liar. Spit it out."

"I'll tell you when it's clear in my head. But I know he can't hurt me."

"You don't know that, Alex. He tried to have me murdered," Elena said hotly, obviously trying to discourage whatever was in my head.

"You don't know for certain it was him."

A hard look came into her eyes. "Yes, I do."

"Good. Knowing will make it even more satisfying to bring him down. But still, Elena, understand he can't hurt me, and won't hurt me. Not yet, because he's arrogant. I'm nothing to him."

"I still don't see why you have to expose yourself."

"I have a legitimate reason for needing a closer look at him." Caught off guard, Elena backed off, staring at me without comprehension. "Don't you see? If he issues Mage Challenge, I'm the one he'll fight. He doesn't know that, but I do. I need to see what I'm up against. While I'm close enough to breathe down his neck, I'll rattle him with hints of the Crownmage."

As I quieted, out of breath and rattled myself, Anders massaged my neck, easing the knotted muscles to blessed relief. "I'm going with you."

"To Ardenna, yes. To confront Ravess, no." Braced for an argument, I grabbed his hands where they rested on my neck. "We'll discuss this later."

He kissed the top of my head. "All right."

I rolled my eyes in disgust at his too easy acquiescence.

Elena started to laugh, though she still eyed me with a fair amount of anxiety. "I'm leaving in the morning if you'd like to travel with me," she offered, glancing over my head to trade a look with Anders.

Another kiss landed with delicacy on my head. "Your choice, Alex."

I turned to Jules, who'd kept quiet for much of the night's conversation. "Can you ask Lauryn to cover my lessons for a few days?"

"Yes, of course. Tell me what she should teach them."

"She's done it before. Lauryn knows what to do."

Green eyes studied me a moment, perplexed. "Every time you disappeared for a few days?" When I nodded, he complained, "Why is it my wife knows so much more than me?"

"Because I trust Lauryn so much more than I trust you." I grinned to soften my words. "Elena, I don't want to be seen with you when we get closer to the city," I said, noting she was still eying Anders. What were they so worried about?

Snatching her cloak from the disheveled pile of books it rested upon, Elena nodded to Jules, and started to get up. "If you're ashamed to be seen in my company, then I'll be sure to keep my distance."

"Idiot." I tugged at her trouser knees. "Ravess doesn't need to know you've been talking to me recently. I'd rather—" Impatient, I shoved Elena back in the direction of the armchair. "Will you sit down? My neck hurts looking up at you."

Puzzled, Elena sank back into the armchair with a graceful movement.

"Listen." I turned to look at Anders. "You, too. I do have a plan, and you're not going to like it, but if I must fight him, I want him caught off guard the day of the Mage Challenge when I show up."

Anders traded another inscrutable look with Elena and joined me on the floor opposite Jules.

I took a very deep breath and faced Elena. "The day you threw Ravess from the throne room, I met him in the hall." Her expression grew blank. "I was there. I knew what happened."

"Why were you there without telling me?"

I toyed with my toes, amazed at how cold they felt. "Because I wanted to give you another chance. You'd angered me." Finding courage, I met Elena's dark gaze and shrugged, trying to act unconcerned, trying to convince myself she couldn't see through my act. "I had to see for myself whether you really needed my help."

Elena sat motionless, pale face elegant and composed in the shadows cast by the crackling fire, waiting for the hurtful words she'd grown to expect from me.

"Anyway," I went on, grateful for the fingers Anders entangled with mine, "Ravess nearly knocked me over in a deserted corridor."

Orphan child.

"He recognized me, threatened me with fire, called me . . ." I faltered, unwilling to say it aloud, staring off into the fireplace, remembering the flames that traveled down the fortress walls, seeking me. Anders squeezed my fingers, encouraging me to explain. "He called me orphan child. Nothing hateful about that, it's a true fact I've lived with all my life, though now—"

Elena knelt beside me before I could react. "I know about your father, Alex. I'm so sorry."

"It doesn't matter."

Lords of the sea, what a lie. Sernyn Keltie abandoned me, and it mattered. It mattered very much.

I continued, keeping my voice steady, "It didn't matter then either except Ravess kept taunting me. He said something else." I met Elena's troubled gaze for one brief moment and then looked away again.

"What did he say to you?" she whispered, shaking my arm. "Alex. Tell me."

Without his words, I didn't have a plan. "He said you pitied me. Always had. That you kept me around because you thought my talent might be useful, even though it hadn't reappeared."

"You don't believe that? If you do, you've no one to blame but yourself," she scolded, scarlet blossoming on her cheeks. "Tell me the truth."

The truth? "I didn't want to believe it."

"But you did. Damn you, Alex, you did, didn't you?"

I caught hold of Elena's sleeve as she started to get up and held her down on her knees until her eyes were level with mine. "Yes, I did because I was still angry and vulnerable. When I thought about it, you idiot, I didn't believe it one bit." As some of the challenge faded from her eyes, I added with a crooked grin, "Ask Rosanna what hurtful words I screamed at her when I was feeling angry and vulnerable. You'll feel better, believe me."

Elena pushed free of my restraining hand and sat back in the chair again. "You're enough to drive us all to distraction. Poor Anders."

"Thank goodness someone understands my plight."

I elbowed the traitor in the stomach with a sharp jab. "Now listen." Jules had a peculiar expression in his eyes. "You, too." When he nodded, I tapped his boot heel. "What's the matter with you?"

"Sometimes I feel I haven't the slightest notion who you are."

"You don't."

"That's a relief. I thought I was going mad."

Anders yanked a strand of my hair. "I just had a nasty suspicious thought. If you're thinking what I think you're thinking, you're absolutely out of your mind. It's too dangerous."

"Don't spoil my fun."

"Fun?"

Elena waved a hand to catch our bickering attention. "Would one of you mind very much telling me what it *is* you're both thinking about?"

"Alex plans to use what Ravess implied about you to convince him he's right. You pity Alex and she's disillusioned with you and—"

Elena lifted a hand to stop his torrent of words. "Why?"

"To catch him off guard when she represents you in the Mage Challenge," Jules answered in a somber tone.

"Elena, listen to me. I'm going to need all the help I can get. If it means making him doubtful the day of the confrontation, than yes, that's my purpose."

"I don't want you near him. He's dangerous."

"So am I."

"And so am I." Anders exchanged a glance with her. "I won't be far."

"That's the only way I'll agree to this." Elena grabbed her cloak again and pushed herself upright. "Understand?"

"Quite, your majesty."

With a stern glare that might have been effective if she hadn't yawned, Elena dragged Jules to his feet. "Come along."

"Yes, your Majesty." With a weary grin, Jules ducked the pillow she sent flying at his head.

"No one listens to me anymore."

"No one ever did," I said in farewell as Elena slammed the cottage door.

Chapter Twenty-Seven

"I really wish you'd reconsider." Elena studied me from the corner of her eye, likely thinking I wasn't aware of her observation.

Guiding my horse back toward the center of the road, I flicked the end of the reins in her direction. "I'm not afraid of him."

Anders snorted on the far side of Elena. "I've found there are few things Alex fears. Her talent was one, until I managed to persuade her otherwise."

"Bridges are another." Elena slanted me another sidelong glance.

"I'm not afraid of bridges."

"We're only a short distance from Jendlan Falls." Elena cocked her head to the side, glossy black hair catching the sunlight. "We could take a side trip, and you could show us the truth."

"I don't need to prove anything to either of you. I'm not afraid of bridges."

"You just don't like them, is that it?" Anders peered around Elena's slender form. "You did admit that the day we took the children to Jendlan Falls and I suggested we have the lesson on the bridge."

"The day you forced me to let you join us." I leaned over to make sure he heard me, raising my voice for emphasis.

"The day you decided to make fun of me." Anders wagged a gloved finger across the head of Elena's mount, which started to grow uneasy as our voices rose.

"Ah, children," Elena interrupted. "You're starting to alarm my horse." Turning innocent blue eyes back to Anders, she kept her face neutral. I knew better. "Then Alex did explain her fear?"

"All she admitted was she didn't like bridges."

"She's terrified of them."

"I am not!" I lowered my voice as Elena's captain turned his head.

Elena laughed suddenly in a rich, warm voice, hinting at old memories. "I spent my summers in Port Alain with the Barlows. At least once each and every summer, Jules and I would sneak up to the falls and lay as flat as possible along the bridge to hide from Alex and Khrista."

"Not very kind," Anders said in mild disapproval, "considering Alex wouldn't come get you even if she knew you were there."

Elena chuckled again, tugging her wool cloak closer to her body as the wind picked up.

The golden opportunity fell right into my lap. How could I resist? Besides, she deserved it. And it did fit in with my plan. I took a deep breath before saying, "And you wonder why I believed what Firemage Ravess said about you."

Elena pulled back on the reins, bringing her horse to a complete halt and setting the rest of the column behind us into various stages of disarray. Challenge flared in her dark blue eyes.

"You're losing your sense of humor." I edged my horse closer to hers, aware of Anders' alert stance.

"You'll forgive me if I find your sense of humor a little difficult at times."

I didn't back down a whit from the challenge in her eyes. "Your reaction might imply a guilty conscience."

Elena's features were stony as she flicked the reins, urging her horse ahead, leaving me side by side with Anders.

"Don't dare say one word."

"I wouldn't dream of it," he lied. "Besides, I don't fancy sleeping on the cold, hard floor."

Elena didn't speak to either of us for the rest of the day or evening, preferring to have her meal alone when we stopped for the night at the inn just south of Tucker's Meadow. I didn't pursue her, and Anders didn't question me. I was weary and thoughtful and wanted nothing but dreamless sleep. But the moment my eyes closed against the lumpy pillow, loud knocking jolted me awake.

"Vengeance, pure and simple," Anders grumbled. "If you hadn't upset Elena, we'd be able to get a decent night's sleep." He groped for a lamp and struggled into his tunic and trousers, tossing my clothes over the bed at me.

"Open the door before she wakes the entire inn." I pulled the tunic over my head and sat up in bed.

Elena was immediately apologetic at Anders' scowl.

"I'm not angry at you, Elena. Come in. It's that damned idiot in my bed."

"Romantic and loving," I muttered, tucking the blankets around my waist to keep out the chill, "just the way I like them."

Elena edged over the doorstep and made her way into the small room, one eye on Anders, who leaned against the wall, arms folded across his chest.

I patted the edge of the disheveled bed. "Sit."

As Anders waved her down, Elena settled at the opposite end, furthest from me. "I couldn't sleep." Elena darted another look of apology at Anders. Not at me.

"Would you rather I leave?" he asked.

"No. I—" She shook her head. "No. Damn it, Alex, why must you be so beastly difficult? You say things in a light-hearted manner, but I know you better. You hide your pain in banter. And you should know, if you don't already, this is one heartache which has no place between us."

I looked away, distressed at the open grief in her eyes. Tucking my legs under me, I sat back against the headboard. I looked up to find Anders watching; waiting for my response as he balanced one leg on the edge of the bed.

"You're partially right. I wanted to unsettle you."

Elena's dark blue eyes widened at my admission. "Why?"

"Two reasons. The first and most obvious, if you'd been reacting with your head and not your heart, was I wanted to give us a plausible reason for not traveling further with you. If word gets around you and I argued, then you can go off tomorrow on your own, leaving us free to follow."

"If I reacted with my head, it wouldn't have been very convincing."

"True."

"Does the second reason involve your desire to wander through the Marain vineyards unescorted?" When I shook my head, Elena grew suspicious again. "Then what?"

I traced a design on the blankets, avoiding her eyes, until she covered my fretting fingers with her own, the Dunneal signet gleaming in the lamplight.

"Was I very difficult growing up?" I met her troubled expression as she kept a firm grip on my hand.

"You always kept yourself a little apart, as though you had no right to be with Jules and me, or didn't want to be," she said, her words slow as she watched me. "Sometimes we couldn't read you. It always hurt us, Alex, because we tried so hard to stop you from thinking like that. If we didn't want to be with you, we wouldn't have. No one forced us." She waited, but I stayed quiet. "And so many times, you'd say something like you said today on the road, hiding behind sarcasm or humor. We never knew how to take your doubts away. We loved you then, and we love you now, and you still can't accept it without questioning us."

I tried to turn away, but Elena's free hand caught my chin, forcing me to look at her. "Don't you see?" I took her hand away, not without gentleness, and wiped betraying wetness from my cheeks. "I never doubted you or Jules. I doubted me."

Orphan child.

"I still doubt myself. Maybe that's why it was easier to blame you for forcing me to try my talent on Jules. Easier to blame you for holding back on your affection and attention if I didn't do what you wanted. But you never did that, not even in jest. I don't know," I whispered, shaking my head as though to clear my thoughts under her silent scrutiny. "If I hold myself back or put the blame elsewhere, then you or Jules or Rosanna can still toss me aside and it won't hurt as much. It won't matter because I don't really belong with you, with any of you."

"Alex." Elena gripped my shoulders as I wept, surprising both of us. "Whatever your father's reasons for leaving you in Port Alain has nothing to do with the rest of us."

"He's nothing to do with this."

"He's everything to do with this." Elena studied me with a critical eye. "Finding him after all these years, knowing he's alive, has rattled the few brains you have in your head and ripped your heart wide open."

"Elena—"

"He may not have been part of your life for twenty-five years, but we have, Alex. All of us, and now Anders, and we're the ones who count. The only ones. Stop second guessing us and trust us for once in your life." Uncertain, Elena glanced over at Anders for support.

Cool sea-gray eyes lightened as he smiled in reassurance. "You're doing fine without my help."

"Idiot." I tugged a pillow from behind my back and tossed it at his head.

Elena finally laughed as the tension eased. "You've no right to call him an idiot, not with the way you think."

"Why don't you slam the door on your way out so anyone listening will really believe you're angry at me?"

"It's obvious you can't take criticism with grace." Elena sat back, leaning against the bedpost, appraising my mood.

"I don't enjoy being called names."

"But you enjoy calling others names."

"That's different."

Elena's laugh was far more relaxed as she stretched forward and grabbed my shoulders again. "You're all right?" When I nodded, she hugged me tight. "Be careful and don't get hurt."

"I wouldn't dare."

Elena disentangled herself from me and stopped in front of Anders, who surprised her by wrapping his arms around her slender shoulders. She returned his embrace with equal affection and headed for the door.

"Don't forget to slam the door." When she rolled her eyes at Anders, I said her name aloud.

"What now, Alex?"

"Thanks."

Her features softened as she nodded once, and then left, slamming the door so hard the window rattled.

"I guess she really doesn't want us traveling with her."

Chapter Twenty-Eight

With the excuse of giving Elena a head start, we arrived in Ardenna three days later. Not far from the residence of Firemage Ravess, we took a small room in a quiet, nondescript inn.

"He doesn't know me. There's no reason I can't go with you." Anders paced back and forth in the neat, sparsely furnished room as I unpacked some clean clothes to ease the wrinkles from them.

"I'd rather he didn't know you. Let him believe I'm alone and pathetic." I grinned at Anders' immediate frown. "Seriously, I'd rather have the security of knowing you're out there if I need you. I'll be fine."

"He's vicious."

"So am I when I need to be."

"That's true." I reached for my cloak and gloves as Anders reached for me. "I'd rather you weren't vicious with me."

"Then behave, old man."

"Promise you'll be careful."

"Yes. Of course." I flung my cloak around my shoulders.

"Alex." He gripped my shoulders and shook me with gentle firmness. "I'm serious. He's dangerous."

"I know." As Anders pulled me close for a kiss, I shoved aside the hesitation and doubt clamoring for attention. "I'll be all right." I wrapped my arms around his warm neck.

"Then why are you shaking?"

"I'm not an idiot, despite what Elena thinks. He terrifies me."

"Good. I was starting to think your head was empty." He grabbed the cloak I tossed his way. "Let's go."

We reached the firemage's residence without incident. The house loomed ahead, darkened but for the lamp in the study at the back. The same room where I found him the last time. I fidgeted as Anders worried the lock free, and then slipped inside after he squeezed my fingers. Waiting at the entrance until my eyes adjusted to the shadows, I focused on the dim light at the end of the long, wide hallway. Assuming that's where he'd be, though we couldn't see him from the outside, I started forward, instinct on edge. Creeping with measured slowness, I kept my arms close to my sides, fearful of entangling them in unseen objects along the corridor. Thick carpeting muffled the creak of my steps. Almost there, I halted to catch my breath and quiet the pounding of my heart. From my vantage, I couldn't see or hear anything or anyone in the study.

I edged closer. Another step. Still no sound. Another step.

Wincing as the floorboard creaked, I held my breath, and then flew across the room as a strong arm whisked me through the narrow doorway. Fumbling to get my bearings, I stopped immediately at the icy touch of steel on my exposed throat.

Firemage Ravess brought the lamp in his hand closer to peer at my face, gasping in surprise. "Orphan child. I'm not surprised you're a thief, needing to steal to keep up with your betters, but I thought for certain you'd have expert skills." With a look of contempt, he added, "How often did Elena catch you robbing from her? Or did she turn away from the truth out of pity?"

I held my peace, the dagger still at my throat.

He stepped back and jerked me upright, throwing me backward into a chair. Dagger held ready, he waved his arms around the shadowed study. "What did you plan to steal from me?" Contempt flashed again in deep, lush brown eyes that had no place in his malevolent face. "Or were you spying for your royal mistress? That makes more sense. She always knew how to use you, while you scampered after her, lapping up the crumbs of friendship she tossed over her shoulder." He set the lamp down, increasing the flame's brightness without any obvious gesture, and ran his finger along the dagger's edge. "Apparently, she still does." Catching me off guard, he immobilized my arms by sheer brute strength and held the dagger against my throat once more. "Although I'm curious, I'd rather you told me why you're here, instead of wasting my time with guessing games."

I kept my face neutral, allowing a hint of bitterness and anger to seep through, my heart aching at how easy it was. "I came to give you news."

"How commendable." The dagger drew a thin trickle of blood along the side of my neck. "Don't waste my time. Tell me the truth."

Refusing to flinch from the pain, I didn't back down, though I wanted to strangle him. "She thinks one of the Crown Council is the Crownmage."

Brown eyes glittered with danger in the lamplight. "Old news." The dagger moved again, sending a thin stream of fresh blood down my collar.

I feigned distress, but was relieved Jules managed to spread the rumor. "How could you possibly know that? She's told no one."

"You trust her? You're a bigger fool than I thought." He trailed the dagger along a bit further. "My sources are my secret. What else?"

Restraining the urge to rip out his heart, I started to tremble, not difficult to pretend with cold steel threatening. "That's all I know."

"Not good enough, orphan child. Why are you really here?"

With no effort at all, which shamed me, I released all the bitterness and anger I'd held inside. "You were right about her, what you said that day in the corridor, what you said tonight." Tears came easily, too, along with contempt to mirror his ugly emotion. "I don't owe her anything." I laughed a little wildly. "She talks in front of me as though I'm not even there. I never saw it before." I looked away, unable to turn too far with the dagger poised at my neck. "I never wanted to." I cried out as the dagger drew blood once more.

"And what do you want from me?"

I shook my head once. "Vengeance. But it's useless. You already know what I came to tell you."

"You want nothing more?" His tone was seductive; his white hair an eerie sight beneath the lamp's flickering light. "I don't trust you for a moment, but I'd be willing to hear more news if it isn't old. If one of the Council is the Crownmage—" The control on his expression slipped, quickly masked in icy contempt as he sighed. "So many enemies. And you, orphan child, just discovering yours."

"I was a fool."

The firemage regarded me with a steady gaze. "Perhaps." Removing the dagger from its bloody trail along my neck, he stood back. "Go now. I've no more time or patience to trifle with you."

It wasn't necessary to hide my relief. "If I hear anything of use—"

"If you have more news, and if that news is not so old, then send word. If not, keep away from me. I've no time to spare for pathetic fools seeking vengeance." With an absent gesture toward the lamp, he caused the flames to rise higher, dispelling the gloom from the shadowed corners. "Now go."

I fled at the dismissal and said nothing to Anders until we were safe in our room at the inn.

"Let me see what he's done to your neck. Bloody bastard." With gentle fingers, controlling his anger, Anders loosened the stiff collar of the tunic. He apologized as I flinched when the material pulled free of my skin.

I gathered my hair out of his way as he snarled another curse. "Hush. You'll wake the entire inn."

He helped me ease the tunic over my head, eyes darkening at sight of the bloodied collar. "I'll get some water. Sit down."

Obedient, I sat on the bed, stained tunic thrown aside, shivering in the chilled room. I crossed my arms for warmth as Anders gathered fresh water and a clean cloth.

"I've no healing salves," he muttered, kneeling in front of me, pushing my hair back and over my shoulders.

"If it were poisoned, I'd be feeling the effects by now."

"I don't trust him." Though his words were harsh, his touch was gentle, holding me still when I winced and pulled away. "Sorry, again."

"If it doesn't look any better in the morning, we'll find a healer for some salve. Besides, it's almost dawn anyway."

"Even if it looks better, we'll find a healer."

"Anders."

"What?" Near-black eyes dared me to challenge him.

"I'm all right."

Anders sat back on his heels and closed his eyes. When I touched his arm, he stared at me for a long, silent moment. "I haven't cared for anyone in a very long time, Alex. And I'm afraid. I don't want anything to happen to you. Not for your mother's sake, but for mine. And this," he touched my neck with care, "is proof I didn't protect you as I promised Elena I would."

"If I felt I was in serious danger, I'd have shouted my head off and the hell with Elena's noble cause." I traced the rough stubble of his cheek.

"I know. Still—"

"Still." I leaned over to kiss him. "If you feel that guilty, then I suggest you make amends."

"When we get home?"

"You're not serious."

* * * *

"Before we go back to the cottage, humor me." Anders turned his horse toward the coast, in the direction of the seawall just outside the town. "The timing's about right."

"For what?"

"You'll see."

Biting back questions and snide comments, I helped Anders settle our horses off the road and followed him toward the center of town, straight for the mage council hall. What was he up to? Anders propped himself on the seawall and held me in his arms, my back to the building. Still, I didn't question him though I had an uneasy suspicion his plan involved Seamage Neal Brandt. No sooner did I arrive at that conclusion, I heard the sounds of children running, free of their mage lessons.

"Perfect timing. I told you so."

I arched one brow in silent query, but never had the chance to speak. Anders drew my head closer for a passionate kiss that left me breathless. Starting to push him away so I could catch a breath and still my pounding heart, I changed my mind as the sound of footsteps approached.

"Your mother was a whore, too, Mistress Keltie."

I bit back rage and turned, held loosely in Anders' embrace, though his fingers made a point of digging into the soft flesh of my arms.

"Did Master Perrin tell you he slept with her when your father wasn't around to keep her faithful?"

"As a matter of fact, Seamage Brandt," I smiled with mock friendliness, "he told me she slept with every eligible man in Port Alain, but you. Somehow, she couldn't quite lower herself to your level."

"That's not how I remember it." Brandt looked beyond me. "Seems you got what you came for, Master Perrin. I hope she's skilled in bed. She's not skilled at much else, including magic."

"Oh, I don't know. She makes a decent schoolmistress. The children apparently adore her."

"If you consider children a reliable source of opinion." Brandt shrugged. "They're easily swayed."

"I should know," I said with bitterness, caught by a dangerous idea. "I was swayed by Elena." I started to push away from Anders' embrace, but he grabbed my waist. "What? Isn't it true?" I snarled at him. "All these years, I thought she was my friend. All these years, I—" Choking back a sob, I freed myself, avoiding Anders' frantic reach.

"I thought you were a loyal supporter of our queen," Brandt said quietly, stepping directly into my path.

"Loyalty to the crown doesn't always mean loyalty to the person wearing it," I snapped, face flushed with rising anger. "I'm tired of being naïve. I'm tired of being used." Storming past the seamage, I ignored Anders' loud plea for me to stop. I headed along the path that would take me home, not daring to walk toward the spot where we'd tethered our mounts.

"Alex . . . Alex, wait!" Anders came running after me, grabbed my arm, and spun me around, planting a loud enthusiastic kiss on my lips. "You are magnificent," he murmured, careful to keep his voice low.

"In bed?"

He laughed, hugging me close. "That goes without saying. I was, however, talking about your little performance in front of the seamage. You might consider teaching the children some play acting."

"Considering you didn't have the decency to warn me what you were planning, we were lucky."

"Nor did you warn me." Anders hugged me again, voice somber. "Though I'd rather Elena didn't know how easy it is for you to convince people you resent her."

I stepped back from his embrace, mindful Seamage Brandt might still be in the vicinity. "It bothered me how easy it was to persuade Firemage Ravess, too." Admitting that uncomfortable truth, I rested my head on his chest. "I don't believe it, Anders, but when I'm vulnerable I find it frightening. What if someone uses it against me?"

Chapter Twenty-Nine

"It seems as though that sea captain in Port Alain better look elsewhere."

I refused to acknowledge Khrista's self-satisfied, smug, nasty comment. Too bad my face didn't agree. I felt a hot flush creep up from my neck. Ever one to take advantage, much like her brother, Khrista snickered at my discomfort as she stood in the schoolroom doorway with Lauryn beside her.

"Your mother always said vengeance isn't attractive."

Khrista laughed. "You don't think I listen to her, do you?"

"Maybe she'll listen to you," I muttered to Lauryn, whose clear blue eyes looked apologetic, but no less amused.

"Sorry, Alex. If I defend you, Khrista will make my life miserable."

"So you'll forgo your kind, gentle, and discreet nature to join in with her snide, ill-mannered insults?" I tossed a book to the opposite end of the table.

"Of course not. I'll just remain neutral."

I muttered an eloquent answer beneath my breath, and Lauryn made a mumbled attempt at an apology before clearing her throat with exaggerated delicacy and fixing me with a pointed stare. "Ah, Alex," she hesitated, as Khrista elbowed her, "we were wondering what's going on."

"With Anders?"

"We're quite aware what's going on with him. At least when you're alone."

"I used to like you."

"You still do." Lauryn pushed on. "But we were wondering what's going on with Elena." She stopped as I narrowed my eyes, misinterpreting her words.

"What Lauryn's trying to say," Khrista cut in before I could utter a word, "is that you go running off to Ardenna with Master Perrin to see Elena without telling us a thing beyond the fact you're going. Then you return with that same Master Perrin wrapped around your finger. Then Elena arrives in the middle of the night, and you go running off again."

I raised a brow at Khrista's admission. Lauryn had the decency to blush, but jumped to her sister-in-law's defense. Clarifying the fact Jules wasn't always a flaming idiot. "Jules told me. We weren't spying. And we saw Elena before you left that morning."

"Did Jules tell you why she came?"

"He said it was your decision to tell us if you wanted to." Lauryn's meek reply was balanced by the spark of defiance in her eyes. "But as I'm the wife of Duke Barlow, I have the authority to pressure you."

I studied the two of them, curious and wide-eyed as the twins. No—worse. "Not a word to Kerrie or Brendan."

"Of course not," they said in tandem.

"Then come in and shut the door."

* * * *

"I'm still Alex." Ill at ease, I frowned at their utter and complete stunned silence, not knowing what to say.

Lauryn knew I'd had mage talent, just not quite what kind. She spoke first, blue eyes thoughtful. "That explains why Seamage Brandt was so friendly yesterday. A bit too friendly, if you know what I mean, though he did make some snide comments."

"We've been discreet."

"He called you a whore, Alex," Lauryn blurted out, looking ready to go after the seamage. "I assume you weren't completely discreet."

"That was Anders' idea." I laughed and told them about our little drama. "We were trying to convince Brandt Anders is only interested in sleeping with me."

"Seems you convinced him, though he's still slippery when it comes to your long-ago magery."

"I haven't flashed lightning across the harbor, so I don't know why he's still sniffing along on that trail."

"Maybe he knows something about your father," Lauryn said quietly, having heard that part of the tale from Rosanna.

"Maybe." I shrugged and turned away, fidgeting with the books I'd thrown aside. "That's not important now."

"It is if it bothers you so much."

"It doesn't. Besides, I'm part of Rosanna's family. No need to seek elsewhere for what I already have, right?" As long as I didn't look at Lauryn, I was safe.

Khrista hugged me tight. "You never need to go elsewhere. I'd get rid of my brother long before that happened."

"If only I could change him into a jackass, it'd make all my training worthwhile." Elena was right. I was doing it again, making light of my heartaches, treating them as mere inconveniences while they ripped me apart.

"I could think of worse fates for my poor husband, but Khrista's right. I've been telling you so all along. So has everyone else." Lauryn caught my eye, and I knew she saw right through my ploy. Lords of the sea, did they all see through me? "I hope Elena won't need your help," she added, helping me straighten out the books.

"Neither do I, but if she does, she'll pay handsomely for it."

Khrista propped a slender leg on the bench beside her. "What if the Crownmage appears and allies with the Ardenna Crown Council?"

"I don't even want to think about it. And neither does Elena, because she knows she'll never find me. I'll be long gone from Port Alain."

"Seriously, Alex." Lauryn squeezed my arm. "What would you do?"

"The best I can, and hope that it's enough."

"With Anders teaching you a trick or two, you'll be well prepared for anything, day or night," Khrista teased, heading for the door.

I tossed a book at her head as she scurried out, missing her completely. "Some days, she's as bad as her brother, or mother, for that matter."

"She doesn't even come close when Jules is being obnoxious." Lauryn picked up the book I'd flung at Khrista, a wistfulness in her tone I couldn't ignore. She straightened out a folded page and set the book in its place on the table, surprising me by initiating the troubling topic. "He runs the very moment she breathes his name."

"He's got a certain amount of responsibility toward her as duke."

"I know all that."

"Then why not let it rest?"

Lauryn's slender body went rigid, though she didn't answer right away. "I try, Alex. You don't know how hard I try, but every time he goes north—" She spun on her heels to face me. "For Elena, nothing ever happened. I don't hold it against her, that wouldn't be fair. She didn't ask him to fall in love with her. But Jules will always love her. I can't change that."

"He loves you."

"Yes." She smiled, as though I were the one in need of reassurance. "Yes, he does. But it's different. I'm not blind, Alex. If Elena wanted him now, offered herself to him, Jules wouldn't hesitate."

"You're so wrong."

"Alex," she laughed, a sound echoing old heartaches, "you're so na-ïve."

* * * *

Days later, fire and ice pierced every inch of my head. The magic sent slivers of pain through the rest of my body all the way down to my toes as I lost my concentration; still worried about Lauryn.

"Stop insisting it's going to work. Go away."

"You're not letting it work."

"I'm not letting it work?" I searched for something to fling at Anders' head.

"You're using Emila's pendant as a good luck charm. Let it go. You should be able to perform the same feats without using it."

"I can't."

"You won't." He ducked as a pillow slammed into the wall behind him. "You're afraid to let go and stand on your own two feet."

"Go away. Rosanna needs help in her gardens doing something dirty and muddy." I turned my back on him.

"It's after supper and early winter. I think Lady Barlow prefers to do her gardening in the daylight, not to mention the spring and summer." He crept behind me. "That's so she can tell the frost-free weeds from her precious ferns." He stroked the back of my neck beneath my hair, careful to stay clear of the thin scar on my neck.

"Stop that." I reached back to smack his hand away.

"You can do it," he whispered into my ear, fingers sneaking back to my neck. "You just have to try harder." When I moved forward to get away from him, he held me back against his chest. Lips replaced fingers, caressing my neck.

"Stop that. If you don't, then I won't stay angry with you. And I'd much rather stay angry with you."

"I know. We'll talk about the pendant later. I'd prefer you in a different frame of mind right now."

* * * *

Trust Anders to play games. Talk about the pendant reared its ugly head from an entirely different, though not unexpected, source.

"You never really told me what happened in Glynnswood."

"Why bother repeating what Anders already told you in sordid detail?"

"I want to hear it from you."

I sat back against the pillows in the armchair closest the fireplace in Rosanna's suite, feet stretched toward the blaze, grateful for the warmth. "You must hear the shouting from your balcony every time we argue about this sore topic. I don't want to discuss it."

"You owe me at least one discussion," she persisted, stretching to pour me another glass of Marain wine. "I'm not quite sure why, Alex, but you do."

Sighing, I tugged my scuffed boots off and tossed them aside. "So you can defend Sernyn Keltie's actions?" Sernyn. Not Father. Never again Father.

"I have no intention of defending him. I understand what he did, and why he did it, and I honored my promise to him all these years."

"But he put you in a rather awkward position," I finished, with a crooked smile, accepting with thanks the glass she held out to me.

"Well, yes. But I'm not concerned about Sernyn. I'm concerned about you."

"Of course."

"Don't be so smug. It's horrid enough you blamed yourself for Emila's death, still do. Now you've got to deal with a father who abandoned you all these years."

234

"I don't have to deal with Sernyn because he was never a father to me, with the exception of making my mother pregnant."

"He always wanted to hear about you."

"Not with such desperation he'd come back and admit he'd been wrong. No, Rosanna," I repeated with emphasis, wagging a finger, "he didn't want to deal with me, and I don't want to deal with him."

"It's affecting your mage talent."

"Pardon me?"

Rosanna studied her pudgy fingers, twirling the half-empty glass in her hands until I started to laugh. "What?" she demanded, looking aggrieved.

"It's difficult to see you hesitant, rather out of character."

The old fire came back to her eyes. "I'm afraid you'll turn me into something horrid."

"If I could, I'd have experimented on your son first. Say whatever you're thinking. I'll hear it sooner or later."

She played with the glass again. "If you accepted your father's heritage as part of your mage talent, you'd be able to use your gift freely without depending on your mother's copper pendant."

"You're so confident I presume the old man convinced you of that."

"As a matter of fact, we arrived at the idea separately, and found ourselves in complete agreement."

"How amazing. Why don't I send him here to keep you company since your relationship is so congenial."

"I think Anders is quite content where he is. And so are you to have him there, even though you won't admit it." Her eyes held the same maternal satisfaction I'd seen in Lauryn's blue eyes when I'd confessed all.

"I only keep him there to prevent Jules from finding me a husband."

"Yes." She raised a glass in a mocking salute. "Of course. No honest affection between you and Anders. That's good, Alex. After all, we wouldn't want you to resemble anything faintly human." When I reached for my boots in disgust, Rosanna stretched out a hand to stop me. "Anders did tell me about your encounter with Firemage Ravess." Her eyes traveled in concern to my neck, though strands of hair covered the scar from her sight. "And Elena."

I looked away, fists clenched at my side.

"Like it or not, your father's affecting your life."

"I don't like it."

She didn't answer for a moment, then rummaged in her pocket and offered me the envelope she'd pulled free. The neat handwriting that scrawled my name across the envelope was unfamiliar. Curious, I took it and sliced the seal in half. Too late. Instincts screaming, it was too late. My eyes swiftly scanned the contents in cold fury.

> *Alex—*
>
> *Forgive my presumption in writing to you, particularly about something of which I am ignorant. It is none of my affair, truly. I know. But I fear you will make my mistake and run from your talent. Please do not. Face your gift as I never had the courage to do. Face it, and use it as best you can to the fullest extent you can. Do not ever let it control you, as it did me.*
>
> *Sernyn Keltie*

Hand trembling with rage, I crumpled the letter and flung it across the room.

"All right, then. Listen." Rosanna's voice was calm. "All I wanted to say was I'm here if you need to talk." When I tugged my boots on without responding, she added quietly, "It's the same for all of us, what

Elena said, but you know that. And Alex," I stopped stuffing trousers into my boots and looked into Rosanna's loving face, caught by her wistful tone. "I'm glad Anders is with you."

I started to say something light, inconsequential, but chose not to, without understanding why. I headed for the door, avoiding the crumpled letter, and stopped.

"So am I."

Chapter Thirty

I was glad Anders was with me to face the coming nightmare.

"Where's our glorious monarch?" I asked Rosanna some days later, glancing around the manor's seldom-used, semi-formal chamber to see who was gathered for an audience with the queen. I'd sent Anders up the Hill alone earlier in the day, promising to arrive after Elena's unplanned meeting with Jules and his Port Alain advisors ended.

Elena had come for me, and I needed the time alone.

Jules was lodged in a quiet corner with Anders, engaged in serious talk I had every intention of avoiding. Khrista and Lauryn, in the far corner by the overstuffed bookcases, caught my eye and waved a greeting. I waved back, noting Kerrie standing shyly by the window, digesting all we'd told him over the past few days.

"She's kidnapped her beloved heir," Rosanna replied, "and dragged him off to find a corner so they could speak in privacy."

"Did the twins behave?" I asked Lauryn as she and Khrista joined us, all three ladies wearing their finest meet-Elena-formally-in-Port-Alain clothes. I chose a fancier version of my usual tunic and trousers, adding a soft leather vest, knowing Elena would appreciate the gesture.

If she'd come looking for a Mage Champion, she'd get one.

"Brendan threatened the boys with imprisonment in the deepest dungeons of Ardenna if they didn't. But truly," Lauryn answered, with more than a trace of maternal pride in her eyes, "I'm not sure who was the more charmed, Elena or the boys." And beyond that pride was an honest affection for Elena, despite the lingering uncertainty about her husband's long-held desire, which never quite left Lauryn in peace. Elena possessed an infuriating talent for gathering loyalty and affection, despite whether one chose to offer either.

As the huge double doors swung open again, Anders sent me a thoughtful nod. Without discussing a word, he understood and respected my instinctive fears this morning and left me alone.

Elena sauntered in, arm in arm with Brendan. Close together, they were so alike, almost twins, but for their age difference. Her glance darted around the room, openly relieved at the sight of me.

"Alex."

"Majesty." I bowed my head in a mockery of court formality. "And enlightened, all-wise monarch of the kingdom of Tuldamoran and everything from the shores of our beautiful—"

"Stop that." Releasing Brendan's arm, she embraced me and then stepped back. Still holding on, she inspected every inch of me, her gaze stopping without hesitation at the thin scar at my neck.

"I only wanted to offer appropriate tribute."

Elena gave me a knowing look, accepting my distraction gracefully. One hand resting on her slender hip, she turned to confront Rosanna. "I thought you taught her how to be respectful."

The old seawitch sighed with heavy drama and looked far too apologetic. "She's been difficult. I'm sorry. But sometimes she's too headstrong. You've no idea."

I looked at both of them in disgust before challenging Elena, poking her shoulder playfully with my finger. "Did you come empty-handed? If you did, you may as well mount up and head back north."

"Of course not." She pointed an elegant finger, wearing the Dunneal crown ring of sapphires, to a rather large assortment of bottles of Marain wine lying in the corner behind Anders. "Even though it's not midnight, I thought we'd need a bottle."

"Need?"

"Well, yes." She released a huge sigh. "Firemage Ravess accused me of treasonous dealing with the Meravan monarchy against my own subjects. Unfortunately, there were witnesses." She paused, gathering her thoughts, or perhaps her courage. "On behalf of the Crown Council, he issued formal Mage Challenge. The issue is my word of honorable dealing with Meravan against his false patriotic rhetoric to save Tuldamoran from my ill-intentioned rule."

Oh hell.

"I'm sorry, Alex."

As Anders' arm rested around my waist, I shrugged. "Then perhaps Jules should open more than one bottle."

Rosanna took charge and hustled the others into comfortable seats. Still watching me with apology in every angle of her slender body, Elena looked up, startled. Lauryn nudged her in the direction of an armchair, though Elena only stood beside it. With an affectionate wink at me, Lauryn pointed to the pile of cushions she'd gathered in front of the fireplace next to Anders. Tamely, to her open amusement, I settled myself in the crook of his sheltering arm.

"By Tuldamoran law, I'm obliged to send word to the Crown Council, as the Challengers, within seven days to declare my decisions for the confrontation." Jules poured us all a glass of the rich, fruity wine as Elena explained, "As the Challenged party, I'm free to make the choice on several details. The first decision is timing."

"Can we postpone it for a few years?"

"I wish we could postpone it forever. But the Challenge must be met within a month's time."

"Then, by all means, set it for the absolutely last hour of the last day. Well, not at night. That might be tricky. What's next?"

"Place."

"A suggestion?" Anders interrupted, waiting for her nod to continue. "With Alex's unconventional talent, it might be best if she has free access to at least two sources of elements."

I turned to Anders and narrowed my eyes. "I presume you've been thinking about this dilemma for a bit and have a place in mind?"

He nodded, sea-gray eyes calm and confident. I envied his confidence. "There's a small valley north of here that runs along the Kieren River."

"Tucker's Meadow?"

"You'd have immediate access to both water and earth. Those you can change to flame and wind if needed. Charlton Ravess, as Firemage, will be allowed a steadily burning fire for his use so the location doesn't offer him any unexpected advantages. It's just a suggestion. It's still your choice."

"It's an intelligent suggestion, coming from you. Besides, it's near enough to the Marain vineyards, should I have the urge."

Elena laughed with forced humor. "Too near."

"Well, all right, I'll wait until I've defeated the firemage so it won't interfere with my concentration. What next?"

"My representative, Alex, if you'll still do this for me." At my immediate, grave nod of agreement, she paused before continuing. I thought she might have wanted to say something else, but changed her mind. "Ravess will be your opponent, as we expected. He wouldn't miss this opportunity to personally throw me from the throne and rub my face in the mud."

"Can we keep my identity secret for awhile?"

"Up until the challenge, yes. I need only proclaim I have a champion. The rules are much nicer to the challenged party."

"Has any good come from the rumors we've spread?"

Glass in hand, Elena paced around the chamber. "From what I hear in private, Ravess is unsettled, for which I'm grateful." She stared again at the thin scar that ran along the side of my neck. "But more than that, the firemage told me in no uncertain terms you'd betrayed me and you'd tried for vengeance and failed."

"I'm sure he said other things."

Her expression was eloquent, confirming my suspicions, though she didn't say aloud what those other things might be. "If he believed what you said . . ." Again, her eyes spoke volumes. "Then he'd think I wouldn't care on a personal basis." She stood in front of the fireplace, uncertain, but with deep apology in her eyes. "That's why I can't see any advantage for him to tell me except to hurt my cause in public by showing my allies could betray me."

"Maybe he's just growing careless?" Jules suggested from his place at Lauryn's side.

Elena glanced at him, considering, before pacing again. "Maybe. But now he's cut off the possibility of Alex going back to him with anything else. He's always mistrusted the other council mages and fears their envy of his position. My spies tell me he's withdrawn from the other council members, destroying their effectiveness as a group, which is useful. But to be honest, I don't think he quite knows what to think."

"That's useful, too," I said.

"Yes. And there's more. Charlton Ravess is afraid the Crownmage, if not a council member, may still appear as my ally and fight him in the challenge. But even if the Crownmage isn't one of the council, Ravess fears he, or she, may approach them to offer help in overthrowing Ravess as council head."

"With Ravess out of the picture," Anders said, "you keep the throne."

"Yes, but then the council can issue Mage Challenge again if the Crownmage agrees to fight my champion. But if none of that happens, Ravess is the only one who can legitimately participate in the Mage Challenge against Alex."

"That goes both ways," I said. "Once you send word of my formal acceptance, no one else can replace me or you forfeit the throne to Brendan."

"But if the Crownmage does exist and offers to help Elena before your participation is formal, Alex . . ." Lauryn's question reflected her hope for an escape for me. "Surely the Crownmage can take your place, since no one knows the identity of the actual champion. Right?"

"Yes, but that wouldn't be honorable," I intervened, before Elena could answer. "Besides, for better or worse, the Crownmage doesn't matter anymore. After we spent all that time and effort arguing about it—" I stopped at the peculiar look in Anders' eyes. "What?"

Anders' smile was coy, but he didn't answer, at least, not directly. "Nothing of consequence, Alex. Trust me. You're right about wasted effort."

Not satisfied, I turned back to Elena. "Is there any way they can refuse to accept me as your champion, because I have such unconventional talent?"

Elena shook her head, stopping in front of the window. "Not unless they forge the original rules. I checked all documents pertaining to the Mage Challenge. The same term is used throughout. 'The Crown's mage of choice.' "

"How does it end?" I asked, gratefully accepting a small refill from Jules. It was a question I'd studiously avoided asking from the very start of this predicament weeks ago. Even though I knew the answer in my gut.

Elena gazed out the window for long moments, dark strands of her hair catching the fading sunlight as she traced a design on the frosted glass. "It continues until one of the adversaries yields."

"If neither yields?" When she didn't answer, I set my glass down and joined Elena at the window, staring out at Rosanna's winter-bare gardens. "Then how does it end?"

Elena turned miserable blue eyes to face me. "If neither yields, the Challenge ends when one mage dies."

From the corner of my eye, I caught Lauryn's sudden movement and Rosanna's answering handclasp. I'd known it in my heart. Maybe it was why I never asked, not that it would've changed my decision.

"I'd understand if you refused." Elena's eyes strayed to the scar at my neck once again, her expression filled with misplaced guilt.

"Don't insult me."

"If it's a risk you're not prepared to take, I can't accept your participation. Brendan's quite capable of sitting on the throne should I forfeit this challenge." She flashed him an adoring smile. "I'm prepared to do that, Alex, before all these witnesses. And I'll still be prepared to do it in Tucker's Meadow."

"Anders?" My gaze remained locked on Elena's deep blue eyes as I crossed my arms and leaned against the chilled window ledge. "Did you know this?"

"Yes."

"Oh hell, Elena, I suppose I knew it, too. I just kept avoiding the issue."

Elena placed a hand on my arm, squeezing it. "I told you I'd understand if you withdrew your help."

"And I told you I'd do this for you."

"You don't have to prove anything, not to me."

"I gave my word as your friend." I dared her to contradict me. "And that means more to me than an impersonal oath of fealty. I'm not doing this to prove anything. I'm doing this because it's right. Ask Rosanna or Anders. Either one of them will tell you I've no choice here because of my own damned conscience. But I'll tell you this," I grinned, to take the sting from my words, "when this nightmare is over, I expect a decent supply of Marain wine."

Clutching my hands in both of hers, she laughed, her grasp shaky. "I'll make very certain you have all the Marain wine you'll ever want."

Chapter Thirty-One

The nightmare turned truly frightening some weeks later.

Anders jumped to his feet when I entered the cottage. "What happened?" He took my face in his hands, examining me for bruises other than the one I felt on my left cheek and the bump at the back of my head.

I shrugged, trembling still, as I had all the way up the cold, dark road. "I don't know."

"Are you hurt anywhere else?" He started to cleanse the dirt from my cheek, stopping as I winced in pain.

I shook my head, confused. "Only that—and a bump on the back of my head. I must have hit the ground when I fell. I was pushed, Anders, and robbed." I heard the panic in my voice, unable to hold back the hysteria that had threatened all the way home in the dark.

"Hush." He wrapped his warm arms around me as I sagged against his chest. "So they've taken whatever coins you carried. As long as you're all right. I'll take you down to the healer in Port Alain. It doesn't matter what they took."

"Yes, it does. They took Mother's pendant," I mumbled, shamed, into his chest as Anders tensed against me. Pushing free of his arms, I stepped away, looking anywhere except at him.

"I'll send word to Jules to have his troops search the woods. Whoever did this, Alex—"

"Is long gone. When the thief realizes what he's taken, he won't wait for an angry mage to come looking for him."

"It's useless to whoever stole it. Let me at least warn Jules."

"No." I held him back, hands caught in his tunic, as he went toward the door. "If you do, he'll tell Elena, and she'll be frantic with worry."

"We'll make him promise not to tell her."

"Much as I love Jules dearly, he'd feel obligated to tell Elena. No. No, please. What if Seamage Brandt was behind this?"

"How could he know? We've been so careful."

"Maybe someone watched us in secret." I started to tremble, sick at heart, ill at the thought of what it would mean for Elena. "Anders?"He drew me closer, careful of my aches. "If the Port Alain council has the pendant, they'll suspect the truth and warn Firemage Ravess."

"It won't matter whether or not Neal Brandt or Charlton Ravess knows the truth. And if they do, they'll believe you a seamage."

I didn't answer, couldn't find comfort in his words.

* * * *

"You're trying much too hard," Anders said the next afternoon, lifting me with gentle strength from the ground and leading me to a chair by the fireplace in my parlor.

"I have no choice." Leaning back against the pillows he settled behind me, I closed my eyes.

"If you push yourself so hard," a familiar voice scolded, "you won't do Elena the slightest bit of good."

My eyes flew open. "Rosanna!"

"Anders let me in while you were, ah, experimenting. You were trying so hard you didn't hear me."

"You told her?" I said, not bothering to disguise the accusation in my voice, particularly when Anders avoided my eyes, busying himself by pouring some hot cinnamon tea.

"Not willingly," Rosanna answered in his stead. "When I arrived just now, poor Anders had no choice but to explain what happened."

"He chose not to respect my privacy."

"Your face was scarlet from trying too hard, and you have a bruise on your cheek. I'm sure I would have noted there was a problem and forced him to tell me." She hastened to add, "I've no intention of lecturing." She accepted a cup of tea from Anders and handed it to me instead. "The last time I saw you was the day Elena arrived. You flee the Hill the moment the children's lessons are over." She accepted another cup for herself. "I was worried about you."

"Now you can return home even more worried."

"Shouldn't Elena be told?"

Anders shook his gray-streaked head, an unreadable expression in his eyes. "It wouldn't matter. Not unless Alex forfeits."

"Why not?" Rosanna asked, puzzled. "Surely someone can take Alex's place if she can't control her mage talent."

"Once Elena declared she has a champion, which she did a week ago, no one other than me," I said in a quiet voice, "can act as Challenged. If I forfeit, then Elena loses without a fight."

"I was under the impression Elena didn't have to reveal the name of her champion."

"She doesn't, and didn't," I murmured. "It's a matter of honor," I said hotly when Rosanna opened her mouth to protest. "I can't let her down. And I won't."

"You won't be letting her down if someone else steps in."

"You've been telling me all along to help her."

Rosanna flushed and looked to Anders, floundering.

"Shouldn't it be Elena's decision?" He knelt at my feet.

"No." I shook my head, feeling stubborn and defiant. "Not yet." When he looked about to protest, too, I shook my head again. "Not yet. I haven't given up."

* * * *

But we'd run out of time.

Jules sent two spirited horses that carried us to the Hill, where Elena's personal guard waited to escort us to Tucker's Meadow. Khrista and Kerrie, along with Jules and Brendan, traveled with us. Rosanna stayed behind with Lauryn and the twins to keep watch over Port Alain in Jules' absence. I dismounted at the manor's main entrance, where Lauryn waited with Rosanna, the twins wide-eyed between them. Lauryn's clear blue eyes watched me with a fair bit of anxiety before she caught me in a fierce hug. Releasing me, she stepped back, started to speak, and crossed her arms instead.

Carey edged closer to me, Hunter, of course, at his heels, both of them acting very unsure of me as I crouched down to their height. Carey was unusually serious as he craned his neck in Jules' direction. When his father nodded solemnly, Carey focused huge serious eyes on my face.

"Father said you're going to fight the firemage for the queen's honor."

"That's what he told me, too," I tried hard not to laugh at the unusually quiet, somber-faced boy. "So, I guess I'd better do my best."

"Even though you're a mage," he whispered, stumbling on the word with a frightened expression in his eyes, "you're still Alex, aren't you?"

Lords of the sea, I never expected the children to be frightened. "Of course, I am." I hugged him tight as he wrapped small, shaking arms round my neck. "And I expect you to have your lessons ready for me the very moment I get back, or I'll throw you into Shad's Bay for whales to nibble at your toes. Or turn you into a horned wild hog or something ugly and gruesome. Like your father," I added, with a wink in Lauryn's direction.

Carey laughed in relief, nudging his twin in the ribs. "I told you she'd still be Alex." He turned back to me. "Father said you're going to thrash the firemage."

"Thrash?" I arched a skeptical brow at Jules, and then at Lauryn, finally coaxing a reluctant smile from her tense expression. Hunter nodded solemnly, and elbowed his brother aside to be included in my hug. I ruffled both curly heads, hugged them once more close to my chest. I leaned on their heads as I stood upright to make them laugh again. Selfishly, I craved their laughter, a sound I needed to hear; a sound I wanted so desperately to come home to.

As though she knew this, and probably did, Lauryn grabbed my arm as I stood and spun me around to face her once again. "I don't intend to keep teaching the children in your place, so you'd better come back in one piece. And don't try to be a heroine, either. I also don't intend to recount your reckless deeds to future generations."

I stared her down, waited a moment. "Anything else you don't intend to do, Lady Barlow?" When she flushed and shook her head, I laughed and hugged her again, turning to find Rosanna eying me.

"Lady Barlow Senior," I graced her with a bow, "I will try my best to, ah, thrash my adversary to uphold the honor of Port Alain and the Barlow name."

"Whatever you do is more than enough to honor our name, and the Keltie name," she met my raised brow without flinching, "because it's the best you have to offer. And you know in your heart you have much to offer." She blinked away a tear as Lauryn rested a hand on her shoulder. "Remember your heritage, Alex, all of it. You'll need it." Before I could protest, the old seawitch hugged me close. "Now go and thrash the wretched traitor and get this ordeal over with so I can have my schoolmistress and gardener back from Tucker's Meadow."

Chapter Thirty-Two

Tucker's Meadow, along the Kieren River, was in the heart of the Marain vineyards. We reached it after a day's steady ride, a long day during which I kept to myself. No one troubled me. Even Anders kept his distance, though I knew he'd jump to my side in a heartbeat if I needed him. Pavilions were set up around a larger central one, flying Elena's Dunneal gold crown in a ring of sapphires. Guards circled her spacious tent, ramrod straight, alert for trouble. As we approached the royal pavilion, people parted to let us pass, curious eyes tracking our progress. The flap of Elena's tent slid open as she stepped into the bright sunlight, dark hair blowing lightly in the riverside breeze.

Elena hid her impatience as we dismounted. She hustled us inside the privacy of her pavilion, greeting each one of my companions, and leaving me for last. Dark blue eyes searched me with unusual intensity, sensing my turbulent frame of mind before too many moments passed.

"What's wrong, Alex?"

I walked away from Elena's keen gaze and wandered the confines of her sparsely furnished tent, which, unfortunately, didn't take very long.

"Elena . . ." I stopped, confronting her troubled expression, unable to admit my failure and my fears.

Anders came to my side and spoke softly for my hearing alone. "Do you want me to tell her?"

I'd have done anything to avoid Elena's disappointment. Ironic, when I fought so bitterly against helping her. I shook my head. "It's my responsibility and my failure." I touched his arm and held him back as he started to step aside, cool sea-gray eyes resting on mine. "But thank you."

He leaned closer to kiss my forehead.

I took a deep breath and turned my back on Anders, meeting Elena's dark appraisal. "I haven't been able to control the talent. Some thief whacked me on the head and robbed my mother's seamage pendant. Maybe the Port Alain mages. I don't know. I've . . ." I took another deep breath, ignoring the appalled look on Jules' face. "I've never been able to control what happens without using it. I know I should have warned you, but I kept hoping that maybe . . ." I crossed my arms to hide my shaking hands. "Oh hell, Elena, I'm sorry."

She listened dispassionately and met Anders' eyes as he stood beside me.

"I'll take her place. No one need know the truth," he said in a quiet voice.

"No," I blurted. "I—"

Elena's voice was steady, no recrimination or judgment in her eyes for either of us. "Thank you, Anders, but it won't be necessary to endanger you, either. Ravess is a vile man and capable of treachery. I'll forfeit at first light tomorrow morning. I'll make sure Brendan's ready to replace me."

"No," I repeated.

"I can't have you risk yourself in a fight where you haven't a chance, Alex. That was never my intent. I meant every word I said back in Port Alain."

"I didn't say I haven't a chance." I leaned against Anders' warmth as he crept behind me, grateful for the touch of his arms as they rested on my shoulders. "I gave you my word to do what I could. I have to try. If I don't, I'll never forgive myself. Or respect myself. Can't you see?"

"I don't want you hurt." Elena traced a finger along my neck. "This scar should never have happened. I won't stand by and see it happen again. I want your word now you'll yield if you think it's hopeless. Promise me," she repeated, searching my eyes for the answer she demanded, "or I'll forfeit the Challenge myself if I see you're in danger. And if you don't wipe that stubborn expression off your face, I'll forfeit now before it even begins."

I nodded in reluctant agreement as she placed her hands on Anders', still resting on my shoulders.

"Go and get some sleep."

* * * *

As though I could sleep.

"I'm sorry," I mumbled into Anders' shoulder, as I tossed for the hundred thousandth time in the uncomfortable camp bed. "I'm keeping you awake."

Turning around to face me in the dim light of the lamp we'd kept burning, he tugged at a lock of my tangled hair. "I hadn't noticed."

"Liar."

He leaned closer to kiss the tip of my nose.

"Anders?"

"Hmm." He moved his lips from my nose to my mouth, holding me close.

"Since I can't sleep," I said between kisses that lasted longer, "and you can't sleep," I caught a quick breath, "because I can't sleep," and another, "perhaps, maybe . . ."

"Good idea," he murmured, running his hands playfully through my hair.

"It might even help," I teased, enjoying the feel of his hands on my neck, waiting impatiently for them to wander.

"Well, then, not that I needed a reason, but if you think it might help you sleep, who am I to be inconsiderate?"

Chapter Thirty-Three

"I hope it helped," Anders whispered close behind me as we stepped from the spacious tent. I squinted against the bright sunshine, staying well under the overhanging flap until my eyes adjusted.

"Even if it didn't, you know it wasn't wasted." I craned my neck around to meet his eyes. "Though it was pretty impressive for an old wretched seamage. One would never guess how decrepit you truly are."

"I try very hard to impress you, Alex, even if it means my brittle bones will ache for days afterward."

"Then let's get this over and done and thrash the arrogant traitor so Rosanna can have her faithful servants back."

Anders touched my cheek before we left the shelter of the tent's overhang. "May the lords of the sea guide and protect you." He hesitated, taking his hand away, and tucking it in his pocket. "And damnation, be careful."

"I will."

We walked in silence toward Elena's central pavilion where she waited, eyes controlled and calm. The dukes and barons of the assembled duchies and territories of Tuldamoran gathered around her like ravenous vultures, waiting to pounce.

Not if I could help it.

Banners snapped in the strong morning breeze to either side of the royal Dunneal standard, Port Alain immediately to the right of the Crown, then Marain Valley, Belbridge Cliff, Thornmarsh, Barrows Pass, Ardsbrook, Bitterhill, Brodie Flats, and the linked tokens of the Ardenna Crown Council representing the four mage talents. Ironic I'd notice the absence of the Glynnswood banner when I'd barely noticed the absence of Sernyn Keltie in my life.

"Who's that?" I whispered to Anders, distracted by the sight of a tall, blond, bearded man, standing a few feet from Elena. "He's watching our monarch with more than a polite interest."

As we edged closer, my adversary, Charlton Ravess, appeared at the entrance to the Crown Council tent. He chose to dress in black leather like myself. The firemage exchanged an inscrutable look with the blond man near Elena. Instinct burning, I turned my face to keep my identity hidden from Ravess until the last moment. He may have heard I'd ridden into camp yesterday, but I prayed to the lords of the sea he assumed Anders was the queen's mage.

Face still hidden behind my hair I knelt with formal respect at Elena's feet. "Your majesty."

"Mage."

Without looking up, I listened as the regal tone of authority Elena practiced on Jules and me as children carried over the heads of her audience. She lowered her voice for my hearing only. "Master Perrin looks as though he didn't sleep a wink all night. I hope you kept him awake for good reason."

"Of course." I glanced up at the unconcerned playfulness of Elena's dark blue eyes, set in a solemn face. "Since neither of us could sleep, we kept each other awake. By the way, he's quite impressive for an old man. I might just keep him."

"So I gathered, and you'd better. Before this idiotic Challenge starts, what were the two of you discussing with such avid interest?"

"Don't peer over your shoulder, but we think you have an admirer."

"Me?" She sounded honestly surprised, as though no one in all Tuldamoran would ever look with favor on her. Because of Jules and that heartbreaking memory? "Is he at least handsome?"

I stifled a laugh and kept my face composed. "Full head of thick white hair, deep brown eyes, older gentleman, dressed in a black tunic."

"Alex."

"Honest, I'm not sure, but I think it's Lord Erich Harwoode of Barrows Pass who can't tear his eyes from you."

Blue eyes danced in an otherwise emotionless face. "Interesting."

"We thought so."

"You would."

Instinct reared its noisy head again. "At the risk of sounding too much like your nursemaid, if he is interested . . ." An eloquent arched brow was the only sign of her attention. "Be careful. We don't know anything about him. At least, I don't. He's only just taken over the duchy from his father."

"Was his eye too lecherous? It'd be nice for a change."

I shook my head, dismissing her jest. "I don't know. Just be careful."

"We'll discuss your instinct after you humiliate Ravess." She stopped my protest, blue eyes abruptly grim. "I can still forfeit the Challenge. It's not too late."

"And ruin my chances of stealing some Marain wine from your overflowing wine cellars? Don't even think of it."

"You'll get the wine either way." Her face lost some of its stony formality.

"My conscience won't be satisfied if I don't at least make the attempt. Elena," I took her hand and pressed my forehead with apparent submission to the glittering Dunneal ring. "My knees are screaming in pain against this hard ground. Now stop chatting. If you want your champion to stand a fighting chance, let me get up."

"Alex, I'm grateful." She gestured me to stand. As I tried hard not to groan aloud, she gripped my hands, heedless of the watching eyes. "Damnation, you idiot. If you're not careful, I'll rip out your heart myself."

I bowed once again before nodding to Jules and the rest of the Barlows. I shot a lusty wink at Anders and turned with deceptive coolness to face my enemy. Rewarded by the sweet, satisfying sound of an angry hiss, I stared at Charlton Ravess, my face calm. Only then was I aware of Seamage Neal Brandt beneath the Port Alain banner.

Maybe neither mage knew about Mother's pendant.

Maybe I had a chance.

"Seems you've been recognized." Elena's murmur sounded close behind me as I studied the white-haired mage who hadn't budged from his spot at the entrance to the Crown Council tent.

A horn sounded to my right, and Elena's steward stepped forward to declare the formalities of the Challenge. I was grateful he couldn't slam the oak staff in my ear, though the horn was jarring enough to wake the dead buried in the old town graveyard.

"Elena Dunneal, Queen of Tuldamoran, stands challenged by Charlton Ravess, Firemage of the Ardenna Crown Council of Mages."

I met my opponent's furious glare with an easy, measuring look, disguising the turmoil in my head and heart as Anders taught me. I coaxed the fire and ice awake, praying with fervor to the lords of the sea to keep an eye open in my favor.

"The Mage Challenge continues until either the Challenged or Challenger yields. If neither opponent yields, the Challenge continues until one mage dies. Representing Elena Dunneal, Queen of Tuldamoran, is Alexandra Daine Keltie, Mage."

Mage.

Ravess didn't bother to hide the hatred and contempt in those deep brown eyes. Confusion flashed across his face, but swiftly vanished. Mage. Let the traitor fret about the orphan child.

"Representing Firemage Charlton Ravess is the Firemage himself."

Not the Crownmage.

"The Mage Challenge begins with a ritual testing by each mage to confirm the presence of talent."

Damn the person who stole Mother's pendant.

With a stiff bow to Elena, the steward stepped back into place.

Elena placed both hands on my shoulders as I faced the field. "I won't tolerate this idiocy if you're in serious danger. Remember that." As I nodded, she squeezed my shoulders and dropped her hands to her side.

Before confronting Charlton Ravess, I needed one more reassurance. From the corner of my eye, I found what I needed. Anders' calm expression revealed not the slightest trace of any anxiety. A smile tugged at the corner of his mouth, one I matched without hesitation. Slowly, I confronted Charlton Ravess. Watching me approach his position on the field, he exchanged an almost imperceptible glance with Erich Harwoode of Barrow's Pass. What was going on there?

I shoved those distracting thoughts aside. I'd time now only for Charlton Ravess and his hate-filled, frost-bitten, hungry eyes. Concentrating on fire and ice, always painful at first until I tamed them, they soon merged into the old familiar presence. Cool warmth drifted through every part of my body, every finger and toe, every strand of hair. Anders taught me how easy it could be, showed me how easy it could be. I pushed all thoughts of Mother's copper pendant from my mind, Mother's stolen pendant, and forced myself to concentrate.

Balanced in the warmth of the morning sun, I stood with eyes closed. My senses open to the Kieren River's dampness just beyond the open border of the meadow, the earth's fragrant greenness beneath me, the wind's cold gust from the river ruffling my hair, and the flame's heat burning at Ravess's feet. I opened my eyes in slow motion and blinked.

"Orphan child."

When I didn't acknowledge his taunt, flames sprouted at my feet. It was a test from Ravess, according to the rules. Who stared with hate-filled eyes at Elena, and then me. The traitor betrayed. His own fault we were here.

Calm.

Envisioning the flames quenched with water, I cursed in silence as wind fanned the flames higher, though managed to keep my face emotionless.

Concentrate.

I inched back from the flames licking too near my boots, focusing on water; on Anders' cool sea-gray eyes. I felt the cool spray from the Kieren River and Shad's Bay beyond Port Alain, reaching even, in my mind, to the Skandar Sea. I groaned in bitter disappointment as a mound of dirt smothered the flames. But the flames, at least, were gone. The Challenge required a test from me before it continued unrestricted.

Focus.

There, the log at Ravess' feet. I saw the flames in my mind, fatal, creeping slowly upward, along his vile body. Instead, I called a strong gust of wind, which did no harm. It died on its own as I released the talent, trying hard to ignore my opponent's blatant triumph. The ritual test barely satisfied with my elemental conjuring, I braced for his attack, and found myself ringed with searing flames. Sweat erupted as the heat's intensity increased, the flames inching closer and higher. I focused on the sea; even weed-filled clumps of dirt would do at the moment.

Concentrate.

I cried out sharply at the gust of wind, my own flameblasted wind, which fanned the fire higher. Enraged and despairing, I called on moist, vibrant earth to snuff out the dangerous flames. I was rewarded with cool, drenching water, which soaked me completely, offering some little protection for a short while.

Ravess snarled at my drenched, shivering figure. He pushed wayward locks of white tangled hair from his face, which bore an expression of uncertainty. Elena had told him nothing, given him not one clue. Wretched beast, let him wonder. Fire and ice reasserted themselves with excruciating pain as I lost my concentration.

Focus.

I needed to attack Ravess now, and focused on the sea once again. I saw it clearly raging around him as the earth beneath his feet turned to crashing, rushing water to drag him away. But flames erupted at his feet instead, distracting him. He leaped agilely as the first flame appeared and snuffed the fire without effort, leaving the earth scorched and blackened. Raising his hands, maybe to frighten me, he sent flames shooting down the length of my body. Clothes still drenched from my last failed attempt feebly kept the flames at bay, hissing and steaming until they began to smoulder.

"Alex!" Jules shouted somewhere behind me as I fought back the rising panic and despair. Elena's voice murmured something unintelligible.

Fearful she'd forfeit, I dared a moment's glance in her direction and shook my head. Pale with worry, lips pressed tight, she nodded once.

I begged the lords of the sea for cool river water, pledged the lives of my unborn children and grandchildren if I could only coax water from the blistering flames. The wind, in heartbreaking mockery, rose in a ferocious gust to defeat me. I shook with dread. Fire and ice pierced my head with unimaginable pain, while the flames sought to destroy the meager leather protecting me.

Lords of the sea, not with fire.

"Thrash him, Alex. Oh please, Alex, thrash him. Hurry!"

I blinked at the terrified words and the familiar voice that shrieked them. Unable to concentrate, I nearly collapsed from the fire and ice that raged through my body. Lords of the sea, is this what my mother suffered before she died?

"Thrash him!"

Thrash him? As ice-cold realization hit, I turned in shock to find Carey crouched at the edge of the crowd, white with fear, perilously close to me. Too close. How did he get here? As Jules raced with frantic speed to snatch him to safety, Carey stumbled onto the open meadow in panicked fright as the flames spread outward, inching swiftly toward the boy. Carey knelt in the dirt, paralyzed with fascinated horror by the approaching river of flame. Jules would never reach him in time.

My heart stopped for one brief raging moment. Sernyn Keltie stood alone, beyond the crowd, mournful eyes shadowing my every move, mouthing something I couldn't hear, didn't want to hear. Hot consuming anger and cold murderous vengeance shoved my fears aside as I tamed the fire and ice, heedless of the sharp sting of the flames licking my skin. Anger surged through me at Sernyn Keltie's betrayal and abandonment, and now witness to my humiliating struggle. I laughed with unbridled bitterness, almost madness, using whatever power his flameblasted blood gifted to me, used it to wreak vengeance and ease my own grief-stricken, guilty pain.

Bastard.

I focused on cool, cleansing river water, reached with my thoughts to the overflowing Kieren River. Commanded it to soak my smoldering clothes and singed hair. And it came. Thank the lords of the sea, it came, blessed icy coolness that hissed, enveloping me in dense fog. I sank to my knees, trembling in relief despite the sharp bite of the cold wind as Jules grabbed Carey back to the safety of his arms. Some distant part of me heard Elena's gasp of relief, Jules' hoarse whisper to his son. From the corner of my eye, I felt the grim satisfaction in Anders' face, with barely hidden relief, and more than a trace of deep affection. Reckless, I shoved all this aside.

Carey's cry still echoed in my head. Thrash him. Ravess? Sernyn? Did it matter? Did any of it truly matter? Fire and ice was no longer painful, but eager to be used, for vengeance if that was my desire. I waited for the fog to dissipate enough to see where Ravess was standing.

"Orphan child." He beckoned with an obscene gesture, brown eyes richly seductive, until he laughed.

I envisioned a lake, deep and deadly, mere inches wider than his slender body. He sank abruptly as the earth beneath him transformed into a narrow, deep well. Floundering and shocked, Ravess sputtered and vanished from sight, grabbing with desperation for the edge of solid earth. He reappeared briefly before he slipped and vanished again.

I focused on flame, and waited, cloaked in cold vengeance. As Ravess' hand appeared and gripped solid dirt with slick fingers, the earth erupted in flame, throwing him back from the edge, submerging him. His head bobbed to the surface, white hair plastered to his scalp, as he reached for the other side. Flames encircled him, but he was a firemage, and quickly banished the danger.

No matter, I'd shown him what an enraged orphan child could do.

Ravess pulled himself from the well, furious. I watched and waited, taking deep calming breaths, conscious once again of Anders and Elena at the fringe of the meadow. I knew Elena's face was pale with strain. Jules held Carey close to his chest, trying to shelter the child from the murderous scene played out before him. Kerrie's arm wrapped tight around Khrista, both of them fretting.

Sernyn Keltie stood motionless, fists clenched at his side, alone. I blinked back tears and forced him from my thoughts.

Muttering to himself, Ravess stood slowly. I didn't wait; couldn't; knowing he'd snatch the first opportunity to strike at me. I focused on blasting, wintry gusts of wind. Through narrowed eyes I watched with grim satisfaction as the tempest rose, dragging the firemage painfully, brutally, along the hard, frost-covered ground. Unable to stand or catch his balance, he scrambled for a lingering tree as the wind tugged him along. He held on tight, fingers bleeding from his taut grip. When I gentled the wind, he collapsed, panting, body sprawled across the open ground.

I stumbled to my feet, body trembling with fatigue, tension and pain, eyes fixed on Ravess' still form, unwilling just yet to tame my hungry retribution. Elena met my reckless gaze with open unease, perhaps dismayed at the beast she'd set free. I shook my head once, not ready to stop. With an abrupt, inelegant gesture, she signaled the steward forward to kneel by the firemage's head. Heavy silence descended as I let the wind die, the steward's voice echoed eerily, stiff in his formality after our brutal exchange.

"Firemage, do you yield?"

White hair slicked back against his head with sweat and water, Ravess raised himself awkwardly on one blood-streaked arm where the leather of his tunic had been ripped to shreds. Hate-filled, deep brown eyes turned in my direction as he struggled to stand, waving the steward out of the way with a vicious gesture.

"Yield to an orphan child?" Wavering, he hissed at the steward, "I will not yield. Not now. Not ever."

Sernyn bowed his head, and I felt his shame across the meadow between us. I turned my face away, waiting with mounting impatience as the steward scurried to safety by Elena's side. It seemed I delayed too long. Ravess took fierce advantage of my hesitation and sent scorching flames my way. I focused without effort now, cool water coming instantly and blessedly to my relief.

"Did she promise you friendship, orphan child?" Ravess' laughter searched with cruelty for the chink in my emotions, gnawing away at my unstable confidence. "I thought you wanted vengeance. Instead, you crawl at her bidding, seduced by promises of undying affection to suffer at my hands. Foolish child." He edged a step closer. "Are you so desperate to believe her silky lies? No one wants you, everyone pities you, and Elena uses you, orphan child, though you're too desperate to see the truth. Her friendship is sweet as long as you have the talent. But if it disappears again—"

I slipped, shaken by the power of his filthy words. On one knee, I braced for his inevitable attack, weary, sick at heart, knowing what Ravess didn't know. Sernyn Keltie hadn't wanted me either, and he was here, watching.

"Alex, no. He's lying." Elena's grief-stricken whisper snagged my attention. I was close enough to recognize unshed tears in dark blue eyes that begged me not to believe his dangerous seductive words. "I'll forfeit." She gripped the steward's arm, fully prepared to stop the Challenge. "Damn you, Alex. I'll forfeit now."

"No."

Ravess poised to strike.

I envisioned the river surging past, heard the water rushing by. I watched with heartfelt appeasement as the earth beneath the firemage turned again to a raging, roaring, uncontrolled stream. The water carried him to the banks of the Kieren River, plunging him under time and again, and without mercy, once more.

I sank to both knees, exhausted.

Ravess snatched a passing log for safety, teeth chattering in the frigid water. I forced myself to wait with cold patience until he anchored himself around the log, steering it toward the riverbank. Without a trace of hesitation, I envisioned the log as flames beneath his head where it rested against the rough wood. Ravess screamed in agonizing pain as the fire sizzled against the skin of his unbearded cheek. The firemage clawed his way frantically back toward the earthen bank. Hate and vengeance consumed his deep brown eyes as he gingerly touched his scarred cheek, raising a trembling hand to hurl flames my way. I struck once again, with vicious coldness, sending a wintry tempest to lift him bodily. The blast flung him down, screaming his anger and hatred, at Elena's feet where he lay still.

I staggered to where she waited, dark eyes fighting to hold a jumble of emotions in check. Filthy, bedraggled, hurting, and wanting nothing more than to be back in my cottage with Anders, I prayed the Challenge was ended. All anger and vengeance drained away. Pushing aside my own confused jumble of emotions, I struggled to maintain some shred of dignity.

Elena slanted a grim look in Anders' direction before meeting my eyes with deceptive calm over Ravess' limp body, and prodded the mage with her boot.

"Firemage," accompanied by another kick, "do you yield?"

His muffled answer was more a bitter curse than an intelligent response.

"My Mage Champion cannot hear you. Do you yield?" She repeated the ritual question in an ice cold voice, prodding Ravess again.

"Yes." Ravess didn't have the strength to raise his blood-spattered, scarred head in my direction. I heard the unforgettable, unforgiving hatred in his harsh voice and shivered.

I scanned the crowd, searching for Sernyn, but he was gone, as though he'd never been. Vanished from my life once again.

Elena's cool triumphant expression turned to alarm as my vision spun with dizziness and my body swayed.

"Anders, hurry."

Barely in time, Anders caught me as I fell forward, grateful for the soothing, cool darkness as I fainted dead away.

Epilogue

"How long have I been sleeping?" I rubbed my eyes like a child, hesitantly stepping in the direction of my sitting room.

"Sleeping for a day and a half, snoring for only the half. Amazing you never once opened your eyes on the trip back home, though we bounced along the roadway," Anders answered with a grin. "You just kept right on snoring, oblivious."

"I don't snore," I said irritably, "you do." I caught my balance with an awkward lurch moments before falling face forward into the cold wall. "What's all this?" I stared at the crates lined against the cottage wall, shrinking the room even further.

"The first shipment of Marain wine from Elena," Anders smiled, lifting a glass in salute, "as promised. You look like you could use a hearty taste."

I shivered as a light cool breeze chilled me. "Can you stir those logs in the fireplace? Please? It's cold in here."

"Of course." He poured another glass of the rich wine, handed it to me, and sat opposite the fireplace, feet resting on a pile of embroidered pillows.

"Anders," I said with mild impatience. "The fire—" And watched in utter confusion as the flames grew higher and burned hotter while Anders sat unconcerned and oblivious in his chair, enjoying the wine.

"How did you do that?" I whispered, eyes wide in shock. "You're a seamage."

Cool sea-gray eyes held my gaze, the barest, almost imperceptible, hint of mischief in them. The icy draft in the room grew stronger until my hair, disheveled and tangled enough from sleep, was blowing freely.

"You bastard." I flung the wineglass at his gray-streaked head, but he dodged it. "No wonder you knew so damned much about the Crownmage. You lied to me."

"I didn't lie, Alex. I just kept the truth from you for a little while. After all, in every one of those hundred thousand questions, you never thought to ask me if I were the Crownmage."

"Why didn't you tell me?" I demanded, shaking with rage and unexpected betrayal, thinking suddenly of Sernyn Keltie. "I trusted you."

"Sit, and I'll tell you."

"Why?"

He sighed as if I were being unreasonable and demanding, though I knew he caught the controlled grief beneath my anger. "My first reason was to wait until I met Elena, and then decide if I should ally myself with her."

"You met Elena weeks ago."

"Well, yes. But then you started displaying the most extraordinary, intriguing talent, and, frankly," he took a deep, lingering sip of wine, "I was afraid you'd use me as an excuse and hold yourself back."

"I could've been killed at Tucker's Meadow," I whispered in betrayal. "Carey could've been killed, and Elena would've forfeited her crown. Don't you give a damn for any of us? For me? Or was I just a fleeting source of amusement for you?"

His eyes lost their bemused expression, darkening with apprehension. "Do you think I would've let either of you be hurt, or let Elena lose her crown?" he asked, hand outstretched in a pleading gesture. "If you do, then I've no place here with you. And I want very much to be a part of your life." I slumped into the chair opposite him. "Do you think I would've let you die?"

"Of course not, you wretched old beast. You'd have lost your most gifted student. But, damnation, Anders, I wish you'd trusted me."

"Ah, yes. Trust," he said, rising to pour another glass for me, the playfulness back in his voice. "I trusted you, Alex. Completely."

I held the glass motionless at my lips, suspicious. "What do you mean?"

He dug into his tunic pocket, searching for something. Pulling a small object free, he tossed it to me. I caught it, and held it before the fire to get a better look. Mother's stolen seamage pendant.

"You bastard." I hurled the second glass at his head and missed again.

"Your mother had better aim."

"I'll never trust you again. Rosanna lied to me time and again; Sernyn Keltie betrayed me, and now you—"

He caught my arm as I started to leave the parlor. "You've no reason to trust me again except for the most important reason. Everything I did was for your sake."

"That doesn't make it right."

"Alex, listen. Please. I trusted you, far more than you trusted yourself. And you proved yourself beyond my wildest dreams."

"I proved I can manipulate my talent to almost murder a man and seek vengeance."

"You proved you can control the talent, and use it when you need to."

I slipped the pendant over my head and tucked it inside my wrinkled tunic, eye to eye with him. "Anders Perrin, if you ever lie to me again or deceive me, whether or not it's for my benefit, I'll—"

He caught my arms and held me away from him, hands rigid at my side. "You'll do what?" He stretched to kiss me with exaggerated caution.

Flaming hell. I kissed him slowly, deeply, then pulled away to make my point. "Issue Mage Challenge."

About the Author

Virginia G. McMorrow has worked as an editor/writer for more than 30 years, after a career in human resources. In her professional capacity, Ginny has worked for business publishers as an editor of books, journals, reports, and newsletters targeted for clients, and now works as a freelance editor/writer. She has also had numerous articles on both professional and writing topics published, along with several short stories. As a playwright, Ginny has had 28 short one acts and one full-length play produced off-off Broadway by Love Creek Productions in a black box theater, as well as two short plays performed on a west coast radio show. She now lives and works in Venice, Florida.

Coming Soon!

VIRGINIA G. MCMORROW
MAGE RESOLUTION
THE MAGE TRILOGY
BOOK 2

Mage Resolution, book two of The Mage Trilogy, continues the saga of Mage Alex Keltie—the most endearing, lovable and infuriating character since Scarlett O'Hara. Her old nemesis returns to trouble her, even as she learns new secrets about herself, her origins, her family and the mystery of Spreebridge that threatens the lives of those closest to her.

For more Information
visit: www.SpeakingVolumes.us

On Sale Now!

KEITH TAYLOR
BARD SERIES
BOOKS 1 - 5

"For lovers of magic, history, and/or swashbuckling adventure, [Bard] is an excellent novel about an earthy and genuinely likeable Irish hero."—Science Fiction Review

Visit: www.SpeakingVolumes.us

On Sale Now!

JACK HILLMAN
GIANTS WAR TRILOGY
BOOKS 1 – 3

**For more information
visit:** www.SpeakingVolumes.us

Sign up for free and bargain books

Join the Speaking Volumes
mailing list

Text

ILOVEBOOKS

to 22828 to get started.

Message and data rates may apply.